The C

by

David Williams

Find out more about the author and upcoming books online at www.lonelyballerina.com
Also at Twitter: @DavidWil8997774 Facebook: www.facebook.com/davieg25

Produced in United Kingdom.

CONTENTS

About The Author

David was born in Leeds in 1963, the second of four children in a single-parent household. He was educated at All Saints Junior and Middle School and Crossgreen Comprehensive. He left school with few qualifications to start work at sixteen in the family roofing business and attended Leeds College of Building. He returned to academic study in 2010 and attained a BA (Hons) degree with the Open University six years later. He is married with four children and lives in East Leeds.

Acknowledgements

Many thanks for the continued support of my family during the writing of this book. None more so than my youngest son Harvey with his intellect, wit and boundless knowledge of internet graphics and technical stuff in general. To my youngest daughter Scarlett for her offer of assistance which ultimately came to nothing but for which I was eternally grateful, the warm, but brief, feeling of altruism was good whilst it lasted. Also my wife Yvonne, eldest two, Rosie and Gheorghe for their succinct, expedient and knowledgeable input plus sisters Karen & Janine and Arkid (aka Gerald) for their continued support and encouragement. Finally to all friends, family and those who supported my debut book *Lonely Ballerina* I offer my sincere thanks. Without this support and encouragement there would be no *The Girl* sequel.

RIP Uncle Patrick

This book is dedicated to the following souls
who drew their last breath whilst sleeping
rough on the streets of Leeds:

Alan Campbell, died on October 11, 2017, age 42
Jeffrey 'Geordie' Hepburn, died on October 13, 2017, age 54
Nigel Whalley, died on December 19, 2017, age 50
Kenneth Howson, died on January 5, 2018, age 65
Fiona Watson (a.k.a. Fiona Swann), died on January 8, 2018, age 56
Ryan Thomas McGurgan, died on April 10, 2018, age 33
Jason Wager, died on July 10, 2018, age 52
Andrew Burnett, died on October 3, 2018, age 27
Lee Jenkinson, died on December 3, 2018, age 43

and lastly

Amanda Skinner, (a.k.a. Sasha Taylor) died on March 7, 2019, age 45, my inspiration behind the character of 'Betty'.

Rest in Peace, in warmth and love; unencumbered.

Information courtesy of LeedsLive: https://www.leeds-live.co.uk/news/leeds-news/10-tragic-homeless-people-who-19097927

The Essence of Humanity

to Be, to Aspire, to Endeavour

CHAPTER 1

The light in the room slowly dims as a soothing black mist descends onto the little sitting-room. The sounds of the television, the ticking clock, and the outward prevailing storm dumb down and dissipate, leaving an atmosphere shrouded in an ice-cold, deathly silence. A chink of light emerges from the far corner ceiling, and slowly draws to the fore, gradually increasing in size as it reaches the middle of the room. A spotlight from above focuses a harsh light onto a figure in the pitch-blackness, a life-sized figure. The figure of a female, old and haggard, is now centre-stage and sits on a revolving barstool. The stiff-backed figure is slumped to one side, emaciated limbs hang loose. Bedraggled hair scraped back into a loose bun. The figure sits stock still on the slowly revolving barstool. The head hangs loose, eyes closed, the face embellished with scarlet-red lipstick and heavy smudged eyeliner. Its skin pale and wrinkled. The figure is dressed as a ballerina. Grey tutu, bodice, loose-fitting tights and scuffed ballet slippers. The listing stiff-backed figure is dead. It sits on the revolving barstool. Zoe observes, she scrutinises, she witnesses. She sees. Slowly revolving, dead, spotlight, velvet blackness, front, side, back, side, over and over, calming silence, revolving, slow. Limp-limbed and stiff-backed. Dead.

*

Zoe sat bolt upright. Just for a second, she found herself

9

in the tiny sitting room of the back-to-back terraced house in East Moor Park. Her heart raced as the image of the dead ballerina whirled around her head before gradually dissolving into the dark recesses of her convoluted subconscious. However, the feeling of deep-seated dread lingered. As her eyes became accustomed to the surroundings she realised she was back home, in bed. The family home that is, her mother's home in Seacroft, a vast sprawling council estate in East Leeds. A sense of relief engulfed her as she recognised the layout of the room, the comfortable double bed, the dated but sturdy wardrobes and chest of drawers. The room was tidy, her mother wouldn't have allowed anything else, and Phil, her common-law husband, had already left for work. She closed her eyes. She thought of the day in front of her. She'd have to rouse Sophia, her seven-year-old. With any luck, she thought, her mother might offer to do the school run and save her the hassle. She'd got therapy at eleven after which the remainder of the day was hers to do as she pleased.

She sighed. *Fuck! I'd better get up. Get Sophia ready. Shower, walk it to therapy...waste o' friggin' time...and then what?* Zoe saw only dark, foggy clouds when she envisaged anything further down the line than the day in front of her. She couldn't see any future mapped out, she hadn't a clue where she'd be or what she'd be doing this time next week, next month or next year. One day at a time they'd said, take each day as it comes. Depression was only part of her problems, but more than that it was the reluctance, the sheer refusal of those around her to listen, to see things from her perspective. She didn't think she needed therapy.

Therapy for what? So I've taken a bit o' crack and

necked a few sherbets! Who 'asn't? I know what I'm doing, I only started taking that shit again to help me get through living down there in that fuckin' hell-'ole. I know what I saw, what I witnessed, what I went through. They think I'm mental, but let 'em think it, I know I'm not...or am I?

*

'Thanks for taking her Mam. Was she alright?'

Zoe slouched on the lounge sofa with coffee at hand and toast on the coffee table. She'd showered and dressed and straightened her long blonde hair. She'd always been of slim build but her time in hospital had rendered her thin, and it was part of her mother's remit to fatten her up. She wore leggings and a baggy sweater and whilst her mother had taken Sophia to school she'd applied a hint of basic make-up to mask her pale and drawn features

'Aye, she were fine,' replied Linda as she looked down and scrutinised the sight of her only daughter. 'What time's your therapy?'

'Eleven.'

'Well you'd better be going lady, that's all I'm saying, it's your last chance, I'm telling ya.'

'I am going, why wouldn't I?'

'I'm just saying that's all. It's about Sophia all this, never mind you. She needs a mother firing on all cylinders, not one with her 'ead in the clouds. Are yer listening lady?'

'Well if I'm being truthful Mam I don't think the therapy is doing me any good at all, I've told you, but for god's sake chill out, I'm going.'

'Never mind being clever. You get to that bloody therapy that's all, else you'll 'ave me to contend wi...that's all I'm sayin'.'

'Alright, put yer eyeballs back we're not playing marbles,' muttered Zoe as her mother turned to leave the room. Linda heard the side-shot and twisted back round to face her. She kept a tight ship in her tidy semi-detached council home and didn't take kindly to receiving any back-chat or chelp either from her two children or any of her three grandchildren. But Zoe couldn't resist squaring up to her bullish mother head-on, with each striving to have the last word. On this occasion, Linda settled for shooting Zoe a menacing glare before leaving the room on her way through to the kitchen.

Linda was in her early fifties, well-nourished and red-faced. She had dark shoulder length hair and could still turn a few heads on the odd occasion she ventured into town all dolled up for a night out with her mates. However, it was only when she spoke that the raw northernness of her personality smacked you in the face like a head butt from an obnoxious bullock. A deep croaky voice with a narrow range of vocabulary, spoken with enthusiastic animation and a flat Leeds accent. Since her husband had passed away some five years earlier she'd gradually retreated from what had been a healthy and robust social life. Now, she kept her home, and herself, going for the benefit of her family. Zoe, Phil and Sophia were living under her roof, with Chris visiting a couple of times a week. His wife Rena and their two kids were over every Sunday afternoon for the traditional family Sunday roast. Linda loved all her grandkids and they loved her, accepting her iron-fist rules as granted and thinking nothing more of it. Chris was easy going with his mother but the feisty Zoe had always been the one to challenge her, ruffle her feathers and test her resolve, just to see how far she could get. She'd always been a daddy's girl and although she loved her mother there was also a deep-seated resentment. There'd been little leeway when Linda had found evidence of drug abuse in the house. Zoe had received one warning, failed to heed the warning, and then she'd been out. No messing. Daughter and partner, on the street, this after living together at the family home for the previous three years. Sophia had stayed on with her grandmother until they'd hastily bought and renovated a small back-to-back property in the East Moor Park district of Leeds. Following that disastrous spell, and Zoe's subsequent stint in hospital, Linda had relented and allowed the small family to return but only under strict rules. Zoe was under no illusions as to the consequences should she slip back into old habits.

*

It was ten-thirty as Zoe poked her head around the corner of the kitchen door. Linda sat at the kitchen table brooding over a mug of tea. The delicious aroma of oven baking floated across the airspace as the manufacture of cookies, pies and cakes continued unabated, as it did almost every day of the week. The baking was predominately for the consumption of her grandkids but such was her reputation for producing mouth-watering concoctions that no one was ever denied a slice of the action.

'Right, I'm going Mam.'

'Right, I'll see ya later.'

'I'll be calling at 'shop on 'way back if you want owt.'

'Well don't be bringing any booze back 'ere, d'ya hear?'

'Don't worry, I won't, I know the rules.'

'Aye, and don't you forget 'em, lady.'

'Tara then.'

'Aye, tara...and be careful.'

Zoe left her mother at the table as she walked down the hallway and out of the front door. The sun was shining and the skies were pale blue with a small cluster of wispy cloud roaming slowly across the heavens. The huge council estate was rousing, blinking in the sunlight and stretching its raw limbs after a cold and harsh start to the new year. Spring was in full stride and with the ominous air of winter now largely behind there was a mood of optimism on the estate. Even with an early-March nip in the air, the feathered airborne community were flushed with the industrious matters of courtship and nest building, their boundless energy and piercing melodies instilling a positive vibe for all who cared to listen and observe.

She walked up the concrete pathway towards a battered wooden gate. The front garden was neat if not showy. The low privet hedge, trimmed twice a year, was now showing the first signs of spring with new green shoots bursting out into the crisp morning air. She turned right and walked down the slight incline of Kentmere Avenue towards Killingbeck.

The estate was predominantly made up of semi-detached and four-block traditional two-storey council housing. Some of the gardens and house-frontages were immaculate, others were overgrown and strewn with rubbish and dog shit, most were bounded by privet hedge. Although the Seacroft estate had an unfavourable reputation from some quarters, those who lived there, and kept themselves to themselves, lived in peace and harmony. For Zoe, she'd been born and bred on the estate and felt at ease in the suburb and walked the streets she knew so well with confidence. She knew how to handle trouble if and when it occurred, and had enough contacts of the required calibre should she require their dubious services. This was Seacroft. A huge housing estate built to replace the inner-city slum clearances after the second world war. Wide roads, an abundance of trees, open grassed areas, green gardens and privet hedge. It gave Zoe a boost to be back home, just when she needed it and the onset of Spring, the sunshine and birdsong helped brighten her mood after her recent period of hell.

*

She stood in the queue at the local mini-market. She'd picked up dog food for Princess, their half-breed Yorkshire Terrier. Phil had purchased the puppy from his mate Andy, both of whom had wrongly assumed the puppy to be female. Sophia had already been sold on the name and so it had been too late to change once the correct sex had been determined after the little bastard had attempted to rodger the little girl's ankles off. Hence Zoe's pet name for the dog as 'Jimmy', a reference to the late and infamous local celebrity, Jimmy Saville.

She checked her phone and looked over her shoulder, her edgy demeanour a product of her wafer-thin patience. She nodded to a middle-aged woman she knew through her mother then again checked the time on her phone and looked out towards the window. She caught sight of a woman staring at her from the other side of the store who subsequently slipped behind the frozen food aisle. Only slightly perturbed, Zoe quickly shrugged it off and shuffled along as the queue shortened. As she approached the counter and glanced up at the mirrored cigarette display cabinet she caught the reflection of the same woman gawking at her, this time from the cover of a different aisle. She turned around, more through annoyance than anything else but once again the woman dodged behind a customer and out of view. However, on this occasion, she got a good enough look to recognise the woman, not by name but by reputation. *It's that silly old bugger from South Farm Road, what's she up to?*

Most districts in any community have an eccentric character or two treading the flagstones and this end of Seacroft was no different. If nothing else the recognition eased Zoe's mind, the woman was harmless and bore no physical or verbal threat. She was just a bit mad. She'd been walking the streets for years with her trademark purple bowler hat and oversized raincoat. On one occasion, as teenagers, Zoe and a small gang of mates had ambushed the poor woman by pelting her with rotten tomatoes they'd found from the bin area at the back of Purdey's greengrocers. They'd found it hilarious, running off and leaving the poor woman to wipe herself down and replace her bowler hat. The thought flashed through her mind that the odd little woman had remembered the incident after all these years and had some kind of reckoning to deliver. However, as she hit the front of the queue and entered into the usual counter chit-chat with the cashier, the bowler-hatted local oddball slipped her mind.

Zoe trudged back up Kentmere Avenue with the carrier bag swinging by her side and stared into her iPhone, oblivious to the environment around her save for the winding black tarmac pathway that would eventually lead all the way home. She tapped on her mobile, unaware of the dishevelled little character puffing and wheezing behind her. She stopped and smiled as she posted what she surmised to be a cutting and witty quip onto the Facebook thread. This slight hiatus in pace gave the bowler-hatted woman, with the ill-fitting overcoat, time to catch her up. Even as she hunched over right behind her, gulping the spring air, the spellbound Zoe still failed to notice her. Eventually, the old woman cleared her throat, which had the desired effect.

'Jesus! What the fuck!' cried Zoe as she swung around to see the dishevelled little character gasping for air and staring up at her.

'I'm sorry love,' she spluttered in between breaths, 'I didn't mean to startle you, I just—'

'What is it? You nearly gave me a twatting heart attack for God's sake!'

'I know love I'm sorry... '

'It's you! You were watching me in 'shop wan't ya. What's up? What do you want?'

'Well, please just calm down m'dear, it's just something I'd like to discuss with you. I'm just a harmless old woman luvvie...I don't mean you any harm.'

Zoe looked her in the eye as she slowly recovered from the initial shock. The woman had a kindly face and spoke with a slightly educated soft voice. She felt a slight pang of guilt, not only over the tomato incident many years ago but of the intervening years when she'd been the subject of much derision and piss-taking from the local youths.

'I'm sorry,' said Zoe, 'You just gave me a bit of a shock that's all.'

'I know I did my love and I'm sorry, and I'm sorry if I made you feel uneasy in the shop, I didn't mean to.'

'Okay, well what is it then? What d'ya want?' Zoe turned off her phone and rammed it into the inside pocket of her jacket before fronting the woman up.

'Well, I need you to stay with me on this me dear, just stay with me, it's not gonna be easy love... ' Zoe now looked down at the woman with the inklings of suspicion. *What's the silly old get on about? Jesus! Has she been on the piss?*

'Go on then...what?'

'Well my love, I'm guessing you're not called Zelda so I'm going for Zoe. Is that it? Is your name Zoe? It's just that I'm getting a big Zed that's all.'

'How do you know me name's Zoe? Do I know you? Do you know me, Mam?'

'No love, I don't know you... or your Mam love, it's...

'

'Well, how do you know me name then,' asked Zoe glaring down at the woman.

'It's your Dad... '

'Me Dad? What d'ya mean it's me Dad, did you know him or summat?'

'I'm getting an en love... '

'A bleedin' Hen! What you on about? Are ya pissed?'

'No love en, an en something...e n...Ben or... '

'Ken! That's me Dad...but he's been dead five years, what the 'ell are you talking about?'

'Ken love, that's it, that's your dad isn't it? Ken, yes love, just calm down, just give me a minute, please... ' Zoe gave the woman the benefit of the doubt and calmed down a little. She maintained a defensive stance with her arms folded and clamped firmly to her body.

'Well go on then,' she said after giving the woman time to catch her breath.

'Well it's your Dad luvvie, he's got a message for you...you see I'm a medium love... ' Seeing the puzzlement on Zoe's face the bowler-hatted lady smiled. 'I'm not mad love, or wanting to do you any harm ... '

'But me Dad's dead,' blurted out Zoe before she realised the absurdity of the situation, talking to the bowler-hatted woman in the middle of the street about her dead father. She rolled her eyes and looked around, but there were no spectators, they were alone, the streets were deserted. Her face flushed up. It would be her normal reaction to fire a round of obscenities, but she felt embarrassed. The oddball woman, close up looked so harmless, so genuine, she couldn't just tell her to piss off. She stood and looked her in the eye.

'No love, you see your dad passed from this plane into spirit. His physical body is no more but his spirit survives and he survives in the same space as us...he's here love...he's all around us, but just in a different plane that's all, a different dimension. Folk like me, in different ways, can tap into this other dimension. We're not mad love.' Zoe stood and offered nothing in return as she attempted to figure out the rationale of the batty old lady.

'Just think of it like this love. Your physical body is a car and your spirit, or soul, is the driver of the car. The driver of the car looks after and maintains the car as best they can to prolong its life, a bit similar to how we look after our physical selves, by eating correctly and not abusing our bodies with alcohol or drugs.' Zoe's right eyebrow twitched. 'And when the car needs repair it goes into a garage, similar as to when, perhaps, we have to go to a hospital to fix physical problems that may arise.'

'Well, what about when you go in hospital for mental problems?'

'Well my love, those with such problems on this plane will receive much the same treatment as those with the same issues in spirit. It's the soul that needs comfort and love in those situations, my love.' Zoe didn't answer. She wasn't getting comfort and love, she was getting tablets and pointless shitty therapy, but she let the woman continue. 'So you see when the car has run to the end of its useful life then it's scrapped and the driver has to find a new car to drive around in. And that's where your dad is my love. He's in the market for a new car, a new body, to continue his spiritual development on this plane. But things don't happen in spirit as they do down here love. There is no time lapse. It could take your dad fifty of our years before he finds the right car, or physical body, to come back into this plane. But he will, as we all will. In the meantime my love he's receiving help and guidance, he wasn't perfect my love, none of us are, but he's watching over you as he does every day. He loves you my darling.'

Zoe didn't know how to react and did what she always did when backed into a tight corner, blurted out obscenities.

'What a load o' bollocks! I'm sorry love but I haven't got a clue what you're on about, 'ens and bleedin' cars and...oh god, I can't handle this I really can't...'

'Just give me a minute love then I'll go and be on my way, I promise. You've been through it just lately haven't you my love?'

'Yeah, I have. How do you know?'

'And you've been on your own haven't you, no support, no shoulder to cry on? No one would listen to you would they my darling?'

This revelation made Zoe take note. *How does the silly old bugger know that? There's no way she could know that.* She now took what she was hearing a tad more seriously.

'Your dad knows this, my love. He's been watching over you and he's been at your side when you've been at your lowest point, and you've been in some dark places haven't you my love?' Zoe nodded. 'He's been coming to me now for weeks, almost every day. At first, I tried to ignore him, I'm getting too old for this. But his sheer persistence forced me to take action and he eventually guided me to you, today, just now in the shop. This is his message to you, my love. He's saying that he wants you to know that he's always watching over you, he's there for you, he loves you and he knows you love him. But there's something else my love.'

'Jesus, what now?' replied a bamboozled Zoe as she wiped away a solitary tear.

'Well, he said you're special love. Sorry, of course, all dads think their daughters' are special, but he's saying that you've got the gift, my love.'

'The gift? What bleedin' gift?'

'He's saying that you're like me love.' Just for a second Zoe imagined herself wearing a purple bowler hat and a scruffy oversized overcoat treading the streets of Seacroft. Her eyes narrowed before she realised what the old woman was saying.

'What? That I'm a medium?'

'Well, he's saying you have the gift love, and that you're one of the special ones, but that you don't know it yet. Everyone has the gift to a certain extent but there are those of us with more of an acute command of the gift, it just needs developing.' Zoe stood there and shrugged her shoulders. She had no words.

'Well what do you want me to do then,' she asked the woman who was now becoming tired and already looked older than she had done just a few minutes earlier.

'Well I can't guide you, my dear, I'm past that now, I'm in retirement so to speak, but one of my ex-students would be able to help.' She pulled out a card from her pocket and handed it to Zoe.

'Paula Jackson, she's a lovely girl, one of my best ever students. She runs spirit circles and a spirit school of excellence and she also organises sittings and does media work. She's got a nice little reputation going and even helps the police on occasions. And she's based in Leeds, over in Kirkstall. Just give her a ring and tell her Brenda told you to get in touch. I don't do it any more, and in any case, us old fashioned mediums still use the dark little sitting rooms with the tasselled lampshades and it would probably put you off. Paula works out of modern buildings and uses computers and all that stuff, she's dragged our industry into the modern age, my love, she'll look after you.'

Zoe looked at the card and then shoved it into her jeans pocket. She didn't know whether to thank the woman or just walk off. She stood there looking at her.

'And do you know what my love?'

'What?'

'I think that you've already been buzzed a couple of times, haven't you? You've been there, haven't you? All confused and no one to talk to. That's what your dad's saying to me. You've already been there, you just need to learn how to harness the power, my love, the gift from god. Oh, and your dad's saying... ' She stopped and smiled at Zoe. 'He's saying that you'll have to curb your language love, they don't like offensive language in this industry.' She laughed and held up her hands, 'It's your dad saying that love, not me, don't shoot the messenger.' Zoe stood and took in a large gulp of air. Shook her head. The bowler-hatted woman smiled at her.

'Well, that's me done m'dear. I've delivered the message and I have to tell you that I'm shattered. I don't know about your dad looking for a new car, I could do with one myself,' she laughed. 'Hopefully, he'll leave me in peace now. He's a good man love and he's with you all the time. I'll be off now, I'm going for a lay down, but please, please contact Paula, please love, for your own sake...and your dad's...tell her Brenda sent you. Well, thanks my love and goodbye.'

A shaken Zoe could only offer a rather weak thank you. The woman turned around and set off down the hill back towards the convenience store. Zoe stared at her. After half a dozen steps the woman turned around.

'Oh, and by the way Zoe, don't fret about the tomatoes, you were all so young, and there was no harm done my love.' She smiled before turning away once more. Zoe didn't react to that last statement. She turned towards home and bowed her head. *Jesus! What the fuck just happened to me? How the fuck did... '* She turned her head but the woman had disappeared from view. No sign of an oversized overcoat or a bobbing purple bowler hat. She stuck her hand into her pocket and pulled out the card. **Paula Jackson. Medium. Psychic development school.** On the card was also a landline number, a mobile number and an address in Kirkstall, on the other side of Leeds. She shook her head. *Silly old bleeder.*

*

She closed the door behind her and dropped the carrier bag at the foot of the stairs before trudging into the sitting room and throwing herself onto the sofa. She hadn't been there five seconds before the booming voice of her mother reverberated around the ground floor of the little semi-detached house. *Aw, fuck...what's up now?* Linda marched into the room holding the carrier bag aloft.

"Ey you, what's this doing on me 'all floor? Eh?'

Zoe sighed. 'Gawd, alright Mother, I'll put it away, just give us a minute, will you. I've just got in, I'm knackered.'

'Never mind knackered, there's a place for bloody dog food and it's not on me 'all floor—'

'Alright, alright,' she protested, 'give us it 'ere an' I'll put it in the bleedin' cupboard.' Linda declined to pass the bag but stood and glared at her daughter.

'And another thing,'

'Jesus! What now?'

'You can get in that garden and sort that dog shite out. I told you when ya came back, and I also told Slack-'ole, that there's no way I'm cleaning your dog's shite up...no way! The little bastard took a dump three times this morning an' it's all over the fuckin' place. Ya need to get the shitty-arsed little fucker seen to, it's not normal. So you can get out there and clean it up.'

'Just give me five minutes will you, and then I'll do it,' tutted Zoe.

'Well, as long as you know that's all... ' Linda turned away and headed for the kitchen, taking the bag with her. The conversation continued, forcing each to raise their voices.

'Well doesn't Tosh shit then?'

'Cats keep their shit to thesens,' replied Linda, 'an' anyroad he knows better than to shit in my garden, else he'll get the twattin' hosepipe right up his arse!'

'Huh, charming. So you're saying it's okay to send your own cat to shit in your neighbour's garden but you won't have it shitting in yours?'

'That's it, you got it girl. Spot on. Linda don't do shit and that includes cat shit, dog shit or any other type o' shit, so just make sure you get out there afore Sophia gets 'ome and get it cleared up.' Zoe sighed, she didn't have the energy to continue this thread of debate and after a moment of silence she again shouted through to the kitchen, but this time in a less contentious tone.

'Maaam?'

'What?' came the muted reply.

'Are you putting 'kettle on?'

'Oh aye, you just make yersen comfy, put yer feet up why don't you, and I'll run around like a little lapdog. I'm not cleaning no dog shite up though, I'll tell you that for nowt.'

'Oooh thanks, Mama,' replied Zoe as she snuggled down into the cushioned backrest of the sofa, 'you're a good un, you know you love me.'

'Hmm,' replied Linda under her breath as she filled the kettle, 'I might love ya but I'm not picking your dog shite up. I told yer both that when yer came back. Yer can clean it up yersens. Mucky little bastard!'

Linda went through the motions of preparing the tea whilst Zoe closed her eyes and took a moment to reflect on the bizarre engagement with the old woman halfway down Kentmere Avenue. She mused over the 'message', but wouldn't allow herself to apportion too much validity to the matter, after all, she thought, it's just a load of old bollocks. She slid her slim hand into her jeans pocket, the card was still there but she declined the temptation to pull it out and re-read the details.

As Linda rustled around the kitchen there was a knock at the door before it was flung open and a large, ruddy-faced woman stormed through into the room.

'It's on'y me,' she shouted.

'Oh, come on in love,' yelled Linda from the kitchen. The larger than life frame of Shelly popped her head around the sitting room door and nodded down to Zoe who in turn nodded back nonchalantly, unable to disguise the slight drop in her demeanour. Shelly beamed as she set eyes on her best friend's daughter revealing a mouth full of large irregular teeth.

'Ello love, you alright?'

'Yeah, I'm fine Shelly, you?'

'I'm good love, is this un looking after you?'

Linda appeared and interjected, answering the query herself. 'It's like 'aving a bleedin' five-year-old again, all I do is run around looking after 'er, but I'm telling you this lass,' she said pointing a finger at Zoe, 'there's no way I'm picking up that dog shit.'

'Jesus! Don't get her going again, she never shuts up about it!'

'Are you still going on about the friggin' dog shit,' bellowed Shelly, 'Just pick it up lass, what's up wi' ya... '

'You can talk ya silly old get, it's Dennis who cleans all the shite up from Winston, you'll never get yer hands mucky that's for sure—'

'It's only shite in't it Zoe, I don't know what the silly old bat's going on about.'

'I agree,' declared Zoe and before Linda could muscle in to defend her corner Shelly tactfully changed the direction of conversation.

'Anyhow, I ain't come round 'ere to talk shit wi' you two, I've come for me purple shawl, you've 'ad it now for three bleedin' weeks.'

'It's upstairs, washed an' dried, I don't know why you're getting all het up over a bit o' wool. It looks like a bloody 'orse blanket anyroad, never mind a bleedin' shawl,' replied Linda with a mischievous glint in her eye.

Shelly looked down at Zoe and shook her head in mock condemnation.   'Cheeky bitch.'

'Purple!' blurted out Zoe. Linda and Shelly stopped and looked down at her in silence.

'What?' said Linda.

'Purple what?' piped up Shelly.

'Purple, that old woman with the purple hat, the purple bowler hat and the mucky overcoat, walks all over Seacroft—'

'Oh you mean Barmy Brenda, that silly old bugger-...I haven't seen her for years,' replied Linda.'

'That's her, Brenda, that's the woman.'

'Well what about her?' quizzed Shelly.

'Why do you call her Barmy Brenda?'

'Cos she's bleedin' barmy that's why,' fired back Linda,' as mad as a box o' frogs that un.'

'Well she knew my name, she said she'd got a big Z, and then she said she was getting an en an—'

'Getting an en?' interjected Shelly, 'What is she, a friggin' chicken farmer?' She and Linda started chuckling.

'No...it was me Dad...'

'Well, your dad wan't a chicken farmer you dopey little bugger, he were a scaffolder—'

'Oh piss off Mam. She said she was getting an en for Ken! Me dad! She says she's a medium.'

'A medium what? A medium 'eadcase? More like a full-weight crackpot to me,' piped in Shelly as she fired an elbow towards Linda. They both cackled in unison.

'Well, she said she's a medium and that Dad'd been watching over me an' stuff. You two can think what you want but she collared me on 'way back from 'shop.'

'Well ignore the silly old bleeder, she's raving mad, she allus 'as been, she's been telling people that kinda stuff for years, palm reading, bleedin' tea leaves and crystal balls, why do you think she walks about with a friggin purple bowler 'at on?'

'Well I don't know,' frowned Zoe.

"Cos she's bleedin' barmy that's why, that's why they call her Barmy Brenda! Oh come on Shell, I can't do wi' this, bleedin' chicken farmers, messages from the friggin dead, come on let's 'ave a brew, she's as barmy as that Brenda is this one.' She ushered Shelly out of the living room and into the kitchen and before slamming the door closed she bellowed through to the lounge. 'And ya can get that shite cleared up before Sophia gets in lady!'

'Piss off, the pair of you,' muttered Zoe under her breath and then with a little more gusto she hollered through to the kitchen, 'Are you making some tea or what?'

'I'm boiling 'bleedin' kettle, give us a chance,' came the muted but shrill reply.

'Plug it in, it'll boil itself,' uttered Zoe, but this time well under the radar so as not to be picked up by her mother. She felt a little foolish. At twenty-six-years old she could stick up for herself but she was no match for the combined dry but crude wit of those two, not when they were in this mood. She felt she'd been taken in by the local weirdo and now she was being ridiculed by the 'Scissor Sisters', as she referred to them. She was just relieved she hadn't mentioned the bizarre analogy of the motor vehicles, that wouldn't have gone down well. She pulled out the card from her pocket and stared at it. **Paula Jackson. Medium. Psychic development school.** She shook her head and felt a tightening in her slim throat. *Why won't anyone ever listen to me? What's wrong with me? You can't do owt right you useless bitch.* She tore the card up and threw it towards the litter bin. *What the fuck is wrong with me?*

*

A white transit van pulled up outside the house on Kent-mere Avenue. Phil jumped out of the cab fuelled with enthusiasm for life even after a gruelling ten-hour shift. The self-employed electrician was looking forward to wolfing his tea down before meeting up with his mates to take in half a dozen pints or so and a Leeds United game. He was thickset, pot-bellied and housed, as was the current fashion, a full bushy beard. He bounced into the house and stretched his arms open to the first person he saw, his seven-year-old daughter, Sophia.

'Hiya sweetheart,' he said as he enveloped the little girl in a firm hug and kissed her on the forehead.

'Did you have a good day at school? and where's Princess?'

'He's in my bedroom, and Nana made Mum pick up all the pooh in the garden.'

'Did she now? Well, she does right 'cos your Mum shouldn't be poohing in the garden should she?'

'No Daddy, Princess's pooh, Nana made Mum pick it up with the plastic bag!'

'Eeeugh!' replied Phil as he curled a lip and pulled a face. 'Glad I didn't have to do it, maybe we'll have to get some little doggie nappies for Princess.' The little girl laughed as her father released his grip and left her to wander upstairs to pamper and fuss over the little cross-breed shit-machine. As Phil was just about to enter the front room Linda appeared from the kitchen.

'Ah, look what the dogs dragged in, old Slack-'ole.' Phil immediately broke out into a broad smile revealing a mouthful of gleaming white teeth.

'Ha-ha! It's me favourite mother-in-law, how are ya

me little darling?'

'Never mind how am I, your tea's in 'oven, where've you been?'

'Aw thanks love, I've been working, do I get a hug then or not?'

'No, do you bollocks, go in there and try putting a smile on laughing Lilly's face will ya, she's sulking 'cos she had to clean the dog shite up from round 'back. I'll bring yer tea through in a minute.' Linda disappeared back into the kitchen but couldn't disguise a smile at the sheer cheek of her 'son-in-law'.

'Diamond,' shouted Phil, still smiling as the kitchen door slammed closed in his face. He hesitated before slowly easing the living room door open and popping his head through.

'Hi, love. Everything ok?' Zoe sat on the armchair with her arms folded. She looked up and grunted. Her gaze then resumed close attention to the TV.

'You should'a left the dog crap for me love, I'd 'a sorted it out.'

'What with 'er on me case every five minutes,' she replied, nodding in the direction of the door. 'We need to get out o' this place, she's doing me bleedin' 'ead in.'

'It's only temporary love,' said Phil, as he entered the room and closed the door behind him. He crouched over to kiss her on the cheek. She offered neither resistance nor any reciprocal token of affection. He sat on the adjacent sofa and turned his head towards her.

'Did you go to your therapy today?' he asked. 'How did it go?'

'Shite. It's a waste o' time, I keep telling you. There's fuck all wrong wi' me but no-one'll listen will they?' Phil looked up towards the door.

'All right love, don't be swearing like that wi' Sophia in 'ouse.' Zoe shot him a fierce sideways glance just as the door opened. Linda entered with a plateful of steaming hot grub.

'Knee or table?' she asked.

'I'll have it here sweetheart,' replied Phil to which Linda plonked the plate onto his lap and handed him a knife and fork.

'Ta me darlin',' he replied, 'yer a good un.'

'Has she told you about the chicken farmer and 'bowler 'at woman?' fired in Linda half chuckling.

'No, what's that all about,' said Phil turning to face Zoe. She remained stony-faced and shot her mother a poison-laced dagger of a look.

'Why what's happened? said Phil, this time turning towards Linda.'

'I'll let her explain, you'll laugh your bollocks off at this one,' she chuckled as she left the room and scurried back into the kitchen. A silence fell onto the living room.

'Well?' said Phil after an uneasy silence.

'Well, what?'

'Well, what the hell's your mother on about?'

Resigned to offering an explanation Zoe sighed and shrugged her shoulders.

'It was that silly old bugger who goes round with the purple bowler hat on. She's been going around for years just walking up and down 'streets, all over 'place... '

'Ah, I know who you mean. That scruffy old woman? Is she still knocking about?' offered Phil, in between forkfuls of mash and lamb stew, 'she's been tramping about round 'ere since I were a lad.'

'That's her. Well, she was staring at me in 'shop on 'way back from Killingbeck and then she grabbed me on 'street on 'way back home.'

'What did she want? And what's it got to do wi' chicken farmers?'

'It's got nowt to do wi' chicken farmers, don't listen to me bleedin' mother. She said she were a medium and when she tried to work out me Dad's name she said she were getting an 'en' for Ken, that's all. It was just those two silly fuckers taking the piss.'

'Who?'

'Me mother and that silly bleedin' Shelley, you know what they're like when they get together. Anyway, she told me all sorts that I'd no idea how she could've known. They call her Barmy Brenda.' She looked up at Phil who by now had a broad grin on his face and was trying hard to suppress an outburst of laughter.

'I get it. Getting an 'en', chicken farmer. Funny.'

'You think it's funny then?'

'Well, you're not seriously gonna listen to her,' he replied, chuckling away to himself and shaking his head. 'Barmy Brenda, Medium and part-time chicken farmer!' He laughed and put his hand up to his mouth. Zoe fell silent and just stared at him full on. With his shoulders now shaking Phil averted his vision towards the television, attempting to recover some kind of composure.

After a while, Zoe looked away. 'You going out tonight aren't ya?' she asked.

'Aye love, just for a couple.'

'Good!'

CHAPTER 2

Zoe sat on the top deck of the No 56 bus which circumnavigated Crossgates, en-route from Seacroft to Leeds City Centre. She slouched on the back seat, holding court over the seven or eight passengers in front of her before shifting her gaze to the outside world, eye-balling the public at large buzzing in and around the busy Crossgates Shopping Area. The way they moved, the way they dressed, the way they carried themselves. She scanned the bingo-junkies queuing outside the Mecca Bingo seeking the thrill of a full house over a burger and a basket of chips. The mooching shopaholics as they hustled in and out of the Arndale Centre, heads down, contemplative. The Big Issue lady in her hi-vis overcoat, and cagey hoodies crawling around like busy woodlice. Older natives shuffling around at a more laboured pace, dragging their trusty wheeled shopping trolleys. Austhorpe Road thronged with motorists, buses and taxis with the intermittent pelican and zebra crossings causing consternation for the less relaxed motorists. However, Zoe's attention soon returned to her fellow top deck passengers, whom she meticulously dissected one by one. *She could do wi' losing a few pounds ... hmm ... you wanna cut down on the Big Macs love. Nice face though to be fair, lovely complexion ... a big lass but that friggin' coat's hideous, it does nowt for her ... could do better. An' them boots are like summat me Nana would've worn. Get your life sorted love.*

Zoe was on her way to meet Katie. Katie was a lifelong friend, the two had been born and bred together on the estate but had lost touch when Katie's family had upped sticks and moved to Ilkley when they were just sixteen. Whilst Zoe had stayed in Seacroft and left school, Katie had studied at Lancaster University earning a degree in Economics. Whilst Zoe had bummed about East Leeds getting pissed and drugged up with like-minded souls, Katie had knuckled down, forged ahead and focussed on a future. But that was then, and this was now. Nearly ten years on and Zoe was beginning to see the light as she searched for a new start, responsibilities towards Sophia being at the forefront of her thoughts. Life hadn't exactly gone according to plan for Katie either, but her current employment as a legal clerk to a Leeds firm of solicitors was steady with decent pay. It had been Linda who'd persuaded Zoe to seek out and make contact with Katie, whom she'd always regarded as a steadying influence on her wayward daughter. They'd been more like sisters than best friends and it had only been when Katie had moved away from Seacroft that Zoe had fallen in with those groups who'd stuck two fingers up to all that so-called 'respectable life' bollocks within mainstream society.

Plastered in make-up that one. What's wrong with her? Bet that jacket cost a few quid. Her gaze moved onto the next victim. *He looks a bit like uncle David. A bit thinner in 'face and a bit more hair ... No, actually he doesn't. Uncle David'd never come out looking as scruffy as that, he looks as though he's just finished a shift on 'bins, mucky old bugger. Sorry, Uncle D.* The bus slowed down and stopped outside the White Swan Hotel about halfway down the

A64 York Road, a busy trunk road leading directly into the centre of town. Zoe took a break from evaluating the integrity and correctness of the unsuspecting commuters and checked out the crumbling building. At one time the pub had rocked to live music and live sports events, especially at weekends. There had been outdoor seating and lush plantation, the place had been alive with the buzz and bustle of a thriving East Leeds pub. But not now. The inside was devoid of life. The now rotting garden furniture lay broken and vandalised outside. The once white-painted rendered facade now weathered, peeling and neglected. The bodged up roof was missing slates with the sapling of an oak tree rooted to the inside of a clogged up, rotting timber gutter. She wasn't sure whether or not the pub was still open but one thing she was certain about was that it reminded her of her time in East Moor Park. Though the building stood on the very fringes of the area she shuddered at the slightest thought of it.

Stood aside the pub was an immaculately maintained detached building. Pristine, white-painted render, immaculate new windows and doors, a perfect drip-dry roof with not a scrap of litter in sight. The cooperative funeral parlour was open, lit up and ready for business.

She turned her attention back to the inside of the bus as it slowly eased out of the lay-by and back onto the A64 into the city centre. A large woman puffed her way up the stairs and flopped onto the first available seat.

Jesus! She looks as though she's gonna collapse. She shook her head before moving on to the next. *He looks alright for his age. Well dressed, neat beard from what I can see. Looks to be able to handle himself as well. Nice bloke. Two kids, a lad and a lass...security guard in Leeds...Trinity Centre, yeah, I like him.* At the front end of the bus, a young girl perched silently on the edge of her seat. A stern-looking woman sat stock still on the row behind her, well wrapped up with an overcoat and thick woollen scarf. The blond-haired little girl leaned right up to the window, captivated by the outside world, silently holding onto the rail with a firm grip. The girl wore only a white dress but seemed unperturbed by the chilliness of the upstairs deck.

*

Katie was waiting having already secured a table in the far corner of the snug little Coffee shop on Albion Place. It was a cold and wet morning outside and the cosy little setting provided for a warm, inviting ambience. The two girls squealed in delight as they embraced and hugged each other. Once the kerfuffle of the reunion had died down and the cappuccinos ordered they stared one another in the face, each beaming across the coffee table.

'Well, look at you ya posh get,' said Zoe shaking her head, 'bloody overcoat, heels and chiffon scarf, you'd never guess you were a Seacroft lass.'

Katie laughed. 'Once a Seacroft lass...and anyway, you're looking rather glamorous yourself.'

'Glamorous? Me? Don't talk so round-shouldered ya silly twat!'

'You are,' she chuckled, 'I'm telling you, and after all you've been through, and your little daughter to look after, you should be proud of yersen.'

'Yeah, whatever,' replied Zoe dismissively. 'Anyway, you're looking better than me love, you always did... '

'No, you were always the good looking one and you still look fab...I'm telling you.'

'Not having it,' returned Zoe before they burst out laughing. It was a game they'd often played as youngsters where they'd big each other up but were unable to accept any personal compliment from the other. It was the first time in a long while that Zoe had felt this relaxed. She was comfortable in the presence of her old mucker, her non-judgmental old mucker, more so than in the company of her mother or even Phil. They spent the next hour catching up on the last ten years, how their fortunes had panned out, their experiences, highs and lows, warts an' all. Katie had been no angel, it turned out. She'd lived life to the full, experimenting with sex, drugs and alcohol during a fast and furious time at university and as Zoe lay her own soul bare, she now, for the first time, had an audience willing to listen. Katie felt sympathy towards her old friend. Even if she didn't understand, or even believe, some of the stuff that Zoe was reeling off, she would never betray her.

By the time the second round of coffee was served Zoe was jabbering on about her recent encounter with Barmy Brenda, whom as kids, they'd referred to as 'Bowler-Hat Woman'. Katie sat mesmerised as she listened to the bizarre tale. Her dark, shoulder-length hair pristine, her immaculate makeup, in the mind of Zoe, classy, not over the top, but just right and complimented by flawlessly manicured nails. She still held a Leeds accent but her life away from Seacroft had softened her tones, and rounded her hard vowels, though in the short time she'd now spent in the company of her old pal she'd already rediscovered some of the long lost estate jargon of her previous life. As they continued chatting Zoe couldn't help thinking as to how lucky she was to have Katie back in her life. She wondered as to how different her own desolate existence would have turned out had they'd kept in touch.

'God, I would've burnt up if she'd said that to me. Fancy, after all these years she remembered,' said Katie.

'Yeah, I know, I were gobsmacked meself, 'specially after all that crap over me Dad an' that. We were little bastards though.'

Katie bit her lip and frowned. 'If me mother knew half of what we'd got up to in those days she'd a killed me. It were your idea anyway, to throw the tomatoes at her—'

'Was it buggery, it were you ya nasty little bitch. It wa' me who found 'em an' it were you who came up with the idea of pelting her with 'em.'

Katie chuckled, 'Aye you're right, it was, little fuckers back in the day weren't we?'

'Aye, we were. Do you remember, there was me, you, Tanya Ramsden and Jamie Tomlinson? We all got a tomato each, I missed wi' mine.'

'Yeah, I think mine hit her, but someone knocked her bloody hat off, it must've been Jamie... '

'Who's now in the nick for dealing,' interjected Zoe.

'Poor woman, I feel sorry for her now.' Katie cupped her empty mug with both hands and bit her lip ruefully.

'Yeah, she seemed a nice old lass to be fair, a bit odd like...but we were such little shits in those days. What about the time we balanced that milk bottle on that old woman's 'andle an' knocked on her door. Poor old bugger daren't open it once she saw it through the glass. An' we just stood there waving and shaking us arses at her. Little bastards.'

'I know. And she must have been in her eighties, poor old bugger. God forgive us.' The conversation stopped whilst the two contemplated the heinous acts of devilment during their misspent youth on the estate.

'So have you contacted this medium yet then?' asked Katie, breaking the silence.

'Ooo no, I'm not bothering with all that shite,' replied Zoe, 'that lot taking the piss. I'm not having Phil and the bleedin' Scissor Sisters on me back, I can't do with it. Owt that lot can come up wi' to put me down they will. None of 'em believe me about East Moor Park, they still think I'm a lunatic.'

'Listen love, old Barmy Brenda, Bowler-Hat Woman, might not be so Barmy after all...'

'What, walking round 'streets with a purple bowler hat on?'

'What about all that stuff you say you experienced in that house in East Moor Park? She might be right, it might have summat to do with what she's saying to you, it might be all connected.'

'I dunno Katie, I just don't know. I'm all confused about everything. I don't know if it was just the sleep paralysis playing games in East Moor Park, or they might be right, it might 'ave been the drugs and drink...I just don't know, I'm all mixed up to be honest, even after being in the loony bin for all those weeks. When they carried me out of that cellar I had such an 'orrible, negative feeling, as though I'd been somewhere really evil, experienced summat I shun't a done. I cun't remember how or why I'd got down there in the first place, but I never, ever want to go through that again...ever...it was fuckin' 'orrible.'

'I know love, but from what you've told me, the two months you spent in hospital, in rehab, did nothing for you. Do you feel any different now than when you went in? Has anything changed?'

'Well no, but...'

'Well that avenue, putting you in hospital, or the loony bin as you call it, has done nothing to help has it? You probably needed the rest anyway, but nothing's been resolved if you still have these negative emotions and nightmares. So what have you got to lose then?' Silence fell on the little corner of the coffee shop. Zoe had no answer.

'I can't anyway, I tore the card up and binned it an' I'm not trudging around Seacroft tracking Barmy Brenda down.'

Katie tutted. You don't need a card you gormless get. We're in 2017, not 1970! What was the woman's name?'

'What woman?'

'The medium that Barmy Brenda told you to get in touch with!'

'Er, I dunno, I can't remember.'

"kin 'ell...well try and think. Listen if your Phil and the Scissor Sisters won't back you up, I will. I can pick you up, take you there and bring you back. I'll stay in the car, don't worry. Let's do it, c'mon, where's your sense of adventure, your fighting spirit, you're a Seacroft lass aren't ya? Now try and remember her name and I'll Google the details.'

'I'm trying to,' replied Zoe as she struggled to focus her attention, I just can't remember...hang on...I remember it being in Kirkstall 'cos the thought of the old stone Abbey reminded me o' 'cellar in East Moor Park.'

'Right then, Spirit Circle in Kirkstall it is,' replied Katie as she entered the details into her phone and then pressed search. 'There's a few here,' she said, 'what about Steve Connell - spirit medium? No, you said it was a woman din't you?'

'Yeah, definitely a woman, with just an ordinary name, nowt fancy,'

'Mystic Marlene: Astrology; Tarot cards?'

'No, it weren't her,' chuckled Zoe.

Kirkstall and Meanwood Spiritualist Church? Paula Jackson, Medium, Psychic development School?'

'That's it!' Pronounced Zoe, 'that's her, Paula Jackson, is she in Kirkstall?'

'Yep, this is her, all the details look, phone number, e-mail and website. Now, are you gonna get in touch with her or not?'

'Well, just let me think about it. I dunno if it might make things worse, especially if that lot find out, me Mam and Phil that is. Forward me the link and let me mull it over.'

'Hmm okay love, I don't want to pressurise you into anything you don't want to do, but I'll support you whichever way you go. I think it's worth your while just looking into it, just to see what's what. I'll be there, don't worry.' Katie slid her hands over the table and placed them onto Zoe's. But Zoe was worried. It was all too much too soon for her, but at least she now had someone on her side, someone she could rely on. Katie, her best ever.

The two friends took in Kirkgate Market and the swanky John Lewis and Victoria Quarter shopping centres before departing on their separate ways. Declining the offer of a lift from Katie, Zoe had insisted on getting the 56 home, even though she'd complained that it had stank of piss on the inward journey. She needed some space, some time to think. She got a feeling that things were coming to a head. *Should I stick or should I fucking twist? Is it now or never?*

The top deck of the number 56 bus stank of piss.

The deck was half full but this time there was no in-depth scrutiny of those around her. This time all Zoe could scrutinise was her inner self-doubt, her inner thoughts and her inner soul.

As she trudged down Kentmere Avenue towards home she looked over her shoulder. There was no Barmy Brenda. In a way, Zoe wished she was able to talk to her, go over the stuff she'd mentioned during their encounter. But she was nowhere to be seen, no purple bowler hat bobbing up and down the streets of Seacroft. Her sanity was beginning to dip, just as it had done during her time in East Moor Park, at 10 Reginald Street, all those months ago.

*

Zoe lounged on the sofa staring at a blank TV screen, pensive, deep in thought. In the kitchen, Linda and Shelley cussed and belly-laughed over a brew and a platter of cupcakes. Sophia entertained herself on her Playstation, with Princess for company in the small box-bedroom upstairs. The day's accumulations of dog shit had been dutifully collected, bagged and assigned directly to the outside trash bin. Phil was out. Phil was in the pub with his mates. Phil was always in the pub with his mates. Zoe looked around the room. Was her Dad there? Was he with her now? Was he watching over her like Bowler-Hat Woman had said he was? She reflected. She reflected on the last year, the last month and she reflected on the last few days culminating in her meeting with Katie. She wasn't getting any vibes of her Dad being present, in any form. She was alone. She continued to reflect. Her reflections stopped her dead. The bus. The journey down to town. The characters she derided, dissected. The bloke. The one with the beard, the strong-looking one. He'd got two kids, she was sure of that. A lad and a lass...a security guard at Trinity. Where the fuck did that come from? She'd no idea, she didn't know the bloke, as far as she could work out she'd never laid eyes on him before, but she knew. She just knew. How she knew, she didn't know. Why she knew, she didn't know. But she knew. One hundred per cent. She looked around the room wide-eyed and bit her lip. *Barmy bleedin' Brenda.*

A short explanatory email to Paula Jackson, Medium, was duly despatched. Zoe figured she'd nothing to lose even though, perhaps, not much to gain.

*

It had been just a couple of days after the e-mail to Paula Jackson that Zoe had received a reply, and now, barely a week later, she sat riding in the passenger seat of Katie's smart electric-blue, mini-convertible. They were on their way to the Friday evening, open spirit circle at the Kirkstall and Meanwood Spiritualist Church. As she gnawed away at her fingernails she wished she'd never agreed to attend but Katie was taking no shit, constantly reassuring Zoe that there was nothing to worry about. If she didn't like it she needn't go again, she'd nothing to lose. Even so, as they drove past the daunting edifice of the dark satanic ruins of Kirkstall Abbey, Zoe's imagination conjured up visions of black-hooded monks in deep chambers, with hollowed-out eye sockets and blood-red crosses and dark cellars in East Moor Park. She didn't like it.

'Fuck it, Katie, I'm not going, pull up...turn back...I don't wanna go.'

'Oh calm down you silly bitch, we're nearly there. Just relax, what's the worst that can happen? A big ghost comes out of the bleedin' cupboard and scares you or summat? What's up with ya? Pull yersen together girl.'

Katie didn't pull up or turn round, but calmly continued towards the Kirkstall and Meanwood Spiritualist Church, just a mile or so further down from the Abbey. Zoe clasped her hands together and leant back into the seat of the car. She inhaled large chunks of air as she attempted to calm herself, but her breathing remained tense, she just couldn't relax, it wasn't her thing to be laid back and chilled. She went through the motions of acting relaxed but her head raged and her internal combustion system chugged away with a slow debilitating disquiet.

The car pulled into the car park with Katie securing a secluded parking spot in the far corner. She switched off the ignition and turned to face Zoe.

'Now then you. Come on, where's your backbone eh? Where's that old Seacroft spirit eh? You never used to back down did you?' Zoe sat still and remained silent. 'Don't forget it's your Dad who's set all this up.'

Zoe shrugged. 'Yeah, right...me Dad...who's been dead five years, still pulling the strings.' But Katie was right about Zoe, she never backed down from anything, but then again, this was something she'd never been faced with before. After a short cycle of strict self-catechization, she eventually decided that she would go into the sitting, and she'd go alone. She didn't need the company of her mate, even though the offer had been made. She owed it to herself and no one else.

'Right, here goes,' she said as she unbuckled the seatbelt, 'wish me luck.'

'Go on girl, you can do it, just be yourself,' replied Katie with a mischievous grin and a glint in her eye. 'Oh and Zoe?' she added as Zoe got out of the car.

'What?'

'Give my regards to your Dad will ya?' Katie started to chuckle.

'Fuck off bitch,' fired back a straight-laced Zoe as she slammed the door closed and walked reluctantly towards the entrance of the tile-roofed, single-storey building. The modern, brick-built complex served several small enterprises and looked more like a community centre than a church or, as Zoe had visualised it, like something out of a Scooby-Doo cartoon. Katie settled back and whipped out her iPhone. She prepared herself for a wait of about an hour, content that she was doing the right thing, helping to steer her old mate in the right direction.

It was less than thirty minutes later that a flustered Zoe flew out of the building and stormed towards the car. Jumping into the front passenger seat she slammed the door closed.

'Come on,' she fired, 'let's get going I'm not coming 'ere again ... '

'Calm down love, what's happened?'

'Fucking idiots!'

'What's happened?' repeated Katie.

'Just come on, let's go, get me out of 'ere.'

'Calm down Zoe love, take deep breaths...now, tell me...what 'appened?'

'It's not my scene—'

'What do ya mean it's not your scene?'

'They started fucking singing!' Katie looked on in astonishment and then started laughing.

'Singing? I thought it was a spirit circle, not a twatting X-Factor audition!' shrilled Katie who couldn't help herself and became hysterical, slapping the palm of her hand onto the steering wheel.

'Oh fuck off you... '

'What songs were they singing? I hope you joined in?'

'Did I fuckers like! They were fuckin' hymns, like the stuff we sang at school. Fuckin' hymns! I'm not singing hymns wi' a group o' strangers. At first, everyone seemed nice but then we all had to sit in a circle and I had to stand up and introduce meself. I felt a right twat! Then we had to say some prayers or summat and meditate whilst we 'eld hands. I'm sure the Pervy old bastard next to me was getting hissen off squeezing me fingers an' then there was a geeky fucker wearing glasses sitting right opposite. I opened my eyes and caught him staring at me, fucking pervert. It's not my scene Katie. An' then the fuckin' singing, I thought, what the fuck, I need to get out of 'ere.'

'Well, what did you think it were gonna be like love? They were never gonna sit in a circle and tell mucky jokes were they, or pass the bloody weed around. It's a spiritualist centre Zoe, it's a religion in't it, they're bound to do stuff like that, if you stop and think about it...and anyway there's nowt wrong with a bit o' singing... '

'Bollocks to that, you go in and sing with 'em if you want but I'm not, fuck it. Come on, just get me out of 'ere, take me home.'

Katie sighed and shook her head. 'Listen, just chill out a bit, why don't we go into town for a drink? Let us hair down, you're all stressed out.'

'Huh, no chance o' that wi' me Mother. She's warned us about getting pissed up and all that.'

'Aww come on. Didn't you say your Phil was always out with his mates? Well, it's only fair that you get out for a bit, come on, you'll shrivel up like a bleedin' prune if you carry on like this. Ring her up and tell her you're wi' me, she'll be fine with that, and that we're just nipping into town for a couple, she'll be good.'

Zoe dithered and squirmed in her seat. 'I dunno...she said if I ever took another drug she'd disown me ... for good. She said she wouldn't have any alcohol in 'ouse...but...I suppose she never said owt about me going out for one.'

'There y'are then. Give her a call and we'll go for a drink.'

'Well, what about your car?'

'Never mind the car. I'll park it up and get me Dad to drop me off for it tomorra. Now stop making excuses, get your Mother rang up. Let's just do it...come on. Put this spirit circle thing on the back burner for now and we'll look at it later. I'll sort you out you bitch if it's the last thing I do, I'm not letting you throw away this 'gift' that Bowler-Hat Woman says you've got, but for now let's just forget about it and swan off down to town.'

The persuasive manner of her friend was too much for Zoe to resist. She begrudgingly made the call and was surprised at how well her mother had taken it. She'd agreed to see to Sophia and as much as demanded that she enjoyed herself with Katie. The scene was set, and as Katie serenaded *All Things Bright and Beautiful* the two friends set off into the dark, towards the bright lights and the buzz of the vibrant city centre. Zoe fired a middle fingered salute in return.

*

Lower Briggate was heaving. Although bang in the centre of the city's gay quarter, such was the vibe of the area that it was a honey pot to all walks of society out to enjoy the start of the weekend. Zoe and Katie found themselves in Queens Court, a delightful little cobbled Georgian courtyard that served as an outdoor area to three bars. To be fair, the courtyard was only delightful during the daytime when one could enjoy a range of continental coffees and exquisite cakes amidst the picturesque, historical courtyard, festooned with luxurious planters and hanging baskets. But this was a Friday evening. Delightful was set aside and replaced with booming as the place throbbed and pulsated to the overwhelming throng of constant chat and babble. The three bars, one on either side of the courtyard and the other situated at the head, were all packed, inside and out, with each blasting out their playlists which hybridized the cumulative buzz and reverberated around the ancient brick walls. Here the girls sported outrageous figure-hugging outfits with short hemlines and slender stilettos. Some of the boys wore even shorter mini-skirts and even higher stilettos. There was young and old, flamboyant and drab, straight and gay, almost every thread of society was represented in the thriving little courtyard, united, standing side by side enjoying the nightlife of the bustling northern city on this crisp Spring evening.

As the consumption of cocktails took on a steady pace it wasn't long before the girls loosened up and found themselves chatting to anyone who would listen. Zoe's head began to lighten, her sour demeanour softened and she found herself smiling and gently rocking to the pulsating music. She wouldn't let herself go just yet. That would only happen when her head began to fizz, crackle and pop, but she was on her way. She was happy, the first time for a long while. She felt a little underdressed in jeans, trainers and crop jacket but she'd assumed her evening would be spent at the spiritualist centre. Katie was dressed more suitable for a night on the town and the thought passed that she'd planned all along for them to descend into the city centre. But the idea was quickly despatched, assigned to her negative bad-mindedness, and the alcohol ensured she didn't dwell on it. As she looked around the courtyard she found many others who were similarly casually dressed. *I wonder if all these fuckers have been to a spirit circle tonight* she mused before Katie popped up from the bar with a tall, fruit infested cocktail. She shoved it into Zoe's face.

"Ere y'are, get that down you?' she declared.

'Fuck me, how much did that cost,' replied Zoe taking in the straw, sipping the strong concoction and wincing immediately.'

'Nowt.'

'What d'ya mean nowt?'

'What I said, nowt.' Katie raised her eyebrows and fired a glance towards a group of about six or seven lads at the other side of the courtyard. 'I think you might know one of 'em,' she continued.

'Eh? Who?' asked Zoe as she squinted over. Her heart dropped a beat as two of the fellas immediately started waving at her.

'Oh fuck, what are they doing 'ere,' she replied as she meekly waved back, devoid of emotion. 'How the hell do you know Phil, you've never met him?'

'Well I have now, but it's his little mate I know from school, remember Andy Wilson? Did you know 'im? He was a couple of years above us and I don't think he's grown an inch since those days.' Katie laughed. 'In any case, he got the drinks in so good on 'im.'

'Jesus! Do I know 'im? The 'orrible little twat,' replied Zoe, 'I dunno why Phil knocks about with 'im, he's a bad influence.'

'Oh c'mon, if he wants to buy us drinks then let him, and your Phil seems a really nice guy, fell on your feet there gal,' she winked.

Zoe stood silent, sipping the drink, careful to choose her response. She ended up not responding at all and looked away. Katie sensed the tension creeping back into the situation and attempted to guide the conversation down a different alley. Again Zoe ignored her.

'You din't tell 'em about tonight did ya? At the spirit circle thing, you din't did you?'

'Course I didn't you silly cow, now come on, get that down ya, there's more where that came from.' She ushered her vulnerable friend further away and out of the line of vision of Phil and his pals. The task of getting her old mucker back on the straight and narrow was, she thought, possibly a stiffer test than she'd anticipated.

The girls continued drinking with the boozy alcohol slowly taking effect. The music blared on and on with Zoe almost forgetting that Phil was in the same vicinity just a few yards away around the corner. It was whilst Katie was at the ladies that she felt a slight tugging on her jacket from behind. She turned around and then looked down. It was Andy, Phil's little sidekick. Andy was about five-foot-three inches tall and not far off the same dimension in width. He wore a plain t-shirt which was clearly stained, combat knee-length shorts and Adidas Samba trainers with white socks. His balding head was shaved and he was mostly covered in tattoos including arms, legs and neck. His round head, sporting an unkempt and bushy ginger beard was reddened and sweaty, his glazed eyes, under thick heavy eyelids, struggled to focus.

'Ey up doll,' he slurred, 'it's me, ya favourite

brickie.'

Zoe looked down at him. *Oh fuck.* She looked over his shoulder towards the toilet area. *Where the fuck's she gone now.* 'Hmm, you alright then? Where's Phil?'

Andy fidgeted nervously. He put his arm around her and pulled her closer.

'Yer what?' he fired.

'I said where's Phil?' *Ya deaf little pratt.*

'Ah, Phil...he's just gone for a pie an' mash...'

'A what?' replied Zoe quizzically.

'A pie and mash...a slash...'

Zoe looked down at the repulsive little character, none the wiser.

'A slash,' he repeated, 'a piss...'e's gone for a piss!'

She stared at him and shook her head. 'I bet that silver tongue of yours gets you loads of women dun't it? You still on your own are ya?'

Andy either didn't hear or couldn't comprehend the exchange and so he stood there nodding his head grinning.

'That lass you're wi',' he drawled, 'she's alright in't she? I remembered 'er face from school but din't remember 'er name...but she remembered me. She's alright in't she? What's 'er name again?' he asked, again fidgeting like an imbecilic psychopath.

'Annie,' replied Zoe.

'That's it, Annie...why don't we go for a curry? Me, you, Phil and Annie, the four of us? She's alright is Annie in't she?'

Zoe pulled her head away and looked around in exasperation. *Fuck me! Where the fuck's she and where's, Phil?* 'She' appeared from behind Andy.

'Ask 'er yourself, she's 'ere,' splurted out a relieved

Zoe. She took a step back. *You deal with the little shit.*

'Ey up Annie love, yer fancy a curry after?'

'It's bloody Katie,' she smiled, 'and I thought you were getting us a drink?'

Andy looked confused. 'I got ya one earlier,' he slurred.

'Well we're not going for a curry sober are we Zoe?'

'Right, if you want one doll, you'll get one...an'... ' He turned and pointed to Zoe.

'Zoe,' fired in Katie. 'She's Zoe and I'm Katie, ok?'

'Right, got it.' Andy stood in front of the pair and swayed. 'Zoe...and...Katie,' he said pointing to them. 'Right, drinks, same as y'ad before, leave it to me...I'll be back.' He turned his back on them and boozily barged his way towards the bar. Katie had him in the palm of her hand. She smiled as she turned towards Zoe.

'For fucks sake Katie, don't be encouraging him, I can't stand the little fucker, he's got that nervous twitch or summat, he gives me the fuckin' creeps.'

'Oh don't be worrying, you don't think I'd let anyone like him anywhere near me do ya? If he wants to buy us a couple o' drinks then let him. He can buy me a curry as well if he wants,' she chuckled.

Zoe tutted and shook her head. She scanned the courtyard but couldn't see any sign of Phil. 'Where the bleedin' hell's Phil?' she muttered.

'I've just seen him, he said he'll be over shortly so stop worrying. I'll handle Fidget the midget. Anyway, here, I've got summat for us.'

'What is it?'

'Here, open your hand.' Zoe opened her hand and Katie placed a small white pill into her palm.

'What is it?' repeated Zoe.

Katie popped her own pill into her mouth and yanked her head back, necking it down with the remainder of her drink. 'It's just a little something to help us chill out that's all, go on, get it down you.'

'Where d'ya get it from?'

'Never mind that, it's not gonna bleedin' harm you is it? Come on, just get it necked.'

Zoe looked at the pill and then looked Katie straight in the eye.

'I told you I wasn't taking owt like this, I put all that behind me, Katie. Me mother'll kill me. I don't want it, 'ere, take it back, I'm not 'aving it. I can't believe... '

'Oh alright then, don't take it, I'm not forcing you. Here give us it back, I'll save it for later.' Zoe welled up and clenched the pill in her hand. She turned away. The whole situation suddenly hit her in the face. The disastrous encounter at the spirit circle, the booze, the throng of the crowd, the pulsating music, Fidget the bastard midget. *Fuck it. Nowt's gonna change in my life. Go for it, why not? Everyone else does, why am I any different? Fuck the spirit circle, fuck Phil and his little prick of a mate ... and fuck me Mother. And if you're watching over me now Dad...fuck you!* She threw the pill down her throat and washed it down with the remnants of her cocktail. She sniffed and as she turned around to face Katie she wiped the tear from her eye.

'I've taken it.'

'I know you have you, silly bugger.' Katie reached over and pulled her friend towards her, hugging and kissing her on the forehead. 'Now come on, let's get smashed, it's only early.' Zoe complied, and in the fullness of time she did as instructed and chilled out. The music blurred into a fusion of heavy bass to an upbeat constant Latino beat. The tones and voices of those around her gradually smothered her soul as they merged into a constant buzzing drawl, dropping on her like an oversized greatcoat of obscurity. Her head began to fizz...it popped...and it crackled.

*

It was 11.30 am when she lifted her head. Phil was somewhere in Yorkshire earning a crust before his afternoon's entertainment at Leeds United's Elland Road football ground. This would usually entail a heavy and bawdy boozing session in town afterwards with his posse of mates, headed by the squat, pugnacious Andy. It was the first thing she realised, once her brain had booted up, that she wouldn't be seeing Phil again until the following morning. She sat up and winced as the blood pressure to her head registered a large throbbing sensation. Though she couldn't remember getting back home to Seacroft, here she was, sat upright in the middle bedroom of her mothers home. The essence of memory, agonisingly vague, percolated to the surface. Queens Court...Katie...Phil and his little mate...music...food, Indian food...throwing up. She couldn't pinpoint any particular part of the night, it was just a hazy blur but she got the familiar, general picture. A negative sentiment stuck in her throat as she rubbed her face with both hands.

'Hi Mum, you've been asleep all morning,' announced Sophia as she bounded into the room followed by Princess. The seven-year-old leaned over to embrace her mother and received a dry peck on the cheek as Princess jumped up on the bed and attempted to gatecrash the little family love-in.

'Get the bleedin' dog off the bed Sophia, go on piss of yer little bleeder,' she growled as she attempted to shove him away.

'Mum! He only wants to play.'

'Well, I'm not in the playing mood so gerrim away from me will ya?'

'Nana wants to know if you're coming to Cross-gates with us, she said she's taking me to the Gelato for some ice cream.'

'No love, I'm not feeling well. You go with Nana, I'll stay here with Jimmy.'

'You mean Princess Mum?'

'Oh, Sophia love just stop wittering will you? Be a good girl and go and get me a glass of water?'

'Nana said she isn't happy about you coming home drunk and she said there's some dog shit in the garden and you've got to pick it up because she isn't.'

Zoe shook her head. Under normal circumstances, if Sophia repeated any of the language she'd heard from Linda, she'd challenge both and make her feelings known. On this occasion, she didn't have the stomach for it.

'Well just tell Nana to keep her bleedin' nose out o' my business will ya and go get me some water please.'

'Ok Mum,' replied the little girl as she bounced out of the bedroom and bounded down the stairs, with the ex-citable, yapping Princess right behind her.

'Nana! Mum said you've to keep your bleedin' nose out of her business,' she pronounced as she reached the bottom.

Zoe dropped her head into her hands. She was de-void of fight. She heard her Mother mumble an ominous come back but she couldn't be bothered entering into a catfight. 'Aw fuck off,' she muttered throwing a slack-wristed two-fingered salute. It was as she dropped her head once more that she remembered. It flooded back to her, crystal clear. The humiliation, the feeling of utter contempt, the old bloke holding her hand, the staring geek. The encounter at the Spiritualist Centre was smack, bang right in front of her, clear as a bell. Her heart sank even further as the negative thoughts and the physical hangover dragged her down. She looked around. She needed a drink, an alcoholic drink. She couldn't have one. She wanted a fix but there was nothing in this house that would give her one. She wanted Phil, but he wasn't there. She had her mother, but she didn't want her. She wanted her Dad.

CHAPTER 3

It was now the beginning of May and the country was enjoying a spell of warm settled weather. Spring was at its glorious optimum as the days slowly chugged through the process of morphing into early summer. On the Seacroft estate, the apple blossom dripped opulently in pastel pinks and delicate whites and the dynamic rhododendrons burst with spectacular clusters of vibrant blooms and lush foliage. Critters in their millions buzzed and crawled and fizzed and skittered, energised by the warming temperatures and the collective air of optimism. Birds of all sizes whirled and darted around the skies searching out and gathering grubs and insects in their ceaseless endeavours to feed a whole population of ravenous nest-bound and needy chicklets. The humans of Seacroft were no less engaged, quietly going about their business, busy with life and saddled with daily chores, contented. Open windows allowed the warm, fresh spring air inside to circulate and freshen up the living quarters. In the opposite direction, jaunty musical vibes from local FM radio resonated beyond the confines of the house whilst the delicious aromas from eggs, bacon and coffee filtered through into the same outdoor space. Unashamed family arguments played out in public amidst cultural, blunt language as animated dogs barked and yelped and idle cats curled up and slept. Washing flapped and struggled to break free from the washing lines as the hard-working Croftites lugged themselves and their shopping bags to and from the local supermarkets. Hoodies on undersized bicycles hung around the estate scheming and goading whilst dodgy tradesmen trolled the streets looking for a quick illicit dollar. It was business as usual in Seacroft.

'Come on love, get a move on, we're gonna be late,' chided Phil, looking down at his watch and leaning on the half-opened sitting-room door.

'Aww pissin' shurrup will you,' replied Zoe sharply as she rummaged through her handbag in search of lipstick. 'I'll be five minutes...you'll have to wait.'

Princess bounded into the room and confronted Tosh who was nestled comfortably next to Zoe on the sofa. The large ginger moggie remained unmoved as the little Yorkie yapped and barked attempting to extract a reaction. Tosh was having none of it. He knew that all he had to do was as much as raise a paw and the little canine would be off with his little tail between his little legs. He sat tight, not having the inclination to move. He closed his eyes.

'Piss off you, ya little bleeder!' fired Zoe.

'Well we're supposed to be meeting the agent in twenny minutes and we've to get there yet, it'll take us half an hour with the bloody traffic.'

'Oh stop going on will ya? You're as bad as me mother,' she replied just as Linda barged into the room forcing her way past Phil.

'Who's as bad as what?' she demanded.

'Him, always moaning, just like you.'

'Just come on now you two, get a move on, you're supposed to be there in ten minutes, aren't ya?' said Linda.' She bent down to waft Princess out of the room.

'Go on ya little shit machine ya nowt else, get out!' The yelping Yorkie scurried past her and into the kitchen.

'I'm sick o' the sight o' you two. I had me house to meself afore you came back, I could come and go as I pleased, just me and the bleedin' cat. I wanna see the back of the pair of ye. Our Sophia's no problem, but you two...'

Zoe had heard enough, she slammed her bag closed. 'C'mon, let's get off.' She shot up and proceeded to march past her mother and towards the front door.

'Aye, go on,' returned Linda, 'take your bloody hook, the pair of ya. An' don't be coming back here tonight saying you an't seen owt you like.' By now Zoe was halfway down the garden path and it was she who now goaded her partner into quickening his pace.

'Come on,' she yelled, 'we're gonna be late.' Phil took heed and stepped past his mother-in-law.

'What we having for tea tonight then, old blue eyes?' he asked with an impish grin on his bushy-bearded face.

'Pigs arse and cabbage! Now go on, piss off and get gone.'

Phil took a step back towards her and offered a cheek. 'Do I get a kiss then?'

'Go to Hell,' replied Linda as she yanked her head away from his and crinkled up her nose. 'Yer big ugly get, go on, just make sure you find summat you like, and tell Laughing Lilly out there to put a smile on her face...afore it cracks.' She bundled him out of the door and slammed it closed behind him.

*

Stuck in heavy traffic on the busy Easterly Road Phil looked down at his iPhone. 'Hopefully, she might be late as well,' he said, 'I hate being late for owt.'

Zoe remained quiet. Since she'd been discharged from hospital she was prone to withdrawing into her bubble and immersing herself deep in thought. These dark bouts hadn't gone unnoticed and had eventually become a matter of concern to Phil. He'd been keeping a quiet eye on the situation.

'You alright love?'

'Yep,' she replied curtly.

'What you thinking?'

'Nowt.' After a slight pause she then took a deep sigh. 'Everything. Me 'ead's all over the bleedin' place, there's nowt seems to make sense. I've been getting really bad 'eadaches lately...and buzzing...inside me 'ead. Thinking a lot, 'specially about me dad.' She fell silent once again.

'What? ...d'ya miss him?'

'Well it's not that, I do miss him yeah, o' course I do, but it's...it's...since that Barmy Brenda said he were watching over me he seems to be popping up inside me 'ead all the frigging time. As if he actually is looking over me, watching out for me. It's as if he's trying to relate summat, but I can't work out what. Does that make sense?' She looked up at Phil.

Phil hesitated. He knew that if he said aloud his real thoughts on the matter then she would undoubtedly kick-off. His reply, to start with, was careful and measured..

'Hmmm, well maybe he is love...but, at the same time maybe you should be discussing this with the doctors before it gets out of hand.'

'And what do you think the doctor might do then?' replied Zoe. 'Give me some more tablets? Increase my medication? Is that it?'

'Well love, that Barmy Brenda woman is renowned for having a screw loose in't she, she's well known for it. And buzzing in your head? And...your dad?' He frowned and looked at her. 'Come on love, that not right is it? You need to see 'doctors, they'll sort it out before it gets out of hand again. Stop fighting against it, stop resisting. When's your next therapy?'

Zoe turned away and didn't respond. She shouldn't have expected anything else from Phil. *Fucking thick-'eaded twat, just keep driving ...moron.*

They were en route to an arranged meeting in Armley with an estate agent to view three properties. After the disastrous episode in East Moor Park when Phil had bought a back-to-back at auction, without the knowledge of Zoe, she'd insisted that on this occasion she'd be an integral part of any decision-making process. Last time they'd been lucky to re-sell the property at the auction market and get most, if not all, the purchase price back. However, the expense and hard work that Phil had put in when renovating the property had not been re-covered, to the express benefit of the new owners. But Phil was still insistent on buying low-cost property, the aim to realise an instant profit by renovation and, wher-ever possible, without the use of a mortgage. East Moor Park was out of the question so he'd explored the area of Armley, with its infamous Victorian Gaol, as an area rich in pickings for low-cost properties which were ripe for 'doing up'.

They pulled up outside 62 Andover Street.

'I thought I said we weren't buying another back-to-back,' said Zoe.

'It's not a back-to-back love, it's a through terrace, it's got a little garden at the back for Sophia.'

'If it's got a cellar then it's out,' fired back Zoe, 'I don't know why we can't just get one near me mother's in Seacroft or Whinmoor... '

'Cos they're too dear love. Look stop bloody moaning will you, we're just looking that's all. She's gonna show us another two after this so let's just play us cards close an' 'ave a look eh?'

Zoe muttered as she undid her seatbelt and climbed out of the Transit van. 'Don't know why we can't bleedin' rent us own place, everyone else does.'

'Cos I'm not renting when we can buy, that's why. I'm not putting my money into some landlords bank account, I've told you that before,' he said as he jumped out of the van and slammed the door closed.

'Oh, so it's your money now is it,' mithered Zoe under her breath, 'wondered how long it'd be before you brought that up.'

'What?'

'Oh just shut it and come on,' she replied flashing a swiping glance at her equally perturbed partner.

They approached the entrance to the property. The door was already opened so they both entered. A smartly dressed woman of mid-twenties in age walked from the rear of a small corridor to greet them. She had brushed back dark hair, soft brown eyes and wore smart designer glasses.

'Hi,' said Phil as he held out his hand. 'Is it Jennifer?'

'Ah, good morning Mr Cooper,' replied the agent shaking Phil's hand. 'I'm sorry, Jenny couldn't make it, I'm Debbie, Debbie Richards. She sends her apologies but something cropped up at the last minute and she asked me to show you around the properties. I hope that's ok. Hello, and is it Mrs Cooper?' she asked turning to offer her hand to Zoe.

'Yeah, no problem,' said Phil.

'Er, hello,' replied Zoe. 'No, it's Zoe, we're not married.' She looked Debbie Richards straight in the eye and as their hands met she immediately experienced a mild buzzing sensation inside her head. There was just a slight standoff as both eyed each other up.

'Do I know you?' asked Zoe as she released her grip on the handshake. Debbie looked again.

'I don't think so,' she replied. 'But then again I was brought up all over the place so...who knows? we might have bumped into each other at some stage.'

'I'm from Seacroft,' pressed Zoe, 'did you go to Seacroft Park High?'

'No.'

'What about Maple Hill Middle?'

'Er, no,' replied Debbie, now becoming a little uncomfortable at the cross-examination. 'No, I lived all over the place as a kid. Middleton, Belle Isle, Cookridge, Horsforth, but never over at Seacroft. I was fostered, so I never stayed in the same place for long before they moved me on,' she said, offering a polite smile but unable to hide the fact that her upbringing hadn't been such a great experience.

'Oh, I'm sorry.'

'Ha! No, it's absolutely fine, no problem.' Turning to Phil she handed him a bunch of brochures bound in a neat and glossy folder and then ushered the pair into a bright and airy front sitting room. She commenced her sales pitch which was all but lost on Zoe. She was spellbound by the woman. There was something about her. The buzzing in her head continued, it made her feel dizzy and weak. She followed Phil and Debbie Richards around the property but the highly-polished spiel fell on deaf ears. She was mesmerised and by the end of the viewing, she'd developed another headache.

'What do you think love?' asked Phil as they finished the tour and looked out of the back door onto the 'garden', which turned out to be just a small concrete yard with an old timber bench stuck in the corner.

'Eh?'

'The house, what do you think of it? Do you like it?'

She had to think on her toes. 'Er, no, not really,' she said. 'It's not what I was thinking of.' She looked up at Debbie.

'No problem guys, don't worry. Just have a chat about it and we've still another couple for you to look at,' replied the estate agent, maintaining a gentle and professional smile. 'You can either follow me in the car or we can meet up at the next one in Granger Street in, let's say half an hour.'

'Yeah, we'll meet you there Debbie,' replied Phil, 'It'll give us a chance to have a drive around the area first, give us a feel for it.'

'Okay, see you there in half an hour,' she replied.

Phil and Zoe left Debbie locking up the property as they climbed back into the van. Phil had already preset the satnav for the next address and so they set off to the virtual guide's succinct and chirpy directions.

'Well,' said Phil after a while as they made their way down Armley Ridge Road, 'What did you think about it love? It wasn't too bad was it?'

'Bloody awful,' replied Zoe, 'No way are you gonna get me in there. Garden you said, it was a fuckin' back yard, Phil. Get real will ya?'

'Okay, okay, calm down,' he said holding up his

palm.

'Where we going now anyway?'

'Here, look through that lot,' he said, pushing the folder towards her. 'I think it's Granger Street, the next one, and this one *has* got a garden, so just be giving that one a once over before we get there.'

Zoe did as instructed and shuffled through the glossy paraphernalia.

'Fuck me, yeah, it's got a garden at the back but it's overlooked by the twatting Prison walls! Look, you can see the barbed wire on top of 'em in this photo. What if the prisoners escape whilst Sophia's in the garden? Eh?'

Phil sighed but had no answer. He ignored her.

'No, that one's out, I'm not standing at the sink all day looking out at bleedin' Armley Nick, what yer thinking?' she asked shaking her head. 'Anyway, I'm telling yer now, there's summat about this Debbie Richards, I don't know what it is, but there's summat about her—'

'Oh, 'ere we go,' fired back Phil, 'Making negative judgements on people. You've only known her for two bloody minutes love. She seems a really nice lass she does —'

'Well, you'd think Rose fuckin' West was a really nice lass if she fluttered her eyelashes at you ya big gormless get, but, if you'll let me finish... '

'Go on then,' he sighed.

'I was gonna say...before you interrupted...not in a bad way, I've just got a feeling about her that's all. Don't know what it is, there's just summat about her, I can't put me finger on it.' At that point, Zoe's phone began to buzz. She yanked it out of her bag and scrutinised the text message.

'Who is it?' asked Phil.

Zoe stuffed the phone back into her bag. 'It's just Katie.'

'What's she want?'

'Just wants to know if I wanna meet up on Saturday night in town for a few drinks that's all.'

'Well I'm out on Saturday with the lads so maybe we could all meet up like we did last time. She's a good laugh is your mate, and she seemed to get on well with Andy.'

'Ugh, friggin Andy. I can't stand the little bastard. He'd got a face like a bleedin' pug for a start off, he's repulsive, gross...I don't know, I just can't do with 'im.'

'Well did you say you were going or what?'

'I said I'd see. I'll think about it, I've got the friggin 'eadache back again now, thinking about that little shit!'

*

Phil and Zoe had returned to Seacroft empty-handed, much to the disgruntlement of Linda. The properties they'd seen had been fair game for renovation, but that was the line Phil had wanted to take. Zoe had other ideas and the tension between the two had taken its toll with Phil deciding to get out of the way and make his way up to the Devon Pub to chill out with his mate Andy and the lads. Zoe had completed her duty of removing and sanitizing the day's deposits of dog faeces, courtesy of Princess, and was now daydreaming in the 'clean' back garden. This was mostly just a rough lawned area with a number of untended, spindly rose bushes jotted around the borders. A small creaking wrought-iron gate at the bottom lead out into the little cul-de-sac of Kentmere Gate. She sat on the wooden bench her father had proudly knocked together out of used pallets and scaffold boards many years ago. It was now past its best and in desperate need of a lick of paint but still sturdy enough to seat two people. It was positioned under a silver birch tree that the family had planted when she and Chris had been small children. It was a place of sanctuary for Zoe, a place where she hoped she could think straight, where she could focus. At the moment her headspace was all over the place.

Here she sat in quiet contemplation of the day's events, her ever-strained relationships with her partner and mother, and her station in life in general. The early evening air was warm, the direct sun still hot. She thought of her dad. Sitting on his bench seemed to bring him closer. She envisaged him stood in front of her smiling and holding out his upturned palms at her. He quietly shook his head. She imagined his voice, urging her forward, go on love, he's saying, what you waiting for? Go. And then she derided herself and her ridiculous imagination. *Silly bitch. He's right is Phil. I can't go on like this, I need to see the doctors. But for what? Even they don't listen ... so what's the bleedin' point?* Her mind wandered back to the disastrous spirit circle debacle. She questioned herself as to whether she'd been a little premature in her evaluation of the situation. *Maybe Phil's right. You need to start thinking a bit more before you start judging. Engage head first ya silly cow! You walked out 'cos they were singing ... Grow up.* This thought immediately brought things into perspective as she relived the embarrassment she'd encountered. She'd been thinking of Brenda and the spirit development circle more frequently of late. The concept of spiritualism had been drawing her in, beckoning her into its mysterious fold. Katie had encouraged her to not dismiss the issue out of hand, to keep an open mind, and she'd already been giving this some serious thought. The others, namely her mother and Phil, didn't even know anything about it. She knew what their reaction would have been. The little white lie that she'd issued to Phil earlier that day whilst they'd been looking at the properties had expounded her thoughts on the matter and now she could think of little else. She had received a text message from Katie regarding meeting up for drinks at the weekend, but that text had arrived a couple of days earlier. The message she'd received during their house-hunting expeditions hadn't been from Katie. It was from the Kirkstall and Meanwood Spiritualist Church, not from Paula Jackson but an assistant of hers, a certain Ruth Wishart. Ruth had asked that she contact her as soon as possible.

CHAPTER 4

Zoe eased her slim frame into the comfortable, tartan-covered armchair and folded her arms tightly. Her suspicious eyes flicked from left to right as she surveyed the coffee shop in front of her. She'd chosen the same one on Albion Place where she and Katie had met just a few weeks earlier. She liked the laid-back vibe and had even sat in the same corner booth as on that first visit. It afforded a perfect vantage point to hold court over the comings and goings of everyone in the shop, staff and customers alike. That meeting with Katie had gone so well and had lifted the gloom that had clouded over her. Unfortunately, the gloom had returned, the dark clouds had once again descended and Zoe was fuelled with apprehension and uncertainty. It was the week following the property viewings. She'd chosen not to hook up with Katie at the weekend, specifically to avoid an awkward and uncomfortable audience with Phil and his mates and in particular the vexatious little Andy. Also nagging away at the back of her fuzzled head had been the small matter of the white pill, thrust upon her, and the loss of memory that followed. Not only was she disappointed with her friend but she felt that she'd also let herself down, she should have, could have, been stronger, stood firm. In any case, she'd resolved that if she was to venture further down the spiritualist avenue, then it had to be of her own volition, not on the back of Katie's persuasive manner, nor through guilt or anything else for that matter. It had to be because she wanted it, and after much soul-searching she'd decided that she did want it, or at the very least she felt the need to explore the concept further. She'd nothing to lose. She was 26 years old and a mother, not a gullible teenager. It was time she started acting like an adult, making her way in life, making her own decisions. Her mother, and partner, were singing from a different hymn sheet. *Fuck 'em, I'll do this without them, I'll do it mesen...for mesen.* And so on this occasion, it wasn't Katie, her oldest friend, whom she'd arranged to meet in this happy, vibrant little coffee shop on Albion Place in the centre of Leeds, it was Ruth Wishart, a messenger from the Kirkstall and Meanwood Spiritualist Church.

*

Having made her way into town straight from another impotent therapy session, Zoe was a little early for her appointment. She sat and waited, persistent in her observation and scrutiny of the general public going about their daily business, both inside and outside the shop. She watched a group of teenagers attired in corporate red hoodies as they pushed a wheelie bin, spilling with free promotional chocolate bars, onto Briggate. Flushed with the exuberance of youth and opportunity they went about their commission happy and unencumbered. She looked on as an altercation developed opposite the cafe, between Police Support Officers and a group of homeless people as they attempted to evict them from a makeshift camp in a shop doorway. They didn't go quietly, giving the officers plenty of grief, and not holding back with the blunt language and animated gesticulations. They eventually left, but not without leaving an extensive clean-up job for the street cleansing teams. The relaxed ambience in the street slowly returned as the commotion petered out and peace restored. She watched and waited. She didn't know if she'd recognise Ruth Wishart, who'd said during their brief telephone conversation that she'd been present at the circle when Zoe had walked out. The only members of the circle whose faces she could remember was the geek she'd caught eyeing her up and the older bloke who'd held her hand, both of whom she'd later referred to as perverts.

As was her propensity she continued to dissect and make judgement on everyone who came inside the shop. She looked up at the wall clock. They'd arranged to meet at noon and it was now a quarter past. *Come on you silly cow, you're late.*

By twenty-five past, Zoe was huffing and puffing and glancing up at the clock almost every thirty seconds. Her mindset was frayed and irritable and she'd decided she was giving her five more minutes and then she was off. *Five more minutes. I'm not gonna be fucked about by a jumped-up lackey.*

Fortunately, it didn't come to that. Just before the deadline, a slim young woman of about thirty years of age and of mixed-race edged her way into the shop. She wore a lime green flat cap back-to-front and a denim jacket. She looked around and as soon as their eyes met she waved and made her way over. Zoe immediately recognised her from the circle.

'Zoe, Zoe,' she said, 'I'm so sorry I'm late love, I missed the bus and had to wait for the next, I should've texted you but I never thought.'

'Er, no, it's fine, don't worry about it,' replied Zoe, her heart beating faster, her cheeks flushed. Ruth took off her jacket and hung it on the chair opposite Zoe. She then removed her scarf and placed her bag onto the table, knocking over an empty coffee cup.

'Oh, sorry,' she said smiling and picking up the cup,' I'm all over the place today. I'll get us a coffee, what would you like love?'

'Er just a Latte thanks,' replied Zoe.

'Right Zoe, just give us a minute and I'll be right back.' She turned around to head towards the counter and bumped into a gentleman who was just making his way out.

'Oh, I'm so sorry,' she said to the old-timer who smiled and put up his hands. Zoe wondered what the fuck she'd let herself into as she watched the awkward Ruth join the queue at the counter only to be told that she'd tagged on at the wrong end. She heard her apologise once again, 'It's one of those days, I'm so sorry,' she said as she shuffled round to the other end of the queue.

Fuck me, what's wrong with the silly cow. I've ended up with a right 'un here. She shook her head and looked up towards the ceiling.

Zoe continued to audit the strange little scatter-brain from the spirit circle, scanning her every move, her every mannerism. No matter how many times she apologised or whoever she bumped into, her countenance radiated positive vibes, she seemed to have a permanent smile, thought Zoe. Her golden hair was plaited and scraped back underneath the cap, her soft, fresh complexion in need of no cosmetics. She wore round wired spectacles, a knee-length cotton dress with a cord type belt around her waist over bright orange leggings and flat-heeled, sensible hush puppies. *Fuck me, she's wearing a bleedin' dress. What if she's a lezzy? Fruity little cow! Trust me to get someone like her. Just let me get home, get me away from this place.* As usual, Zoe's overactive and negative mindset immediately forged equivocal assumptions which painted the worst possible scenario and cast a cloud over the whole proceedings. Her nerves surfaced, she became edgy, but she had to sit it out, there was nowhere for her to go. She sat tight and gave herself an internal, hard grilling. Self-discipline would see her through...or that was the plan. Eventually, Ruth returned with the drinks without causing any further rumpus. Zoe blew out a huge sigh as the coffee was passed over to her.

'It was Cappuccino wasn't it love?'

Almost giving up on any will on her part to intake her next breath of air Zoe nodded in agreement. 'Yeah...thanks that's good.'

Ruth smiled and sat down. She began to organise herself. She moved her bag onto the floor by her side. She shuffled her chair closer to the table. She took off her glasses and checked her plait before moving her bag back onto the table and then rummaged around her jacket pockets for a pen. She rubbed the back of her neck and then lifted the bag back onto the floor to retrieve a notepad. As Zoe looked on in astonishment Ruth then proceeded to wipe down the front of her dress before clasping her hands in front of her and placing them on the table. She looked Zoe straight in the eye.

'Sorry about that love,' she said smiling. 'Now, I bet you're wondering what all this is about aren't you?'

I'm wondering what you're all about, you dippy little cow. 'Er, well, yeah, I am really. I were a bit surprised when I got your text last week, but to be honest I'd been thinking about the circle thing for a while now. I might have been a bit hasty when I walked off the other week, I'm sorry about that. It just didn't seem to be my thing that's all.' This first verbal interaction helped to ease the knot of anxiety that had been building up in Zoe's stomach all morning.

'That's no problem, Zoe. The open circle's not for everyone and we understand that some people take longer than others to get into it and pick up on what we try to deliver, what it is we do, so don't worry over that love. Now, let's get down to business...Brenda Cartwright.'

'You mean Barmy Brenda?'

'Oh Zoe,' replied Ruth in a soft assuring manner. 'Barmy love? Oh, she was always lovely to me Zoe. She looked after me like a mother when I first got into this and she used to do heaps for charity when she could. She'd give you the coat off her back if she could love, there wasn't a nicer person going. Why do you call her barmy?'

'Well, she's been walking around Seacroft with a bleedin' purple bowler 'at on for years,' insisted Zoe, 'She collared me on the street, and said she'd been in con-tact wi' me dad, who's been dead five years, and that she was retired. At the time I thought she were mad. Purple bowler hat? In Seacroft?'

Ruth hesitated. 'Oh I see...you've actually met her? but anyway Zoe love, you can't judge a person by what they wear on their heads. I wear a green cap on mine but it doesn't make me barmy does it?' Zoe stared at her. A Seacroft-laced quip dripping with vitriol hung from the tip of her vicious tongue, awaiting liberation. The darling was subsequently sent to the gallows as she somehow managed restraint. After a slight pause, she replied.

'Ok, well I don't know her that well, I'll give ya that, but that's what she's known as around Seacroft, Barmy Brenda, that's all I know. I've only spoken to her that once and to be fair she didn't seem a bad old lass once we were face-to-face.'

Ruth looked deep into Zoe's eyes. 'Yeah...she's lovely love...I can assure you.' She spoke softly with warmth and compassion. There was another small impasse before she continued.

'Anyway, what's happened love is that Brenda has contacted Paula about you.'

'Why? ... What's she said?'

'Nothing to worry about. Brenda and Paula go back years. It was Brenda who mentored Paula from when she was a teenager and they still keep in contact with each other, even though, as you say, she's retired now. So apparently Brenda's still receiving psychic vibrations about you, and she's anxious that we don't let you slip through the net.'

'Bleedin' hell,' muttered Zoe, scratching her head.

'Nothing to worry about love. You see we all have psychic abilities. Everyone does. Everyone in this cafe, everyone out on the street - everyone. Some more than others. Most, like me, have limited psychic ability and I choose to develop mine, but most don't, most people are unaware that they have any psychic capabilities at all. But, at the end of the day, no matter how much development I undertake, and it's an ongoing process, I'm never going to be a Brenda Cartwright or a Paula Jackson, I'm not in that league love. But you do have the potential to be. Brenda thinks that you're one of the Special ones.'

'Special? Jesus! I know a few special ones from 'estate, they're either in 'nick, in rehab or on the bleedin' run. What do you mean special?' replied Zoe, half smiling. Ruth gave her a look. Without saying a word she made it clear that the use of such language was neither necessary nor appreciated within the circles into which she was attempting to recruit Zoe.

'Well love, she thinks you've got the gift. And Brenda's usually spot on with things like this. And her word is good enough for Paula.'

Zoe thought for a second. This sounded like serious stuff.

'Well what do you do then, where do you fit into all this?'

'I work for Paula part-time. I organise her calendar, I'm a bit like her PA and book her in for sittings, demonstrations and shows all over the country. I go with her sometimes,' she said smiling. 'She also does TV and Radio and she's booked in for a four-week tour of Australia next year. Unfortunately, I'm not with her on that trip, I'm looking after things back here, worse luck,' she said with a wry smile.

Zoe continued to take it all in and remained silent. It was like a different world from the one she lived in. TV, tours around the country, Australia. And for such an outwardly scatterbrained character she was taken by the way Ruth spoke, the slightly deep but soft, warm voice, confident but no hint of aggression or negativity. She was unused to being in the company of such gentle creatures.

'So they've asked me to hook up with you and just try to put your mind at rest with some of the stuff you might not understand. I was thrilled when you agreed to meet up. It'll be my job to ease you into our world and to allay any fears or misconceptions you might have, and it doesn't matter how long it takes or how many meetings we might need love. I'm here for you, we don't like to see natural talent go to waste, but at the end of the day, it has to come from you. You need to want to do this. We won't get anywhere if you enter this business under duress, or because you think someone else wants you to do it. It has to come from here love,' she said placing the palm of her hand over and patting her flat chest. '... and a willingness to learn. You've got to want it, Zoe.' She looked at Zoe and waited for a response. Zoe didn't know what to say. She wanted to blurt out everything about her miserable life, the headaches, the buzzing and all that awful stuff that had happened in East Moor Park. But she didn't know how. Ruth picked up on her struggle.

'Ok love, I'm with you. Why don't we start at the beginning? Just take your time.'

It was a slow start from Zoe. She felt uncomfortable opening up to a stranger. She shuffled around in her chair, rubbed her cheek and she toggled her coffee cup. But once she started there was no stopping her. From the clicking sounds in the dead of night she'd first experienced as a young girl, and which had continued ever since, to the visions and phantasms and the sense of a malicious presence she'd encountered over that past three or four years. From the sleep paralysis and ghoulish apparitions to astral travelling and onto the horrors she'd experienced at Reginald Street. The lost hours and out of body experiences, mental conversations with people and entities she didn't even know, being woken up by a shaking and tugging to her shoulder or a violent shout in her ear. The aliens, she told her about the little grey aliens and the tall thin ones. The bouts of headaches and buzzing from within her headspace, the swirling masses of nonsensical junk cascading into and around her head making her weak and dizzy. She left no stone unturned as she rattled off every encounter and experience she could remember, and as she did so the heavy burden of weight slowly slipped from her slender, knotted shoulders.

Afterwards, she felt liberated, lightened and free. At last, she had someone to talk to who was on her side, on her level and who would listen with compassion and without sanctimony. By the time she'd finished offloading her life of tribulation and misery, she sat back. Her cheeks were flushed and her forehead clammy as she breathed a huge sigh of relief. She was jiggered.

'Well, that's quite a story love,' said Ruth, 'no wonder you've been so confused all these years, I feel for you, I really do. But do you know something Zoe? All that stuff you've just reeled off to me love, everything you've had to put up with all those years, it's not that unusual. I can relate to almost everything you've told me, honestly, you're not on your own love. All those years and I bet at times you've been thinking you were going out of your mind haven't you love?'

'I have,' replied Zoe, 'at times I've thought I was mad, and so has me Mam and the bleedin' doctors. I'd never dare tell me mates owt about it as they'd have just taken the piss. Even now, Phil, my partner, just doesn't listen, thinks he knows best. I've really been on my own trying to make sense of all this crap going on in me 'ead all this time. I've even thought about toppin' mesen.'

'I know love. It must have been hard for you. But we'll get you sorted, with a bit of work and compassion. It's all about love you know.' Ruth smiled whilst continuing to look deep into Zoe's eyes. 'And it's not only about making connections with those on the other side love.'

'What do ya mean?'

'Well, we do a lot of voluntary work in the community for instance. We raise funds for local charities and stuff like that. Once a week a group of three or four of us come into town on a Saturday night to help with the homeless. We hand out blankets and stuff, food and water and things like toiletries and such. We work with the crypt and other organisations in the city centre, just to help.'

'Well half of 'em aren't even 'omeless are they?' interrupted Zoe, 'druggies and beggars aren't they?'

'Well, that might be Zoe, but at the end of the day love, they're here on the streets, and whether or not they've made good or bad decisions in whatever paths they've taken on their journeys getting here, they need help. We all need a bit of help at some stage in our lives love.'

'Ok,' replied Zoe, 'so what's the end product then? Where's this all leading to. I don't mean to sound tight, but...what's in it for me? You know, all this pathway that we're going down together and all this charity work and stuff with the beggars, where's this all gonna take me?'

Ruth paused and then looked up at Zoe. 'Well love, we don't do this work for material gain, that's for sure. Yeah, Paula makes a good living out of this but she started off years ago doing private sittings for free, her motivation was to help people, to ease their pain and suffering. That's the only motivation you need in this industry, it's all about love, compassion and honesty. And just like in any other industry, the bad eggs will always come a cropper, they always do.' Zoe looked on and listened. She didn't speak but her suspicious mind was ticking away like a clockwork toy. *Alright, I get the message. Who are ya? Mary bleedin' Poppins?*

'Can I just ask you love?' said Ruth, 'and tell me if you don't want to discuss, but, how's your life been since you left school? Apart from the frustration of not understanding the stuff that we discussed earlier. Have you been happy? Sad? Not quite right? Unfulfilled, out of line? Out of sync?'

Zoe looked on. She decided there and then to be honest and upfront with this woman. There was no point in holding anything back.

'Well I'll be straight with you, apart from Sophia, the last ten years of my life have been hell. I've been a druggie and a pisshead. I've thieved and shoplifted, I've been in rehab twice and me own Mother's booted me and me family out 'cos o' the drugs. I could say that I mixed with the wrong crowds, but to be honest, I was as bad as the rest of 'em, and more often than not, it was me, I was the ringleader. I've been a right twat to be 'onest Ruth. And this is where it's got me, no-fucking-where that's where. I'm growing apart from me daughter's father and I can't get on wi' me Mam. I've had enough and I want to change. I want me life to change, for the sake of me daughter, before it's too late. I want to do right by her, sometimes she's the only thing that keeps me going.' Zoe's eyes moistened. She buried her head into her hands. Ruth reached over a placed a reassuring hand on her arm.

'Come on love. Sometimes fate works in strange circles. There was a reason for your little encounter with Brenda, no matter what you think of her.' Zoe lifted her head and wiped her eyes as Ruth continued. 'And there's no place for drugs and alcohol in this field love. But from where you've been, and where you've come from that'll make you stronger and wiser. Use your past as a foundation to build your future love, in a positive way. I can tell you're a strong and wily person, you just need guidance love, and that's what we're trying to help you with. Your mind, body and spirit are misaligned Zoe, and that's why you're all over the place. Drugs, alcohol and negativity fuel this misalignment and the result is an unfulfilled life, one of acute misery, never being at one with yourself. Together, we can get you back on the straight and narrow and give you a purpose in life. To help others. Not everyone has the abilities to do this line of work, but you have, so that will be our purpose from here on in. From here, where we are now, to there,' she said pointing upwards. 'We'll get those psychic energies of yours flowing in the right direction love, you only have to believe. The hardest prison to break free from is the one we put ourselves in, up here, in the head,' she said tapping her forehead. 'We need to free you up ... and we will.'

'Fuck me, Ruth, you are Mary Poppins, you dotty bugger!' Zoe laughed and wiped her tears away and even Ruth couldn't hide a smile as once again she shook her head at the choice language used by her new recruit.

The two newly acquainted friends slowly warmed to each other and chatted freely over the next half hour or so. Zoe felt liberated at being able to talk to someone on her level without having to resort to arguing and negativity. The odd little character opposite was not the type she'd normally become involved with. A little old fashioned, a bit dull to listen to maybe and as dotty as a duchess at the dogs, but there was something about her. Her words were spoken confidently, she was strong internally and above all Zoe was beginning to think that she could trust her. Usually, when she placed her trust in others it came back and slapped her square in the chops, but she got the feeling that this time it was different.

From Ruth's perspective, she knew she had a job on her hands. She recognised that there were a few rough edges to sheer off and soften before this rocky little Seacroft diamond would shine intensely enough to make a difference. But that had been her brief, and she'd agreed to take on the project. It wasn't going to be an easy road down which they were going to venture together, but as scatty as her outward demeanour may be to some, she was made of strong stuff, and she was up to the task.

*

It was time to leave. The meeting had gone well as far as Ruth was concerned and she was happy she'd made some progress with Zoe, her natural positivity told her it was a challenging project but one that she was determined to see through. She lifted her bag onto the table and began shoving leaflets, papers and other bits and bats back into it. There was no order, it all got shovelled in. She stopped and looked around. She searched the tabletop, and then under the table. She removed all the junk from the bag that had only just been piled in.

'What 'ave you lost Ruth? Is it yer phone love, cos you've just put it in your jacket pocket?' Ruth checked her jacket and confirmed that indeed her mobile was safely tucked in there, but it wasn't the mobile she was searching for.

'No love, it's not my phone, it's my blooming glasses. I'm sure I had them with me because I remember dropping them and picking them up off the floor when I came out of the house. Where are they for goodness sake?'

Zoe looked on in astonishment. 'Ruth!' she fired.

Startled at the tone of Zoe's voice Ruth stopped and looked up. 'What love?'

'They're poking out of ya top pocket you dizzy bugger, they've been there all the time since you took 'em off when you first sat down!'

Ruth grabbed the glasses and brought them up to eye level. She smiled. 'Oh, I am sorry love,' she said putting her hand over her mouth. 'I'm as daft as a brush sometimes.'

'Sometimes?' What yer like ya dotty cow ya nowt else?' she shook her head and couldn't hide a smile. They shared a moment.

The two of them stood facing each other on Albion Place. It was almost three in the afternoon and the town centre was buzzing.

'Well Zoe, I've so enjoyed getting to know you and I'm really looking forward to us working together. Make sure you read through all that stuff I gave you love, and if you've any queries just give me a call or a text. And don't forget, if you need a chat, or a shoulder to cry on or anything before we meet up again, you just get in touch.'

'I will...and thanks. I've enjoyed your company too, a bit of an eye-opener, but I'm glad I came, I wan't gonna, but I'm glad I did.'

Ruth leaned over and gave her a hug taking her by surprise. Zoe wasn't a touchy-feely person by default, she felt a little awkward and stiffened up but she went along with it. Ruth was a lovely person she thought, so she cut her a little slack. The coffee shop was almost at the junction with Briggate and it was here they took their separate paths. Ruth turned left to head up to the Headrow for her bus. Zoe turned right and headed down towards the Trinity Centre where she planned on treating herself to a new pair of trainers. She'd only taken three or four steps before she heard Ruth's soft apologetic tones once more. 'Oh, I am sorry love, here let me help you.' She turned her head to see Ruth helping an elderly woman pick up items of shopping that were now scattered over the Briggate precinct. She turned back around and headed down Briggate chuckling, she'd had enough of this Ruth bloody

Wishart for one day.

Briggate had been the lifeblood of the centre of Leeds for centuries. At this time of the day, it was fully pedestrianised with state-of-the-art retractable, terrorist-proof bollards guarding every entrance to the street and surrounding shopping areas. The place was teeming not only with shoppers but a host of street vendors selling everything from street food to plastic phone cases and brightly coloured cheap tack, skilfully designed to hook in the kids. Placard toting Evangelicalists and born-again Christians preached their wares at the top of their voices. Every thirty yards there was a different musical drone, from a North American Indian Chief playing beautiful pan-pipe music to jazz, reggae, swing and even a talented student from the music college beating away on a set of upturned plastic buckets, cartons and containers. The whole place was alive and buzzing. The hot sun sat high in the sky emblazing the full length of the street with a sense of radiant positivity. As she walked down towards the bottom end towards the Trinity Shopping Centre she thought about her meeting with the dotty Ruth. Her mindset was at ease. The lovely weather and the positive meeting had made her feel warm inside, a light at the end of the tunnel. There was a future. She walked towards a white-bearded, dark-skinned old fella who, with his eyes closed, gently gyrated whilst playing harmonious and beautiful soothing tunes on his beloved saxophone. For the first time in her life, Zoe approached a busker and threw a handful of change into his case. She received a thankful nod and he received a warm smile to complement his well-earned remittance. She sauntered on past Marks and Spencer's, where a homeless woman sat on the adjacent stainless steel bench. She too had her eyes closed and two large bags stuffed with belongings by her side. She must be boiling hot wearing that heavy coat in this heat thought Zoe. The woman had a shock of white frazzled hair and listed slightly to one side, her head slightly bowed. She may have been asleep thought Zoe, or she may have been jettisoned to another plane aloft the soothing saxophone music. Either way, it didn't diminish her own positive outlook as she made her way down the bustling street with an uncharacteristic spring in her step. *Must be that Coffee shop.*

Zoe was oblivious to the small girl that had tracked her down Briggate. The same one that had stood outside the coffee shop for an hour, awaiting her departure. The barefoot girl, of about six years of age, wearing only a long white nightdress had followed Zoe through the bustling crowds. Her pale, sad face unnoticed in a sea of vibrancy and optimism. She'd followed Zoe until she reached Marks and Spencer's and then she stopped. Zoe turned into the snappy Trinity Centre and out of view.

CHAPTER 5

'Come on Hun, try and keep up.'

Sophia, loaded with a SpongeBob backpack and lunchbox, dawdled behind her mother. Zoe didn't have the patience to dawdle over anything. If she embarked on any task, she wanted it done there and then, no messing. The problem with Zoe was getting started in the first place. She'd spend ten times the amount of time thinking about a task in hand than the time required to complete it. Procrastination was her biggest bugbear, but once she got started, she was off and wouldn't tolerate anything less than rigid expediency.

'Mum?'

'What love? Come on, keep up,' she replied walking at a brisk pace without breaking stride.

'Can we stop at the paper shop for some sweets?'

'Sweets? What do you want sweets for? They're bad for your teeth love.'

'Well, Bethany Gobshell gets sweets every day on her way home from school. She told me. Her mum buys them for her.'

'Well you're not Bethany Gobshell and I'm not Bethany Gobshell's mum am I?'

'Aw Mum. Can I have some?'

Zoe looked over her shoulder. 'Well, have you been a good girl at school today?'

'Yes.'

'Have you been brushing your teeth properly?'

Sophia rolled her eyes. 'Yes Mum, I have, now can I have some sweets please? ...from the paper shop?'

'Come on, 'urry up, I haven't got all day love, I've gotta life to lead.'

'Well, can I then?' continued the little girl as she increased her pace and grabbed her mother's hand.

'Can you what?'

'Mum! You know what! Can...I...have...some...sweets...please?' returned Sophia, now getting quite cross with the teasing antics being meted out by her mother.

'Did you tidy your bedroom this morning?' continued Zoe.

'Mum! Stop being tight, yes I did. Now can I have some or what?'

'Well, just let me have a little think about this then. Sweets is it?'

'Yes Mum, you know what it is, stop teasing me.'

'Hmmm, let me think. Sweets eh? Hmmm, okay love, well let's see...sweets...paper shop...Bethany Gobshell...yep, I've had a little think about it now love and I think I've reached my decision.' There was a pause.

'Well? can I have some then?'

'Have some what?'

'Mum!'

'Oh, you mean the sweets?'

'Yes mum, the sweets.'

'Er...no luvvie, you can't!'

'Mum! screamed Sophia as she stopped dead and threw her mother's hand away in disgust. 'Why not? Why can't I have some? Bethany Gobshell can!' It was too much for Zoe, who burst out laughing and turned towards her daughter before dropping to her knees.

'I'm only kidding sweetheart, come here and give Mama a cuddle,' she said holding her arms out. Her eyes glazed over with the sheer hilarity of the situation.

'It's not funny Mum,' protested Sophia, her own eyes now welling up.

'Oh Lighten up Sophes love, you're getting to be like your nana,' said Zoe still chuckling as she stroked the girl's cheek and stood back up,' No tears now...or no sweets.' The tears stopped immediately, but Zoe couldn't help herself. They continued up South Parkway but after just a few steps she looked down at the little perturbed expression on the face of her daughter. She burst out laughing again. Sophia looked up at her mother and with her little lips pursed and her little forehead furrowed she shot her an icy stare through her narrowed little eyes, the sight of which set Zoe off once again. But Sophia was a gentle creature at heart and any negativity towards her mother was short-lived. She stuck her tongue to the inside of her cheek as she attempted to stifle her giggles, but she couldn't hold out and eventually succumbed to joining in with the amusement. They laughed together. She could never remember her mum being this happy, and certainly not laughing with tears in her eyes. She liked it, it gave her a warm feeling inside. She was glad her mum was happy even if it had come at her expense, and she was glad she was getting the sweets, the delights of which, she could share with Bethany Gobshell at school tomorrow. The happy mother and daughter held hands and both wore broad contented smiles as they continued their way up South Parkway from school and on towards the parade of shops on Kentmere Avenue.

*

It was a month after Zoe's initial meeting at the coffee shop rendezvous with Ruth and since then they'd met up a couple more times. They were building a solid relationship from the foundations upwards, it was the only way, Ruth had explained. If they were going to work together their relationship had to be based on trust, integrity and respect, perhaps values that hadn't exactly been on the forefront of Zoe's *essential morals for life* list. But she was determined to give it a go and had even begun the process of drip-feeding snippets of this new phase to her life to her mother and Phil. Neither seemed that interested, but at least they'd got past the stage where they were constantly taking the piss. She was seeing less and less of Phil. On the weekends when he wasn't working away he spent them with the lads in town, or up at The Devon, taking in Leeds Rhinos and the Super League, now that the football season had ended. Even during the week he often didn't make it home until the early hours, steaming drunk and then up and off at the crack of dawn for work. Though he provided well for the family, and they were still on the hunt for their own house, their current situation, at Kentmere Avenue, remained at times a very lonely place for Zoe. On the plus side, her general demeanour had much improved since she'd been seeing Ruth. She'd researched the subject of spiritualism via Google, but Ruth had suggested that she pare back on the internet searches, and instead concentrate on the methods of development that they'd discussed, and the books and paraphernalia she'd provided for her. She explained that there was as much bad stuff on the net as good stuff and, for now, it would be prudent to give the Google search engines a wide berth. For Zoe's part, she'd been practising the art of meditation and breathing techniques. Ruth had gingerly advocated yoga in conjunction with meditation in an attempt to bring Zoe's body and spirit back into alignment. But that hadn't happened. Zoe imagined the scene if her mother discovered her in full meditation mode whilst in the lotus position. She'd left that one on the shelf for now.

*

'Mama!' shouted Zoe through to the kitchen where Linda was loading up the dishwasher after dinner. Phil's evening meal was still in the micro-wave where it would stay until he came home, not before ten was the usual.

'What now?' came the muted reply before 'Mama' bundled through the door and into the living room. Linda knew that the use of the word 'Mama,' instead of 'Mam' meant that Zoe wanted something from her. 'What do y'want?'

'Would you mind, on Saturday if I went out for a drink wi' Katie in town? It's just that I 'aven't seen her for a bit and I keep knocking her back when she asks me.'

'No, I don't mind, but you know the rules. Don't be coming back 'ere pissed up, you're a mother to your daughter don't forget, and if you start with them substances an' drugs again, don't even bother coming back at all,' she fired, pointing a threatening finger at Zoe as she lounged on the sofa.

'It'll only be for a bit, but I'm gonna try to keep in touch, I don't wanna lose her again like last time. She's the only real mate I've got and I 'ardley see Phil these days.'

'Hmm, don't think I 'aven't noticed love. To be honest, I think he's taking the piss, he 'ardley ever sees our Sophia. He's never out o' 'pub, I'm beginning to see through 'im now, a different side to 'im. You keep your eyes on 'im lass, mark my words. It's alright 'im giving you money to buy yerself and our Sophia stuff, and giving me money towards food and 'bills, but he should be spending more time with his family. Just saying. And Shelley agrees wi' me.'

Zoe sighed. It had nothing to do with Shelley, but she let it fly over her head. She'd been getting on better with her mother of late and didn't want to rock the boat.

'To be fair he works all week, and quite a few weekends Mam. It's just his way of unwinding that's all. He says I can go out with him anytime if I want to, but I'd rather just stay at 'ome. Can't do with drinking every night - do me 'ead in.'

'Well, I'm just saying that's all. Anyroad, 'is dinner's in 'microwave, whenever he decides to float in. An' yeah, get yersen out wi' Katie o' Sat'day, it'll do you good. At least I know you won't be getting up to owt when you're out with her. She's a lovely lass is Katie, always has been, I've always said that. Why don't you ask her over for tea or summat? It'd be nice to see her again.'

'Okay, I'll ring her tonight...thanks, Mam.'

'Well, I don't mind minding our Sophia, she's no trouble to me at all, but just don't take the piss lady, you know what I mean.' replied Linda as she gave her daughter a look and turned to leave the room.

'Alright, you've said it once,' replied Zoe under her breath, 'I know.' But Linda had now disappeared back into the kitchen to await the impending arrival of her scissor sister in crime, Shelley.

Zoe sat in the sitting room. It was here that she'd been spending quite a bit of time alone. It was where she practised her meditation when all was quiet and so with Sophia upstairs and Linda preoccupied in the kitchen she thought she might as well give it ten minutes. She eased back into the sofa and shuffled herself into a comfortable position laying her hands flat onto her thighs. She closed her eyes and initiated the breathing technique as tutored by Ruth. A deep intake, a split second hold, and then a smooth exhalation. She envisaged the air entering her lungs and the oxygen being distributed to every extremity and corner of her anatomy, replenishing and injecting life and vitality. She then imagined all the toxicity in her body being pushed out and expelled, her lungs cleared of years of vile negative shit, cleansing every cell, atom and particle of her body. She was soon into her rhythm and once she reached a level of consistency she relaxed, sat back and opened her mental airwaves. There was usually a bunch of shit swirling around her head at this stage and she'd been practising on how to separate it and allow the buzzing sensations to come through. On this occasion though, she was already picking up a fine background vibration. She remembered the mantra Ruth had taught her on the onset of vibrations, and that was to concentrate, bring them to the fore. And this she did. She thought hard and positive whilst maintaining consistent breathing and focus. She imagined the cosmic powers of the whole universe being channelled and flowing through every vein and artery in her body. A blurred image slowly manifested in her mind's eye. She concentrated, she channelled her mental energies, and slowly the image became clearer, it came nearer and nearer. A photograph. A picture. At first, she couldn't decipher the nature of the image but it looked old, dated and worn. It slowly came into focus, a figure. A single figure, a beautiful image of a woman in a dress, a canary-yellow dress, 1950's style. Without warning, as if someone had slammed a rubber stamp into her head the word ALICE was superimposed on the photograph. And within a couple of seconds again the act was repeated, this time the word BRIGGATE was painfully rammed into her brain with such a force that it made her jerk backwards. She moaned. Then a tapping, a knocking. Another knock, but this she recognised as a knock on the front door - she immediately zapped out of the trance. By the time she'd realised what was going on Shelley had already walked in closing the door behind her. She wiped her feet and poked her nose around the living room door.

'Come in Shell,' said Zoe wearily, 'oh, you're already in. Y'all right Shelley?'

'Less o' the lip you,' she returned, smiling. 'Yeah, I'm good love ta, you? She in?'

'Good thanks, yeah just go through, she's waiting for ya.' Shelley closed the door and went to meet Linda in the 'bakery'. Zoe shook her head. *Trust Shelley to storm in. Just when I was getting somewhere. Silly cow.*

Her heavy, aching head was now hot and throbbing. She was pleased despite Shelley's untimely interruption. This was the first time she'd attempted to control the vibrations and be able to implement the methods and processes suggested by Ruth. Instead of attempting to escape this temporary mental aberration through negativity and fear, she'd remained in control, applying positive energies in order to harness the situation for her own use. She was pleased about this. *One small step. My first.* She thought about the image she'd seen in her mind. The impression was that the image of the young woman was not Alice in person. But the Alice part was in some way separate, as if it was Alice who held the photograph, or who had possessed it, took it or coveted it. She didn't know why, but that was the overriding feeling now stuck in her gut. She dropped her hot, throbbing head into her hands. The experience had left her feeling tired and drained. She swung her legs and feet up onto the sofa and buried her head into the soft cushion. She deserved a kip and within two or three minutes she was zonked, floating the heavens, insulated from the savagery of reality, high upon a celestial cloud of peace and tranquillity.

*

It was about an hour later. Linda and Shelley sat at the kitchen table enjoying their nightly natter over a glass of wine or two - or three. The door opened and in walked Zoe. She looked at the pair of them, each wearing unholy grins.

'She's 'ere look, Seacroft's answer to Derek Acorah!'

'Oh shurrup mam,' replied Zoe.

'Ey, don't you talk to your mam like that lass,' chipped in Shelley, 'she'll 'ave you over 'er bloody knee lass —'

'An' you can shut it as well you old lush,' hit back Zoe. Both Linda and her friend put their hands to their mouths in mock aghast.

'You see Shell, this is what I've gotta put up wi, wi' this un,' said Linda shaking her head.

'Oh button it, Mam, you've both had a few by the looks of it, you're turning into a right pair o' piss 'eads, the pair o' ya. Anyway, I've just spoken to Katie on the phone and she's already going out with her mates around Ilkley so it looks like I'll be stuck in on me own this Saturday, so you won't need to mind Sophia, but thanks anyway.'

'Oh good, you can stay in wi' me and Shell. We're having a cheese an wine night aren't we love?'

'We are, and it'd be lovely to share your company,

Zoe. You can cut us toenails for us and read us tea leaves as well if ya like,' returned Shelley as both she and Linda burst out laughing.

'Well thanks for the offer ladies but no thanks, I'd rather slit me throat. Anyway just listen up you two will you. What would you say if I asked you about 'an old photograph of a woman in a yeller dress?' Linda and Shelley looked at one another.

'What the hell y'on about yer silly bugger? 'Ave yer gone daft o' summat?' said Linda.

'It doesn't mean owt to ya then?'

'Not to me it dun't love no,' said Shelley just as perplexed as her friend.

'What if I mentioned Briggate?' The stunned Scissor Sisters sat motionless with blank expressions.

'Okay then, well what if I threw in the name of Alice?' Again Linda and Shelley looked at one another whilst Zoe closely observed their reactions.

'Alice?' said Linda.

'Alice?' repeated Shelley. They then blurted out in perfect unison: 'Who the fuck is Alice?' and immediately burst out laughing and hit a high five between themselves over the kitchen table.

'What?' exclaimed Zoe

'It's that twatting Chubby Brown fella,' laughed Shelley.

'Who the 'ell's Chubby Brown?' Zoe looked on in astonishment at the response she received from such a seemingly innocuous question.

'He's that little fat comedian from up North somewhere, he's a mucky little get,' replied Linda.

'Funny though,' said Shelley.

'Oh, he wa'. I used to watch 'is videos wi' ya dad

when you kids were little. He 'ad me in stitches—'

'He did me, I went to 'Arrogate to see him wi' Dennis and their Mick an Angie. I never stopped laughing, he's a right fucker he is—'

'Well, just hang on a minute you two. What's this Chubby Brown bloke got to do with owt?' asked Zoe.

'The song, *Who The Fuck Is Alice?*' it were one of his songs,' said Linda. 'It's on one o' them videos, I think I've still gorrem somewhere—'

'Wait on,' interrupted Zoe, 'just forget this Chubby bleedin' Brown bloke for a minute, take him out of the equation. Now, does the photograph of a woman in a yeller dress and the name Alice mean owt to either one of you?'

'No,' they both said in unison and shook their heads.

'Right then, that's all I wanted to know. I'm off now. Enjoy the rest of the wine ladies and goodnight.' She left the room to the sound of the Scissor Sisters cackling and digressing over the legendary antics and one-liners of Royston 'Chubby' Brown. *Should 'ave known not to try an experiment wi' them two gormless twats, 'specially when they've had a drink. Just stick to the book lass, little dotty old Ruth'll show you the way. Learn to walk before you can run.*

*

Zoe pulled back the curtain and looked out of the sitting room window. She tutted.'Where the bleedin' 'ell are ya? I've gotta be there in ten minutes.'

She checked her bag once again to make sure she'd left nothing she might need for the evening. There was nothing else she could think of. Mobile, keys and a twenty-pound note, just in case. That was all she needed and all were safely tucked into the inside pockets of her leather crop-jacket. She also wore a thin sweater, jeans and trainers and she'd tied up her hair in readiness for a night of action. She'd also slapped a bit of makeup on but now didn't know whether it was appropriate or not. But fuck it, she'd have to go with it, the taxi was due any minute. She felt like nipping into the kitchen for a swift glass of wine with the Scissor Sisters, just to calm the nerves, but she'd promised Ruth that under no circumstances would she ever turn up under the influence when they were working together, so she'd better not. She paced the room and looked out of the window again. Nothing. She rang the minicab firm up and was told her ride would be there in five minutes. *Fucks sake.* She sat down on the sofa and checked her pockets once again.

It was Saturday night and it was her first night of volunteering. Except she hadn't exactly volunteered herself, it had been Ruth who had volunteered her. She'd reluctantly agreed to it after being turned down by Katie with the dubious prospect of a Saturday evening in the company of her mother and Shelley being the only other option. It had been a last-minute decision and one she was beginning to regret. As was her nature, she prejudged everything in the negative. Handing out stuff to rough sleepers spelt confrontation, dealing with drunks and pissheads in the city centre meant anxiety and grief. But her biggest worry was meeting up with Simon. Simon was the geeky kid who she'd sat opposite during the circle meeting at the Spiritualist Church, the one she'd caught staring at her. Not only that but the arrangement was for him to give both Ruth and herself a lift home as it would be two o'clockish before they'd be finished. *Better not try owt on the geeky little twat else he'll get a fuckin' Seacroft slap, straight off.* Ruth had attempted to allay her fears saying how lovely a lad he was. *Everyone's fucking lovely according to you Ruth.* "He's a teacher at a local primary school and he was probably staring at you because he liked you." *Yeah, well I don't fuckin' like him so he'd just better watch 'is step.*

As she anxiously awaited her ride into town she questioned her judgement in agreeing to this volunteering and also the bigger picture of getting involved with Ruth and the spiritual development school in the first place. She then heard Ruth's dulcet calming tones echo around her head. "When negativity overtakes you just take a step back and take three deep breaths. Don't let negative thought prevail. Oust it by positive thought. Think of white light, love and positive energy. Banish hesitation and replace it with conviction". *Fuck me, easier said than done Ruthy baby, easier said than done.*

*

'Lovely to see you again Zoe. Ruth's been telling me all about you. I'm Simon, looking forward to working with you,' he said, extending his hand forward. Zoe offered a weak hand in return.

She nodded. 'Yeah, me too,' she said meekly, as Ruth rushed over to hug her.

'It's great to have you onboard Zoe love,' she gushed, 'I'm sure you'll get plenty out of it 'cos there's lots of people out there who need our help. It's warm tonight but you can imagine what it's like in winter and don't forget that it's not for us to judge whether or not they should be out here, we just do our bit to help.' She smiled, but it was all a bit surreal for Zoe. She was usually on the other side of the fence getting pissed up and acting like a twat, and now here she was, behaving herself, all sensible and caring, helping people. She felt more attuned to the dossers on the street than she did to the big 'love in' and the group of volunteers she was now a part of.

They had met in Dortmund Square which was just off The Headrow at the top of Briggate. There were about twenty-five or thirty volunteers from all walks of life and charitable organisations throughout the city. The group would be split into smaller groups of three or four and each assigned an area of the town centre. Each group would be given the use of a small four-wheeled trolley with which to distribute the aid and giveaways and then head back to Dortmund Square to replenish the stock as and when needed. That was the concept of the plan. Ruth, Simon and Zoe had been assigned Briggate and surrounding pedestrianised area which included Commercial Street, Albion Place, Lands Lane and King Edward Street. Ruth had already retrieved their loaded trolley and just as they were about to make their way down to Briggate she stopped.

'Oops, sorry, just a sec, forgot to sign the sheet, won't be a minute guys,' she said before darting back to the small Luton Van that served as HQ and which held the night's stock of charitable goods. Zoe and Simon exchanged a glance.

*

They'd been going for about an hour and had just returned from Dortmund Square with the second trolley. There'd been little uptake on the blankets due to the mild evening but the flasks had gone down well. Packaged sandwiches and fruit donated by businesses across the city, bottled water and a host of general stuff including pre-packed parcels of toiletries and first aid items were proving popular and in much demand. Up to now Zoe had pushed the trolley and stood by watching and learning how Simon and Ruth approached and spoke to the street people and the way they interacted with them. The commission was ticking away quite nicely and on the whole, the homeless community seemed appreciative of the help and charity they were receiving. Zoe wondered what all the worry had been about. There'd been no issues with anyone, including the Saturday night drinkers and even Simon seemed to be ok. A bit drippy for her of course. All the guys she'd ever mixed with, before Phil came along, had been physically strong, streetwise and full-weight bastards. Simon was pleasant and quietly spoken but didn't look like he could fight his way out of a soap bubble never mind handle the rough and ready characters on the streets of Leeds. But he seemed nice enough, perhaps she'd been a little hasty in her judgement of him.

On this second run, Ruth had decided that it was time to give Zoe the experience of first-hand contact with the client. She was required to approach them, engage in small talk and ascertain as to whether they were in need of anything, apart from a home of course, with which the team could help. Zoe took it on board and got her chance whilst they were halfway up Albion Place. In the last shop doorway before the intersection with Lands Lane, there was a couple bedded up for the night. Ruth stood in the middle of the street with the trolley and nodded towards the doorway which was about twenty yards up and on the right from where they stood.

'Go on then love. Let's see what you can do, and just be yourself, they won't bite,' said Ruth.

Zoe smiled weakly and grabbed a bottle of water from the trolley. She approached the doorway which was in relative shadow, away from the streetlights. The occupants were totally covered inside a cheap, king-sized sleeping bag, but a slight movement told her that they weren't asleep. She looked around for Ruth who gave her a reassuring nod and then indicated that she should go ahead and give them a nudge. Reticent to start with she took the plunge and reached over, jabbing the nearest occupant with the bottle of water.

'Excuse me,' she said, 'do you want some water?' There was no answer so she poked the occupant again, this time a little firmer. 'D'you want some water?' she repeated.

The sleeping bag was pulled back and a rough-looking character with greasy hair sat up. 'Yer what?'

'Do you need some water or a cup o' tea?' asked Zoe.

'Fuck off!' The wild-eyed and bewildered doorway dweller glared at her.

This took Zoe by surprise, she hadn't expected this response. 'I'm just asking if you need—'

'Fuck off I said, are ya deaf?'

'You fuck off!' returned Zoe, the heckles on her neck now standing up and the rage within her belly beginning to swell. She never reacted well at being told to fuck off. Another head popped up from beneath the sleeping bag, that of a young woman.

'What's up? Piss off ya silly bitch,' she pronounced, scowling at the intruder.

'Fuckin' make me ya little slut!' replied Zoe who had now dropped the water and stood in front of the pair, hands on hips, ready for battle. Ruth bounded over and put her arms around Zoe turning her back into the street and away from the doorway.

'Come on love,' she said, 'just leave them to it. Come on.' She succeeded in ushering Zoe back towards the cart where Simon was now waiting. Ruth made to return to the homeless pair to make the peace.

'Sorry about that guys, we're just making sure you're all right that's all.'

'What the fuck's it gotta do wi' you?' cried out the gravelly voice of the rough sleeper. 'Just fuck off, the lotta ya,' he growled.

'All right love, we're just trying to help,' asserted Ruth, standing up to the guy, 'there's no need for all this is there?' She turned her back on them to the sound of more profanities but she wasn't going to be shaken. She got back to Zoe and smiled. 'What we gonna do with you love, I don't know?'

'Well he started it, I only asked him if he wanted any friggin' water and he told me to fuck off,' explained Zoe.

'I know he did love,' said Ruth.

'So I told him to fuck off.'

'I know you did love. I heard you,' she smiled.

'And then that little bitch piped up—'

'I know she did love.'

'I think he was giving her one anyway, on the bleedin' street,' continued Zoe, 'dirty little bastards!'

'Well, it has been known to happen, love,' replied Ruth, 'Come on, let's go have a time out and get a coffee, they're on me.' She handed the trolley to Simon as she put her arm around Zoe. 'Come on, forget about that, you're doing great.'

'You alright Zoe?' asked Simon, 'Not everyone on the street always wants us help, we just let 'em get on with things. Some can be quite nasty but most are good. You'll be fine, just stick together.'

'I'm good thanks,' said Zoe. She was a little bit shaken if she was being honest. But what she couldn't work out was the reaction of Ruth and Simon. In her world, a confrontation like that would result in a cat-fight or at least an aggressive standoff. In their world, it resulted in smiles and a coffee. It was something that she'd have to get used to.

*

They'd finished the bottom of Briggate, the main hub of activity for city centre street people, especially in and around the busy MacDonald's restaurant. Since the confrontation with the disagreeable rough sleeping couple, things had calmed down a little. Zoe had stepped up to the plate and dealt with a number of streeties and in a manner befitting that of a sympathetic volunteer. She still wasn't sure if this was exactly her scene, but she persevered. It was as they made their way back up Briggate to end the night's work that Zoe stopped at the entrance to the Marks and Spencer's store and peered down onto the occupant. It was the same old woman, with the shock of white hair, that she'd seen a few weeks ago. Then she'd been slouching on a bench just further up from the store, with her eyes closed. This night she was sat up in the doorway, wide awake and gripped a bottle of whisky with both hands. She was wrapped in a blanket and sat stock-still, her sad and dulled eyes exhibiting just the bare minimum signs of cognizance. She didn't move when Zoe approached her, nor did she even acknowledge her presence. She stared out onto Briggate, blankly, as if waiting for someone or something. Her face was grey, her focus distant. Zoe lowered herself and attempted to engage in conversation. She received nothing in return. It was while she was bent over that she started to experience a slight buzzing sensation in her headspace. She stood up but the vibrations continued. She shook her head and stared down at the woman, now wasn't the time to start getting involved in zoning in and all that crap and so, leaving a bottle of water and a sandwich, she took a couple of steps backwards and turned away.

'You all right over there love,' shouted Ruth from the centre of the precinct.'

'Er, yeah. All good,' replied Zoe as she slowly retreated away from the woman and as she did so the vibrations faded away to nothing. She caught up with Ruth and Simon as they made their way up to the top of Briggate. Behind them, on the bench just up from the M&S store doorway where the old woman was pitched was a young girl. The girl looked lost. She wore no shoes and was dressed in a dirty white nightdress. She knelt on the bench with her arms hanging over the back and her chin resting on the backrest. Her sad eyes followed Zoe as she walked up Briggate and into the distance.

*

As the group approached the top end of the boulevard they noticed a pair of rough sleepers in the doorway of the Yorkshire Bank. They hadn't been there earlier and so must have been moved on from somewhere else. It would be the last call of the night and so Ruth gave the honour of serving them to Zoe. She took the last of the sandwiches, water, a parcel of toiletries and the last flask from the trolley and then grabbed a blanket for good measure, which she threw over her shoulder.

'Go and take the trolley back, I'll see to these and meet you up at the van.'

'You sure you'll be ok love?' asked Ruth.

'Yeah, I'll be good.' She approached the doorway leaving Ruth and Simon to return the trolley, do the sign-offs and get ready for home. An older woman of roughly mid-sixties in age sat on a battered camping chair with a blanket over her knee. There was now a chill in the air with the time approaching 1:30 am. The woman wore a baseball cap and a grubby parka-style coat. She stared into the ground through dark, hollowed eyes. Aside her, wearing a thin anorak and a beanie hat was a young man of maybe mid-twenties in age. He was of slim build with a wild countenance, gaunt and unshaven. He too looked down as he huddled into the corner for warmth. A tattered trolley bag and a couple of other plastic bags were stuffed into the doorway beside the chair.

Zoe stooped down to address them. 'Hi guys,' she said, 'Just wondered if you could make use of these?' She held up the sandwiches, water and flask. The woman's black eyes flashed up at her and then turned towards the younger companion. He stared back and then looked up at Zoe.

'Is she talking to us,' croaked the old woman with hardly a tooth left in her mouth.

'What? ...Are these for us?' asked the young man, 'for nowt?'

'Well only if you want them,' replied Zoe, and then not wanting to end the night in a similar confrontation to the one she'd been involved in earlier she added, 'but if you don't it's fine, I can take them back.' The woman looked at her incredulously. She was lost for words. As Zoe looked on, the woman bit her bottom lip and then her eyes moistened.

'No lass, don't take 'em back, we'll 'ave 'em' won't we Rich?' said the woman, her eyes now glistening in the dim street lighting.

'Oh Nana,' said the young man, 'come on, don't start, you'll set me off.' He edged over and put his arm around the old woman.

She looked up at Zoe. 'It's a lovely gesture lass. We an't 'ad much t'eat all day 'ave we Rich? I'm alright, I don't need much, but 'e's been bloody starvin' 'an't ya lad? What's yer name lass?'

'Er, I'm Zoe,' she replied, taken aback at the level of gratitude shown towards her just for the sake of a hot drink and a sandwich.

'Well I'm Ada lass, and this is me grandson Rich, he looks after me don't ya lad?'

'We look after each other Nana. Me Nana's nearly seventy and she won't go into a home cos she won't leave me...she's a stubborn bugger...an' I can't leave her, so 'ere we are.'

'Yer an angel,' said the woman, now with a twinkle in her eyes, as she looked up to Zoe. 'We've been on 'street together for nearly a year now in't it Rich? Since you lost yer job? We lost us flat through debt, an' it wan't ar fault, wa' it Rich? But do you know what lass? In all that time, all those months and weeks on 'streets, this is 'first time anyone's come up to us, talked to us, see if we're alright, or to offer us any 'elp or owt lass, in't it Rich?'

Rich couldn't get a word in, but Zoe smiled and listened whilst the odd little woman shared their story. She described how they regularly moved around West Yorkshire taking in Bradford, Leeds, Wakefield and Huddersfield but that they were originally from Halifax.

"Ere y'are lass, are yer gonna 'ave a drink with us?' asked Ada as she turned around and pulled a half bottle of rum from her shopping trolley. Zoe politely declined, explaining that she'd love to but that she wasn't allowed whilst 'on duty'. She spent the next five minutes just talking and listening to them and she sensed the positive effect this simple altruistic act had upon the desperate couple.

Ada's eyes now sparkled in the crisp Leeds air, her dark, wrinkled face a sea of gratitude. Aside was her smiling grandson Rich, brimming with a newfound faith in the human race. Zoe handed over the blanket and pulled out the twenty-pound note from the inside pocket of her jacket.

'I've got to go now but here, take this,' she said reaching down and handing it to Ada. 'It'll get you a breakfast and a hot drink each in the morning.' Rich looked on in astonishment.

'No, no, we cun't take yer money lass, yer've already been too kind to us, 'an't she Rich?' replied the old woman. But Zoe was adamant as she forcefully placed the folded up note into Ada's old hands and wrapped her cold and hardened fingers firmly around it.

'Take it, I insist,' she said.

'Oh lass, yer an absolute angel, God bless you and ya family love,' said the old woman with tears in her eyes. She pulled Zoe's hands towards her and planted a kiss on them before passing them over to Rich who gave an equally sincere and warm double handshake.

'You've put a smile on me Nana's face so thanks for that love,' he said welling up himself.

Zoe walked away from the pair with a lump in her throat and close to tears herself. This humbling experience was what Ruth had been talking about. The feeling inside when you're able to make a difference to someone, a positive difference. This was what she meant. She'd been spot on again, she could see that now.

*

It had been a long night and one which had ultimately

proven to be rewarding. Zoe was glad that she'd come along now. It had been a night of ups and downs but it had ended with that beautiful encounter with Ada and her grandson Rich. It had been a moving and tender interaction and one which she'd never forget. But now she was tired and as she made her way back to Dortmund Square to join the rest of the volunteer brigade she looked forward to getting home and climbing into her cosy bed back in Seacroft. She got to the top of Briggate and turned left onto the Headrow. As she looked over the road to find a safe crossing she stopped dead in her tracks. Her heart dropped to the floor. The sight that was now playing out thirty yards away on the other side of the road made her feel sick. She could hardly believe it. She didn't want to believe it, but there it was in clear view. She began to shake and felt a lump in her throat, like a chunk of coal lodged solid, blocking her windpipe. *What the fuck!*

By the time she'd caught up with Ruth and Simon, it was obvious by her red-rimmed eyes and agitated demeanour that something had upset her.

'What's up love?' asked Ruth rushing over to offer her support.

'I'm fine Ruth, I've just gotta get 'ome that's all.'

'We usually stay for a coffee with the volunteers love, but we can get you home now if you want. Has something happened love, did anyone upset you on the street?' Simon hovered around, obviously concerned but not yet confident enough with Zoe to interject direct.

'You stay, I'm gonna get a cab,' said Zoe as she broke down in tears. Before either Ruth or Simon could say a word she'd turned her back on them. 'I'll call you in the week,' she cried before scooting away and disappearing into a labyrinth of dark, murky back streets and out of view.

*

The sound of a car engine running outside the house followed by the strike of the taxi door being slammed roused Linda as she dozed in the armchair. She'd never retire to bed until Zoe returned home, and had sat up waiting before eventually nodding off. The door flew open as her daughter stormed in and burst into tears before slamming it closed behind her. Linda sat up with a start.

'What's up now? she demanded. 'What the hell—'

'Don't fucking start wi' me Mam, I'm telling yer now. Can ya please just go out an' pay for 'taxi?'

'What's up with ya? ...I an't said owt. What's up?' You tell me now, 'ave you been drinking, or teken owt else lady?'

'Fuck off Mother, just don't talk to me, don't come near me,' replied Zoe, now in hysterics. She flopped down onto the sofa and buried her head into her hands.

'Bleedin' 'ell, this is all we want in't it at this time o' 'morning,' said Linda shaking her head. She grabbed her purse and ushered outside in her dressing gown to settle up with the taxi driver.

She re-entered the house and closed the door behind her. 'Now then, what's up?' she continued, 'tell me for god's sake, what's bloody happened?'

'Nowt, just leave me alone,' replied Zoe.

The commotion had awoken Sophia and she came running down the stairs.

'Mum, what's the matter?'

'Nowt love, you just go to bed,' replied Zoe in-between sobs, but Sophia wouldn't go back to bed. She went over to console her mother and wrapped her arms around her. She turned to look at Linda.

'Have you been swearing at Mum again Nana?'

Linda opened her hands. 'What? I 'aven't said a word luvvie no, it's nowt to do wi' me.'

'You're always swearing at Mum Nana, and telling her off,' said the little girl. Linda shook her head and sat back in the armchair, folding her arms.

Zoe tried to compose herself for the sake of her daughter. She managed to do so and convinced her that she was ok and that she could go back to bed. And that it hadn't been anything to do with Nana.

'Sleep in my bed wi' me tonight love if you like,' said Zoe, 'I'll be up soon, go on love, you go up.' Sophia kissed her and then made for the door but not before giving her nana a cursory glance before she did so.

Convinced that the problem was not borne out of drink or drugs Linda set about settling her daughter and decided that the best and first course of action was to make them both a cup of tea. She disappeared into the kitchen, leaving Zoe to ponder over the evening's proceedings and the distraught ending to it. She wiped her tear-stained face and sat on the sofa staring down into the carpet. Tosh had had enough, the commotion was too much for him and he was tired. He slunk out of the room to seek sanctuary elsewhere in his little semi-detached abode.

Linda re-entered the living room with two mugs of steaming hot tea and a plateful of cake. She placed them on the coffee table and sat down next to her daughter.

'Now then young lady,' she said, 'you tell Mama what's wrong wi' yer and who or what's upset you. And I want the truth, try pulling the wool over Mama's eyes and she'll know straight off.'

After some gentle cajoling Linda managed to eke the story out of her daughter. She described how she'd looked over the expanse of The Headrow to make her way across to meet the others only to see her partner Phil, and her best friend Katie necking on the street corner. He'd been all over her like a cheap overcoat and Katie had lapped it up for all she was worth. As Zoe had watched on, almost unable to believe what she was seeing, they'd turned left up New Briggate, hand in hand, heading no doubt towards the numerous bars and nightclubs in that lively quarter of the city centre. She'd been devastated.

'I've no one now. My partner, the father of me daughter, and me mate, who I thought wa' me best friend, me only friend. Gone. I'll never fucking trust anyone, ever again. The cheating bastards ... how could they? The lying cheating bastards. He said he was working away this weekend, and her...the conniving little slut.'

'Ok love, don't be getting upset again,' said Linda. 'I get the message, and don't you dare be thinking you've got no one, you've got me and our Sophia an't ya? And your brother, our Chris. We're all here for you love, an' we always will be.' For the first time since she was a little girl, her mother wrapped her arms around her and kissed her on the head.

'To think all this time he's been lying to us. Your Dad'd fucking kill 'im if he were alive today. The bearded fucking shit-house the nowt else...and that two-faced cow, I always said she was a sly little bastard, wait 'till I catch up with the pock-faced little bitch.'

'He can't come back 'ere Mam. If he comes back 'ere I'm off. He'll have to go, I never want to see the fat bastard ever again...but he's still Sophia's dad...fuck me what am I gonna do? What we gonna do about money?' She burst into a fresh tirade of tears.

'Don't worry love. This is your house, not his. And

we'll manage, don't worry your cotton-picking socks off, we'll get by. He won't be coming back 'ere don't you worry about that. I'll sort the bastard out.'

'Well, what are we gonna do? He'll be coming back tomorrow? continued Zoe her demeanour rising to hysterical once again.'

'Leave him to me love. I'll sort it.'

'What am I gonna do Mam?' she cried, her voice muffled as she buried her head into her mother's bosom.' Linda spent the next five minutes gently rocking her daughter, just as she had done when she was a little girl. Consoling, rocking, easing out the pain. Mother and daughter.

'We'll get by love, and I know you're upset now, but when this is over, you'll be back stronger. We're not gonna let a jumped up cretin like him or that little bitch reduce you to this, are we? We're stronger than that love, mark my words.

Linda eventually managed to pack Zoe off to bed, but she stayed up. Her mind whirred away like the computer exchange of an international PLC Bank. There was no way she was going to stand by and let her daughter be defiled and humiliated like this, not by those two cheating bastards. Linda had been born in East Moor Park and raised in Seacroft. This unique combination of DNA gave the woman a granite determination, the heart of a bareknuckle prize-fighter and an inner core of steel. Game on.

CHAPTER 6

Leeds city centre. Briggate. The early hours of a Saturday morning in the middle of June. The street pre-dates even the mediaeval town of Leedes, starting as a bridge over the River Aire. Brigg (gate), Gata (street), became Briggate with twice-weekly markets being held there. Briggate became the area around which the town would grow and prosper, predominantly through the cloth and woollen industry for which it would become known throughout the world.

Perhaps the hustle and bustle of a Friday night on Briggate during the 17th and 18th centuries may not have been too different to that of the contemporary. Drunken brawls would have been commonplace after a bawdy night in any one of the hundred or so candle-lit, atmospheric little hotels and inns around the area. It would have been a lively Briggate both day and night as it served as the main artery, off which branched a network of hundreds of dark and dank connecting yards, alleys and ginnels. Here, domestic living spaces sat aside back street industries such as butchering and weaving and jostled alongside the cramped workshops of carpenters, watchmakers and cobblers. Tiny backyard inns and dubious hotels sat side by side, opposite, above and below one another. It was reputed that the rats outnumbered the Briggate residents by three hundred to one as they scavenged for scraps of food in competition with flea-bitten stray hounds and battle-hardened moggies in the back alleys. The area would undoubtedly have been a dangerous one to be out and about during the dark early hours.

However, by the twenty-first century, this ancient history was lost on the present-day population. Briggate, pronounced 'Briggit' by Leeds loiners, became synonymous with city-centre shopping, the spine of the town and, after hundreds of years, still its bustling premier street. By 2017 the whole expanse of the street was now pedestrianised, open to motorised traffic for commercial deliveries only and closed to all but those on foot from 10.30 in the morning. High street retail giants now fronted the ancient thoroughfare with shop after shop, store after store, coffee houses, fast food outlets and everything in between, offering the modern shopper a multitude of choice in which to flash their cash and flex their cards. Little trace of the history and traditions of the old street remained. Gone were the maze of tunnels and yards, ginnels and alleys, built up and over, or demolished and crushed, life expunged. A handful of the yards and alleys had been developed into grand Victorian shopping arcades, but most had been completely removed. Most, but not all. There were still perhaps a score or so of these original squat and squalid little alleys remaining, now frequented by just the few. Unseen from the sophisticated modern-day shopper, and for those dispassionate towards discounted perfumery, fashion trainers or the purchase of a vegan sausage roll, these atmospheric little dank alleys and yards, just feet away from the main Briggate drag provided a direct link back into Georgian Leeds. Amongst the spent gas lamps, ancient brickwork and age-old worn cobbles some of these back alleys had changed little in almost three hundred years. The rats remained of course. The sense of depravity remained. The dark shadow prevailed, as some areas had been denied a ray of natural sunlight for centuries. By 2017 there was only one sector of the population that chose to frequent these dark backwaters of central Leeds. The feral undesirables of modern-day society. Homeless, druggies, beggars, tramps, call them what you will, but in cities around the world they were on the increase, and Leeds was no exception.

*

'I want me fuckin' money Foxy ya bastard!' screamed Yazz, a wizened little soul of less than five feet tall and barely 20 years of age. She carried a Geordie north-eastern twang and wore an oversized trench coat, jogging bottoms and dirty trainers. Her tired, grey face was sour and desperate, her teeth bad and neglected for one so young. Her hair was scraped back revealing a pitted and scarred forehead with cheap make-up stuck to her pale features. It was 3:30 am and she lurched in the middle of Briggate with a sleeping bag wrapped around her shoulders and which trailed on the granite block-paved precinct behind her. Screeching obscenities at the retreating Foxy, she was half cut, floating like a feather and couldn't give a cat's cock-hair at the attention she was attracting. 'Ya little fuckin' twat! ...Come back! ...ya WANKER! ...WANKER!'

Foxy, himself half-cut and buzzing like a stunned hornet, shuffled in the opposite direction muttering to himself. Of a similar social ilk to Yazz, albeit from local stock, he was of a different temperament and shunned attention. Lugging his bedclothes behind him he slouched into the shadows seeking refuge from the manic rantings of his so-called street partner. He ducked into a dark, narrow alley, the entrance of which was almost invisible to those not familiar with it.

'Foxy! Ya little cunt! ...I'll fuckin' kill ya!' shrilled Yazz, but Foxy had disappeared, he'd gone. It wasn't the first time that he'd manipulated the young, naive and vulnerable Yazz, and it wouldn't be the last. As she slumped onto the nearest stainless steel bench she collapsed in tears, but her street-fighting credentials ensured that the obscene language continued unabated and with just as much vigour. A large stooping figure, dark and silent, emerged from the shadows of an adjacent doorway. He watched and observed the situation before manoeuvring towards her and easing his huge frame onto the same cold bench.

'The little bastard!' she continued, unaware of the lumbering giant who now sat right beside her. 'Foxy!' she bellowed between uncontrollable sobbing, 'Ya little twat!' Her voice trailed off as her energies began to wane.

'What's up Arlass?' asked the giant. Yazz flinched as she turned towards him.

'What the fuck? You nearly gimme a fuckin' 'art attack.' She turned away from him before dropping her head into her hands.

'What's up?' he continued, 'what yer crying for?'

'Nowt,' came the glib reply, 'Nowt you can 'elp me wi' anyway.'

'Well how will ya know if you don't tell me what's up,' pressed the stranger.

'What's it to you anyway, who the fuck are ya? It's that little bastard, he's done it again, it's every bastard night,' she said before he could even think of answering her first question.

'Done what?'

'Ripped me off again, like he does all the fuckin' time,' she continued. 'I get rid of all he asks me to and I don't get a penny, It's me who has to go round town and sell it, not 'im, me, and I get fuck all! An' I've been wi' three of his...shitty clients tonight...and I only charge a tenner a go but he has to look after the money, I never even get to see a penny, the slimy little bastard. FOXY! Ya little bastard, where's me money,' she screeched, her shrill voice echoing down the long, cold street.

'It's no use shouting and bawling, he's gone, he'll be miles away by now, you're wasting your time.'

'Aw shut the fuck up mate, who are ya? Me dad?' The giant didn't answer but looked down at the pathetic sight in front of him. Sensing his stare Yazz turned to face him. 'Who the fuck are you anyway? What do you want? Where ya from?'

'Just up from Manchester for a bit. It's Mitch.'

'Mitch? Mitch from fuckin' Manchester eh?'

'Aye, that's it...Mitch...from Manchester.' Yazz looked him in the face.

'Well, what ya doing over 'ere then? Mitch from fuckin' Manchester.'

'Just checking it out, fancied a change.' He left it hanging right there but Yazz was too far gone to express any further interest, wafting her hand in his face.

'Oh just piss off will ya?' She closed her eyes and went to lay on her side, curling up on the bench.

'Hey, hang on, you can't just go to kip 'ere, what if it rains?' Mitch from Manchester shook her by the shoulder. It had the desired effect as she summoned up the strength to sit back up and open her dog-tired eyes.

'Three 'undred quid that little bastard owes me,' she said before drowsily looking up at Mitch. 'You still 'ere?'

'Where do you normally get yer 'ead down?' he persisted. 'I'm on me own 'ere, come on, show us where we can get us 'eads down.'

'Fuckin' 'ell, he'd love that would Foxy, the little shit, me bedding down wi' a total stranger...from fuckin' Manchester! Are you out of yer 'ead or summat?' she slurred with glazed eyes and a swaying motion.

'What? That little bastard you were with earlier? I'd kick his arse wi' me eyes closed, don't worry about 'im.'

'Yeah, and the others... '

'How many others,' he said.

She looked up at him and with great effort replied, 'there's a pack...about six of 'us. There's Jester and Pikey and Woodlouse and...oh I don't fuckin' know. What is it yer want Malcolm...from fucking Manchester...are y'after a bit or what? Eh? ...It'll be a tenner wi' 'money upfront...an' that slimy little twat in't getting owt.'

'It's Mitch, and right now all I wanna do is get me head down.'

Yazz had had enough. She stood bolt upright. 'Oh for fucksake come on then, you can carry me twatting bag.' The hulking giant rose, already with a large backpack strapped over his shoulders and picked up her bag. She looked up at him.

'You're a big fucker you are,' she said, 'come on, follow me, I'm knackered. I'll sort that little cunt out in the morning.'

She turned and trudged up Briggate, in the opposite direction to where Foxy had sloped off. The looming stranger from across the Pennines loped after her before they both disappeared into the shadows, melting into a dark, stinking ginnel, out of sight.

*

Mitch opened his sleepy eyes to the sound of hissing. He sat up realising that he was in unfamiliar territory. He rubbed his eyes and looked around. Dark brickwork on all four sides with just a thin grey strip of sky stretching from right to left. He was hemmed into a corner by three dirty-green commercial wheelie bins and his pitch stank of stale piss, body fat and general disgusting gunk. Through the gap in the bins, he watched a small stream of frothing, hot golden liquid permeate and trickle down the slight incline, slowly meandering through the rough and ancient cobblestones. As realisation set in he gradually retraced his steps back to the encounter with Yazz on Briggate in the early hours. The shuffling sound of clothes preceded her sudden appearance as she stumbled around the corner stuffing the hem of a woollen sweater into her jogging bottoms. She looked down at Mitch.

'So you're awake then?' she said

'No, I'm still asleep.'

'Funny.'

She sat down onto a blanket that was laid out on top of a multi-layered pile of cardboard and reached over to drag a plastic bag from her pile of belongings. She began rummaging through.

'Well,' she said, without looking at him.

'Well, what?'

She cut him a sideways glance. 'What you doing 'ere? What do you want? You got any spice? Crack? Any booze? You got owt?'

'Don't do spice, crack or any o' that shit. Might have a bottle o' summat though.'

'O' what?'

He dragged over his backpack, opened the top flap

and began rummaging around. He yanked out a bottle of white wine and handed it over to Yazz with a straight arm.

"Ere, this un's on me,' he said. She immediately grabbed the bottle and then looked him in the eye before proceeding to remove the twist top. She guzzled her first swig of the day as Mitch grabbed another bottle and did the same.

'Sorry about the glasses,' he said smiling, revealing a ramshackle set of yellowing teeth.

'I'll get over it.'

Each gave the other a look as they attempted to weigh up the situation, both unsure of the other's motivations and designs.

The next half hour was spent with Mitch probing the mindset of Yazz, with Yazz skilfully deflecting every attempt but continuing to glug away on the free booze. She began her daily routine of ablutions. She cleaned her face with face wipes before re-applying make-up. Her matted, wiry hair was vigorously brushed back and tied. After brushing her teeth she rinsed out her mouth with bottled water and spat out the remnants.

'How old are ya then Arlass?' asked Mitch

'Auld enough,' she replied.

'Where ya from?'

'Newcastle. Why?'

'Just wondered.' After a pause, he continued. 'How come you ended up down 'ere then?' Yazz dug him another icy stare. 'OK, just asking,' he said holding his hands up. A period of silence followed before Yazz eventually broke the ice.

'What ya doing today then?' she asked.

'What do you mean?'

'Where you going? What you planning on doing?' she fired back hastily, her response tailgated by another fiery glower.

'Well I ain't gotta meeting with me bank manager 'ave I?' replied Mitch indignantly. 'Thought I might hang out wi' you and your mates.'

'Well think again. They don't take to strangers.'

'Well I'm not gonna harm anyone am I? What are they, a pack of hyenas or summat?'

Yazz looked at him. 'Huh, you're not far off there.'

'Whatever,' said Mitch with a shrug of his shoulders. 'What about Foxy and that money he owes you. Ya want me to get it off 'im?'

'Doubt you could do that. He's a slippery little bastard, but no leave it. I'll sort it meself.'

'Your shout,' replied Mitch before taking in another large gulp from the bottle. 'Let me know if you change yer mind.'

Yazz continued to plaster on the make-up, ignoring Mitch and making short work of the early-morning liquid breakfast. He watched closely as she began to round up her belongings. Sanitary-ware, tissues, make-up, a purse, a cheap phone, packaged hypodermics, half a packet of strong mints, condoms, a photograph of a family in pose, underwear, nail polish, hairbrush and toothpaste. All were scooped up and thrown back into the Tesco's aptly named, 'Bag for life'. She also had a backpack stuffed with clothes, but it was the 'Bag for life' that held everything Yazz needed to survive on the street. It *was* her life.

Once the wine had been consigned to history Yazz stood up and slung the backpack over her shoulder. She wrapped her sleeping bag around her neck and picked up her Bag for life, leaving the hotel bedding and cardboard mattress to the devices of the binmen and street cleansing services.

Looking down at Mitch she nodded. 'See ya then,' she said without a hint of emotion. Mitch avoided eye contact but acknowledged her with a slight nod, remaining silent. She then turned her back on him and proceeded to labour down the little cobbled alley and through an archway towards the chink of light at the bottom of the yard which opened directly onto Briggate.

Mitch looked up at the grey skies above him and mentally began the process of formulating a plan for the day. He didn't have one, he didn't know anyone in Leeds and didn't know the layout of the area. He'd have to start from scratch. He heaved a sigh and then looked up as what little light there was suddenly became a degree darker. It was Yazz.

'Come on then. Get yer arse up, I'll take you down to the group, but I'm warning ya, they don't take to strangers easy.'

Mitch immediately stood up and grabbed his things, eagerly stuffing his sleeping bag into his backpack.

'Nice one Arlass, right, I'm 'ere, just giz us a minute.' At six-foot-eight, he was a mountain of a man and easily dwarfed the diminutive Yazz. Dark featured with black curly hair and swarthy unshaven complexion he looked rough and unkempt. Even taking into consideration his massive head he had one hell of a snout and judging by its twisted configuration it had undoubtedly taken a few knocks over the years. He wore military-style camouflaged trousers and jacket and a ragged beanie hat over his greasy locks. His huge frame stooped over as he looked down at Yazz, his grey-green eyes laden with uncertainty. 'Right', he said, 'let's hit the road.'

As they exited the seedy little yard the sunlight hit them smack in the face as they both blinked, shielding their eyes from the early morning sunshine. Briggate was already buzzing with commuters, workers, shoppers, window cleaners and delivery vehicles. The Council litter pickers were out in force and the distinctive little blue electric vehicles of the LeedsBid Street Rangers were already fizzing in and around Briggate and surrounding streets.

'Right,' said Yazz, 'We usually meet outside HOF which is right at the bottom, opposite Maccy D's.'

'HOF?' replied Mitch

'House O' Fraser,' right at the bottom on the left, but if they've been moved on they'll be over in the little shop next to MacDonald's. But first I wanna take you somewhere. Just follow me,' she said, looking around and over her shoulder. They started walking down the side of the wide precinct with the sun peeping around the grandiose Victorian architecture at the bottom end. It was warm and bright with the air of early summer injecting an extra bounce in the stride of those around, an extra smile and an air of optimism. Within fifty yards Yazz turned right and yanked the giant inside the entrance of another dark yard.

'Come on,' she said, 'urry up.'

'Where we going?' he replied, 'Where ya takin' me?'

'You'll find out, just be quiet and shut the fuck up.'

Within a few yards of the entrance to the yard was a pub, with a sign overhead claiming to be the oldest in Leeds, and past that was a number of fire doors, and bricked up doorways and windows. Halfway up the yard

Yazz once again looked over her shoulder. The coast was clear. She pushed open a large sheet-metal lined door to her left, entered a dark ginnel and yanked Mitch in after her. She indicated for him to close the door and whispered to him to be quiet. This passageway was much narrower than the main yard and also much darker. They shuffled down the little ginnel and the further they got the filthier the conditions, with debris and rubbish discarded and neglected over many years. They walked down a slight decline and on a slight curve to the right. Deeper and darker as the stench of neglect filtered through their crinkled nostrils. They reached a point at which Mitch thought was the end of the ginnel, it was dark, damp and it stank, but Mitch had thought wrong. Yazz now ducked down under a low brick arch and carried on. 'Come on,' she said quietly, 'watch yer 'ead.'

'Hang on, where you taking me? I don't like this. You setting me up ya little cow?' He stopped and refused to go any further.

'Come on you prick, what am I gonna do? Knack ya?' He reluctantly followed and struggled to stoop his large frame under the arch, mumbling under his breath. Ten yards further on and the ginnel came to an end. Yazz now turned to her right and started yanking a metal chain through the body of a rusting six-foot-high wrought-iron gate which opened up into another dark narrow passage. As they passed through the gate she turned to Mitch.

'Ere, wrap that around 'gate,' she said passing him the chain. 'Early warning system.'

He did as he was told and then proceeded to follow Yazz, with hesitance, down the passage by walking sideways such was the narrowness of the gap. He now realised that he was quite a distance away from the bustling street of Briggate. It was deathly silent and dark but he carried on, putting his trust in the spiky little waif he'd met just a few hours ago. After struggling down the narrow passageway for approximately 20 yards the area opened up into a rough square. Mitch looked up. The square was formed by a patchwork of old brick buildings four and five storeys high and was dimly lit by a small portion of the Leeds sky high above. As his eyes became accustomed to the light he saw a large metal structure in one corner of the square and as he looked up he realised that it was an iron spiral staircase. Probably a fire escape of some description, he thought. Judging by the age and condition of the metalwork he assumed that it had lain unused for many years.

'Come on,' whispered Yazz, 'up 'ere.'

'What? We're going up?' he replied.

'Aye, come on, an' stop being a prick,' she said quietly as she began to clamber up the rusting stairway. She turned around and stared down at Mitch. 'And for fuck's sake be quiet!'

Mitch followed her submissively and with trepidation, wondering whether his judgement had been correct in approaching her in the first place during those early hours. She reached the top first and Mitch lumbered after her, surprised at how solid the structure was bearing in mind its perceived age and condition. Panting, he reached the top and was bewildered at what he saw. A steel-meshed landing gantry of about eight-foot square with a handrail and a sloping wooden canopied roof overhead. He looked around to see three or four bags stuffed with possessions, a small rug, a foldable camping chair and a number of towels, blankets and sleeping bags hung over the side of the handrail.

'Wow! A proper little den you've got 'ere Arlass eh?'

'Aye, but just keep it to yersen. No-one knows o' this place, no-one, not even that little bastard Foxy, so just don't let on. You 'ear?'

'Yeah, I 'eard ya, but it's not a bad little spot this, why din't you come back 'ere last night then? It's better than that shit-hole we ended up in.'

'I just use it now and then, maybe a couple o' times a week, when I need a bit o' space or when Foxy's pissed me off like an' I end up on me own. I was off me 'ead last night and I never come 'ere in that state. If I came 'ere every day I'd get seen and if any o' that lot got wind of it, well, that'd be me. As things stand there's only me that uses this place or even knows about it. And now you.'

'Well, why 'ave you shown me it then? Why 'ave you brought me 'ere?'

'I don't fuckin' know,' she said dismissively, 'you can leave some o' your things 'ere if you want, instead o' carting 'em around. Just nip up now and then but don't come 'ere all the time. You can get into 'Arrisons yard from 'other end o' Commercial Street if it's busy on Brigate. But don't let that lot see yer. If they turn on you, and they might if they don't take to you, you can always get out o' 'way for a bit up 'ere. I call it me cage, cos it protects me from them scumbags and that lot out there.'

'From what lot out where?'

'The fuckin' world, that's what. It's shite out there, full o' cunts an' scumbags.' She sat down on the rug and laid down her bags. Mitch followed suit after removing his backpack.

"Ave y'anymore booze?'

'Fuck me Arlass, do you ever stop? I've just got a

bottle o' cider left and then that's that.'

'Come on then, get it out, then we'll go 'ook up wi' them fuckers.'

Mitch shook his head but reluctantly yanked the plastic 2litre bottle from his bulging backpack. No fucking wonder he can't stand up straight carrying all that around thought Yazz, as he removed the top, took a hearty swig and then handed over the bottle. Both took a second to eye the other up, still gauging the integrity and motivations of each other. Mitch looked up from his crouched stance and was surprised to see how much lighter it was at the top of the cage compared to the bottom. The air up here was clean and breathable, not like the dank, stinking foul air they'd been taking in at ground level. He looked down and could see nothing except the dark form of the buildings with long ago bricked-up windows, a square of black at the bottom with the rusting iron structure rising towards the salvation of a clear blue sky, a symbol of hope amid the rabid desperate world beneath them. There was absolutely no sound. They were sat in the heart of one of the biggest and busiest cities in the country but not a sound could be heard. There was no bird call, no traffic sounds, no nothing.

'If you time it right on a nice day it's not a bad little suntrap up here,' said Yazz. 'Just for a couple of hours, afore 'sun moves over.'

Mitch looked behind her at a huge ancient wooden door which, judging by the rusting hinges, cobwebs and encrusted bottle-green paintwork, had not been opened for over fifty years. 'Who's that there?' he asked nodding towards the door at two small photographs pinned to it.

'That's me an me little sister, and they're me Nana an' Granddad,' she said.

'What about your parents?'

'What about 'em? Never knew me proper Mam, and me Dad and the bitch who replaced 'er were both drunken bastards. We lived wi' me Nana and Granddad but she died o' cancer and then me Granddad got put away for thieving.'

'So what 'appened then?'

'Well, we had to go back to me Dad's din't we. And me two step-brothers. Two right wankers there. I lasted two nights an' thought fuck it, I'm off.'

'What happened to your sister?'

'She was only two at the time, I could hardly bring her down to Leeds wi' me could I? As far as I know, she's still wi' me dad. No idea who her mother wa' but me dad wa' shagging all over 'place. Probably got bairns all over fuckin' Newcastle. She just appeared one day at me Nana's and I were told that she were me sister. She'll be nearly eight be now.'

'What's her name?'

'Lilly,' replied Yazz.

'Do you miss her?'

'Course I fuckin' miss her! But there's nowt I can do about it is there? So stop it with the interrogation for fucksake! Who the fuck d'ya think y'are like, the fuckin' coppers?'

Mitch smiled. 'Calm down and chill, you've got a right little temper there Arlass.'

'You fucking calm down an' chill ya big prick!'

'Be quiet, I thought you said we have to be quiet around 'ere,' said Mitch smiling.

'You be fucking quiet,' she repeated. And fucking quiet they were for the next ten minutes as they both continued to glug on the cider, passing it over to the other.

Very orderly given the tension within the cage.

*

With backpacks shed and loads lightened Mitch and Yazz silently sloped back up the dark passage, gently closing the rusting iron gates behind them, making sure to re-wrap the chain to make it look as though it was properly locked. They then silently made their way up the dark incline of the rubbish-strewn, stinking ginnel and gently opened the door into Harrison's Yard. Yazz poked her nose out. The coast was clear and so they edged out, closed the door and then turned right, sliding past the entrance to The Old George pub and back out onto the brightly lit concourse of Briggate. Yazz carried her Bag for life and Mitch carried a smaller backpack over his broad shoulders as they began their journey down the stretch of Briggate, towards the bottom end where the pack of hyenas had already congregated in their daytime lair, just aside Maccy D's.

The community of rough sleepers integrated un-easily with the mainstream business owners of the street, each going about their own affairs despite the other. As opening times for some of the stores approached, the proprietors and floor managers had the unpleasant task of removing the occupants in time for the onset of cus-tomers. Depending on the inclination of the lodgers this could be a smooth operation or a little more protracted, with the occasional intervention of the police required. Getting them out was one thing, cleaning up after them was another. Although some rough sleepers would hap-pily clear up their mess and leave the doorway as found, others would move on leaving the place a stinking mess. Apart from rubbish and food waste they'd often leave soiled clothes, hotel bed sheets and sleeping bags saturated in piss. Occasionally human excrement would be covered over with cardboard and left in addition to blood and discarded sharps. If the stores were lucky the clean up would be caught on the rounds of the street cleaning teams or by the patrolling LeedsBid Street Rangers. If not they had the insalubrious task of cleaning it out themselves.

There was such an eviction taking place just outside the entrance to Harrison's yard. A white-haired older woman swathed in coats, blankets and sleeping bags heaved herself from the doorway of M&S and grabbed two large plastic bags spilling over with more blankets and the like. She wearily trudged the few yards to the nearest stainless steel bench and took up an encampment there, where she yanked the bags up onto the bench and slouched over, half leaning half laying on them. Mitch stared at her as he and Yazz approached.

'Who's that?' he asked.

'I call her Betty, but some of the others call her the bag-lady, no one knows her real name,' replied Yazz. She's been here for longer than anyone can remember, even the older ones. Most of the oldies move away from Briggate 'cos it gets a bit too lively for 'em, they get down to the Dark Arches or somewhere out o' 'way, but Betty stayed put. You won't get owt out of her, keeps herself to herself. She'll say 'ello to me every now an' then, but that's about it.'

'Aye aye Betty,' said Yazz as they got level with her. The woman just about managed a grunt of sorts without moving her head. 'Y'alright pet?' nodded Yazz without breaking stride, and got the same response. They carried on walking past. Mitch stared at the desperate woman with her shock of white hair, deep socketed yellow eyes with black circles and pale sickly features. There was nothing in her eyes, no spark, no awareness. They were flat...they were dead.

'She dun't look well,' he said.

'She'll be reet. She's like that on a morning. Never ventures out o' this end o' Briggate but she gets well looked after. The bloke from Marks and Spencer's gives her free coffees on a morning and she's the only one the security at Maccy D's'll let use the bogs during the night. Rest of us either have to wait 'till morning for a crap or go drop one in one of the alleys. Wouldn't worry about her.' Mitch wasn't worried but couldn't help looking back at her as they continued their way down Briggate towards Maccy D's.

*

A group of five rough and desperate characters lolled about in the first shop doorway up from the MacDonald's restaurant on the corner of Briggate and Boar Lane. They'd already been ousted from the House of Fraser doorway. This shop was vacant and so they had a much longer window in which to occupy the unit before being moved on if they were moved on at all. Foxy sat in the middle with his back against the glass doors. He surveyed the scene from this vantage point which enabled him to see the comings and goings of everyone in the vicinity, the police, street support and other potential troublemakers. He looked much older than his twenty-six years. His face was gaunt and pock-marked with piercing deep-set, dark eyes. His thin lips gave him a permanent sneering countenance. Shoulder-length, greasy hair was brushed back and set into a ponytail. Around him, a posse of like-minded souls, each with a sordid back-story and each on a daily survival mission.

Foxy's beady little eyes flicked from right to left. He caught sight of Yazz loping down the street towards them with the giant figure of Mitch looming after her.

'Ey up, what's going on 'ere,' he said as he lifted his head towards them. The whole group looked up and stayed silent. The whole group that was except for Scotch John, who stood a couple of yards away from the pack and faced the middle of Briggate. He was stooped over, insensible and barely able to keep balance, the stark result of his interaction with Spice, of which he was a frequent user. As he bobbed and tottered Yazz approached the group with Mitch maintaining a short distance behind.

'Look what the cat's dragged in,' piped up Woodlouse who was stood up and leant on the glass frontage.

'Fuck you,' retorted Yazz before turning to Foxy.

'Give us a cig slime ball,' she said holding her hand down towards him, 'And I 'aven't forgotten about me money—'

'Get yer own fucking cigs—'

'You took me baccy off me last night ya little cunt,' retorted Yazz, her anger rising.

'Just sit down will ya and stop the fuckin' shouting bitchlet.'

'Just give me me fuckin' baccy Foxy,' pressed Yazz.

'Sit down 'ere.'

No, I won't, I ju—'

'Siddown!' demanded Foxy his voice rising in authority as his eyes flashed up towards her. Yazz hesitated and then sighed as she surrendered the verbal tug of war and resigned herself to the usual status quo, that of submitting to the forceful nature of her street partner.

'Move up Jester,' she said to a quiet and vacant looking young lad, as she nestled down between him and

Foxy. Pikey, a wiry twenty-year-old sat astride a small bike that looked far too small for him and felt the need to zoom off into the middle of Briggate. He rode it around in a large circle and then skidded back to where he'd originally started from. Mitch looked on feeling uncomfortable, not knowing how to stand, where to put his hands or whether or not to say anything. He wanted to rip Foxy's head off for the way he was treating Yazz, but he'd been pre-warned against interference of any kind.

Foxy pulled out a tobacco tin, took off the lid and picked out a pre-rolled cigarette. He then whipped out a lighter from his pocket and lit the cigarette on Yazz's behalf before handing it over. She took it from him without emotion and slid it in her mouth taking her first drag of the day. Foxy then grabbed a can of cider from his bag and waggled it provocatively in front of her.

'Give us it 'ere ya twat,' she said as she grabbed the can, yanked the ring-pull and immediately started guzzling.

'See,' said Foxy quietly, 'Share an' share-alike. We said we share all us stuff din't we? That's what we said.'

'You still owe me three 'undred quid, don't think ya getting away with that ya little get.'

'Three 'undred quid,' sniggered Foxy, 'Yer off your fuckin' rocker you are lass.' Yazz fired him a sideways glance and carried on drinking and dragging on the roll-up.

'Anyway,' said Foxy looking Yazz straight in the eye, 'Who's this bloke y've brought down 'ere then?'

'Mitch...he's from Manchester.'

Foxy didn't look up at Mitch but remained stock-still and focussed on Yazz. The rest of the gang, except Scotch John who was now comatose lying flat out on the street, all looked up at Mitch. He shuffled his feet nervously.

'What does he want?' asked Foxy, still staring at Yazz.

'I don't know, fuckin' ask him,' she fired, rolling her eyes and knocking back another glug of the cheap cider.

Pikey whirled away on his bike. 'Ooo! There's gonna be a fuuucking fight!' he pronounced at the top of his voice gleefully as he completed another almost perfect circle and arrived back at the exact starting point.

Foxy turned his head slowly and looked up at Mitch. Sensing the rising tension, Jester shrunk further back into the doorway. After a while, Foxy spoke.

'So, what you doing round 'ere then pal?' Mitch looked at him and then at the rest of the clan. He couldn't understand why Yazz had warned him away from them. He could smash 'em all, he thought, there was only the silent Woodlouse who looked as though he could handle himself but he was twice his size.

'Just checking it out,' replied Mitch. 'Why?'

'Just asking pal...just asking. Where ya from?'

'Manchester.'

'Hmm...Manchester eh?'

'Aye, Manchester, if that's alright wi' you.' Mitch stood his ground, he wasn't going to be shoved around by this arsehole. He looked over at Woodlouse who nodded his head. Mitch reciprocated and stood with his hands in jacket pockets.

'Alright by me pal,' said Foxy quietly but with a sneering arrogance before he turned his gaze away.

The restless Pikey darted off again. 'Fooook,' he shouted, 'It's kicking off! It's kicking off big time!' This time his circle of turn terminated at the Greggs store opposite where he fervently enlightened another group of streeties of the impending scrap between Foxy and the 'new lad' from Manchester. But he was wrong about things kicking off. Instead of continuing the conversation, Foxy started gently chiding Yazz, totally ignoring the presence of Mitch. Jester shied away from even looking at the new bloke and Woodlouse sat down next to Foxy and opened up another can of cider. Mitch was left standing there feeling awkward and foolish. He looked down towards Yazz for moral support but she didn't even acknowledge his presence. By now, with the alcohol she'd consumed since early morning, she was in the state she was most comfortable in. Her head was fizzing as the edge of her demeanour was rounded off. Mitch decided he needed to escape from the highly stressful atmosphere and eventually sloped off, without saying anything further. He drifted past the pack, past Maccy D's and turned right onto Boar Lane out of sight.

'From Manchester eh?' said Foxy quietly to Woodlouse without turning to face him. 'Then why the Scouse accent?'

CHAPTER 7

There was an empty, dead silence in the house on Kentmere Avenue. It was like the quiescence before the sacramental funeral ritual. The period where mourners await the arrival of the hearse and loiter in edgy silence, convincing themselves that matters will be over and done within the not-too-distant future. Linda and Shelley sat opposite at the kitchen table, each clasping a mug of tea. The table was covered by a spotlessly clean and ironed cotton tablecloth. A ginger-cat themed teapot sat in the middle, along with the usual assortment of cake, buns and other fancies. It was a calm, warm morning as Linda looked out of the kitchen window over the back garden and down onto Kentmere Gate. This area of Seacroft was built into a slight gradient of the Aire Valley which gradually fell away to the rear of Kentmere Avenue. The natural topography surrendered a sweeping view of the city centre in the distant background. Given favourable conditions, this panoramic vista could be breathtaking, especially on a crisp and cloudless winter's evening when the city centre was lit up for Christmas or on Bonfire night when the firework celebrations would light up the Leeds skies for miles around. On a clear day, it was possible to see, with the naked eye, the iconic Emily Moor mast which stood almost twenty-five miles away. The grade II listed building was the tallest freestanding structure in the country, standing taller than the Eiffel

Tower, but there was no sign of it today. There was a warm, expectant haze hanging over the city. The only recognisable landmark was the distant clocked tower of the famous Leeds Town Hall. The rest of the cityscape was a maze of hazy grey tower blocks as they grasped towards the skies competing and gasping for fresh air amid the skeletons of huge mechanical cranes which buzzed about the city skyline like giant, shackled dragonflies, forced into hard labour.

Zoe and Sophia had been dispatched over to Chris's house in nearby Crossgates for the day. Linda had insisted that they take Princess for good measure. "Give Tosh a bit o' peace and let the little fucker crap in someone else's garden", had been the rationale behind that one. Shelley looked up at the kitchen wall clock.

"Kin 'ell, is that the right time?' she said. 'How much longer is 'e gonna be? I've 'dinner to put on, you know what Dennis's like if 'is dinner's not ready when 'e gets home from 'club.'

'Stop bloody mithering. He'll be here soon...just shurrup and drink yer tea.' Shelley tutted and shook her head but complied and continued to silently sip her steaming hot drink. Within a couple of minutes, it was Linda's turn to allow impatience to get the better of her.

'Where the bleedin' 'ell is he?' She got up and stormed into the front room, muttering further obscenities as she did so. She pulled back the curtains and scoured the outside, checking for activity. Tosh was curled up on the window-sill, sunning himself. He looked up at his mistress and yawned, opening his jaws like a python at a piglet emporium before licking his lips and burying his head back into his fur-lined midriff. He closed his eyes as Linda shuffled back into the kitchen.

'Right, 'e's 'ere,' she said.

'What?'

'He's 'ere. 'E's just pulled up.'

'Aww Gawd,' replied Shelley.

'Just let me do the talking. It'll either go smoothly...or it might get messy, one or t'other. Either way, 'e's out. Got it?'

'Got it...OUT!'

The front door flew open and in bounded Phil. He didn't notice the two packed holdalls and large, bulging bin-liner at the bottom of the steps. He opened the living room door and peered inside. Empty apart from Tosh. He then made his way to the kitchen, opened the door and walked in. He cast his eyes onto Linda and then Shelley, he smiled.

'Now then ladies, me favourite little juice boxes the pair of ya,' he said with a huge grin on his bushy-whiskered face. 'Any chance of a kiss-kiss?' he beamed. They ignored him. 'Anyone know where Zoe is?' he continued, unperturbed. The Scissor Sisters remained poker-faced.

'She's gone over to our Chris's wi' Sophia for a bit. She'll be back later,' answered Linda, flagrant in her determination to avoid eye contact.

'Just I wa' thinking of 'aving a ride over to Temple Newsam for an hour before dinner that's—'

'Listen, can you just give me a minute wi' Shell and then I'll come in an' see ya. There's summat I wanna go over wi' ya. Just go into 'living room, I won't be a minute,' said Linda her dour monotone still in no way alerting Phil to the impending showdown.

'Ok honey chops, everything okay?'

'Aye, everything's fine. Just give us a minute will ya?' Phil smiled and disappeared before closing the door behind him.

'Ooo I'd love to smash the sickly bastard right in 'is face,' whispered Linda as she brought her fist up to her chin and shook it. 'I'll fuckin' unny chops 'im.'

'The grinnin' twat'll be grinnin' out of his arse bi 'time we've finished with 'im,' replied Shelley. 'Come on, let's get it over an' done wi', I've a joint o' brisket waitin' for 'roast tin.'

The two of them rose in unison and made their way through to the living room with Linda leading the way. Shelley closed the door behind her and stood guard. She was a big woman, almost six foot in height, and carried her considerable weight very well. She cast an imposing figure as she stood sentinel, arms folded, sinister, steadfast.

Phil had already tickled Tosh's belly and having received zilch acknowledgment in return he was now slouched on the sofa. Linda approached him and stood before him. Phil looked up, first at Linda and then at Shelley. For the first time, he sensed there was a problem.

'Now then lad,' said Linda. 'Where were you last night?' She stared him directly in the eye.

'What?'

'Are ya deaf? ...I said...where were you last night?'

'Well, you know where I wa' Lind. I wa' in Birmingham, working.'

'Birmingham eh?' Linda looked over to Shelley who remained stock still save for the raising of her eyebrows.

'And when did you get back to Leeds?' continued Linda.

'This morning, why, what's up? What yer ask—'

'What time this morning?'

'What? What do you mean what time?'

'Are you fuckin' deaf, daft o' just plain stupid? I said...what time did you get back into Leeds this morning? Well?' Phil looked hesitant.

'Er...well, I set off first thing, dropped the lads off and came straight here, why what's—'

'You're a fucking liar!' bellowed Linda. 'A lying bastard, that's what you are.'

'What do you mean?'

'What do I mean? You know full well what I mean you simple 'eaded twat. You were seen in town last night wi' someone!'

'It wan't me Lind, I were in Birmingham...with the lads, it musta been someone else—'

'Don't fucking Lind me ya lying, conniving get, cos you were seen with that little trollop Katie wan't ya? Or wa' that a case o' mistaken identity as well. The pair o' ya, all over each other on the fuckin' Headrow. What a fuckin' plank, a cheating, fuckin', thick, plank.' Phil knew the game was up, he attempted to reason with his captors.

'I can explain Lind, it's not what it looks like—'

'You're not what yer look like, you lying, two-faced fuckwit yer nowt else!' Linda was now getting into some real stride, her Seacroft juices began to flow.

'Just let me talk to Zoe,' protested Phil, 'I'll sort things out with her.'

Linda saw red at his attempt to manipulate the situation, she lunged forwards and slapped her head right up to his, their foreheads now touching.

'Listen, yer simple bastard,' she said through gritted teeth, 'Zoe doesn't even wanna see you again never mind talk to you. It was her who saw the pair of ya. How do you think that made her feel? Eh? You think you can just wade in and smooth things over do ya? Well, think again twatbag because you're fuckin' gone. You're outta here buster. You're history, you'll never lay yer slimy 'ead down in this 'ouse again, so get yer things, and fuck off!' Phil squirmed on the sofa and managed to wrest his head away from Linda's.

'I'm not going anywhere. I live 'ere, me name's on 'electoral register, you can't just kick me out—'

'I couldn't give a cat's cock 'air if yer name's on 'fuckin' milk register, thick 'ead, you're out, now, today!' screamed Linda now flushed with adrenaline, her pulsating veins running amok as the red mist descended. She grabbed hold of Phil's beard and ragged it. 'You cheating bastard, if her father had been alive 'e'd 'ave fucking killed ya. Are ya listening?' She continued ragging his beard left and right. 'Do you understand ya thick bastard?' she raged. She'd lost it and Phil reacted by grabbing her arm and yanking it away.

'Fuckin' get off me you silly cow,' he said as he shuffled to the other side of the sofa attempting to escape her rage. As soon as Shelley saw him grab Linda's arm it signalled her entrance into the ring. She waded in like a prop forward smashing into the pack. Like a tag wrestling team, Linda was pushed away and it was now Shelley's turn to loom over the tortured Phil who squirmed on the sofa beneath her.

'Don't you fucking lay a finger on her you slimy little cod-faced fucker, else you've me to contend wi'. Now get yer bags and piss off, like she said.'

'I'm not going anywhere, I live 'ere, I'll sort it with Zoe,' he continued.

''Ave you got a learning difficulty?' asked Shelley with a wide-eyed, manic stare. Phil looked up at her quizzically.

'Eh? ...No,'

'Do ya fuckin' want one?'

'No.'

'Well fuck off then, like she said, an' before you start thinking o' resisting or laying a finger on me, let me ask you this. Do you know the Chadwicks? From the Skelwiths?'

'No,' replied Phil shaking his head and fidgeting over the sofa like a man laying bareback on a bed of hot coals. He did know of the Chadwicks from the Skelwiths, a local crime family. He was lying.

'You're a liar,' countered Shelley. 'And do you know Billy Chadwick?'

'No,' replied Phil. He did know Billy Chadwick, an active member of the said local crime family and a notorious not-to-be-messed-with meat-head.

'Lying bastard! Everyone knows Billy Chadwick! Well let me tell you, that as we speak Billy is with my Dennis at Seacroft Working Men's, and Billy will be coming back to my fuckin' 'ouse for 'is Sunday twatting dinner and sitting next to 'is partner, my fuckin' daughter. Do I need to go any further? Get me drift?'

The mention of the Chadwicks convinced Phil that the game was up. He protested that he didn't know of them, but he was lying. He did know of them, he knew of them very well, and he knew what they were about. They were the last bunch of 'Croftites he wanted to mix it with. He held his hands up. 'Alright, alright, I'll go,' he said, 'just back the fuck off will ya? Fuckin' lunatics. What about Sophia? When can I see her?'

'Never mind that, just fuck off. Go on, your bags are in 'hall,' snapped Linda, still breathing heavily. He got up and lunged for the door before grabbing the two holdalls.

For Linda and Shelley, the crux of the job was complete, the eviction had gone according to plan, but they weren't finished there. They knew how to kick an adversary in the teeth when they were down. Tosh remained unmoved on the living room windowsill as Phil staggered out of the front door with the Scissor Sisters continuing the on-slaught. Each lashed out at the back of his head as he attempted to duck out of their reach.

'Fucking wanker!' muttered Shelley through gritted teeth.'

'Thick bastard,' followed up Linda.

It was now more for show than anything else, they knew that having the reputation of the Chadwick family on their side there'd be no retaliation.

With the open windows, the commotion from inside the house had attracted a small gathering. Neighbours stood at the end of their gardens watching on and a group of four or five hooded youths, one on a bike, stood in the middle of the road captivated by the clamour. Linda and Shelley followed Phil up to the end of the path. He slammed open the rear doors of the transit and threw the holdalls in while at the same time Linda heaved the black bin-liner over the gate.

'And don't fucking come back!' she bellowed, purposefully putting on a show for the neighbours, wanting to humiliate him to the extent that he'd never dare show his face again in the neighbourhood.

'What's happened Arlass?' asked one of the hoodies, barely a teenager in age, as he sat astride his bike.

'Never mind Arlass ya cheeky get, go on, on yer way,' asserted Linda. The bin-liner had collapsed onto the pavement with an assortment of clothes and smalls spilling out onto the ground, forcing Phil to scramble about retrieving them.

"Ave yer been booted out mate?' asked hoodie-boy, seemingly the leader of the group who was now jeering and revelling in the street-side drama. 'Ha-ha, he's been fucked off,' he grinned to his mates.

'Fuck off you, you little cunt before I fuckin' do ya,' growled Phil.

'You can't even do these two old slappers ya silly bastard,' countered the youth.

'Ey, who you calling slappers ya cheeky little get?' said Linda, wagging her finger at the lad, 'just keep out o' this you.'

'Sorry Arlass,' replied the kid grinning.

'Aye, an' yer can take them mucky knickers wi' yer an' all,' shrilled Shelley as she spotted Phil ramming items of underwear back into the bag.

The youth screeched with delight. 'Aye get yer skiddies off of our street you shitty-arsed fucker,' he turned to his mates who were all in fits of laughter. 'Ha-ha, look lads, it's Sid the skid.'

'I've told you yer little twat, shut the fuck up,' retorted Phil jabbing his finger at the mouthy hoodie-boy. He threw the bag into the back of the van.

'An' I'll tell ya summat else an all shall I,' said Shelley, determined to get her money's worth before he was gone.

Phil stopped, now flush-faced and flustered, he turned and faced the two women. 'What? What d'ya wanna tell us?'

'That common little floozy you went wi', do ya know why she left Seacroft?'

'Well?' he replied, 'Go on then.'

'She was shagging every Tom, Dick an' fuckin' 'Arry

on 'bleedin' estate, that's why. Got herself pregnant twice, had two abortions and she still wun't stop. She's nowt but a slutty little shagging machine. She is, and always 'as been a mucky, dirty little trollop! You were made for each other, so go on and piss off, go an' get yer sticky little dick checked out afore it falls off!'

'Oy! Put yer sticky little dick back in yer shittied up knickers,' sneered hoodie-boy to the continual sniggering of his mates.

'Ey, that's enough from you lot,' chided Linda.

There were now more neighbours dotted about as well as passers-by who'd stopped to witness the scene and which only served to crank up the pressure on Phil, all he wanted to do was get the hell out of there.

'So fucking what. Big deal,' he replied to Shelley before turning his back on them.

'Go on, fuck off,' shouted the kid on the bike to which Phil reacted with a two-fingered salute. He jumped in the cab and as he did so the kid rode up and kicked the back door of the vehicle. This riled Phil, he wound the window down and stuck his head out.

'I'm fucking warning you ya little bastard,' he snarled. The kid rode away and skidded back to the safety of his mates.

'Come on then,' taunted the kid, beckoning Phil to come and join him for a ruck. 'I'll take ya!' Phil ignored him and started the engine up.

'Ey you, pack it in now that's enough,' said Linda to hoodie-boy. But hoodie-boy wasn't finished yet and went back up to the transit to give it one parting stamp with the heel of his foot. Enraged, Phil jumped out and ran to the back of the van. Hoodie-boy and his followers scattered.

'I'll fucking kill you, ya little cunt,' growled an agitated Phil. He returned to his cab as Shelley shot her final volley.

'Get to 'VD clinic and get yersen checked ya cheating bastard,' she shouted, but Phil didn't hear the parting shot, he was off. Cut to shreds, he put his foot down and within seconds he was storming up North Parkway, his goal to get as far away from Seacroft as he possibly could.

The kids had had their fun and slowly dissipated. Linda and Shelley looked around at the neighbours who remained silent but shook their heads in support of whatever cause their two neighbours had been upholding. The Sisters turned around to walk back into the house.

'Well that's that then,' said Linda. 'Thanks for that love.'

'No problem, I enjoyed it,' replied Shelley.

'I didn't know she'd had two abortions.'

'Who?'

'Katie, Katie bleedin' Ackroyd, the little trollop we've been on about.'

'Oh, is that 'er name? No, it wan't 'er. Must o' been someone else,' replied Shelley dryly.

Linda shook her head. 'What yer like?' Come on, lets 'ave a cuppa then you'd better get back to yours afore that joint o' brisket turns on yer.'

CHAPTER 8

It was around seven in the evening. Briggate. A Friday night. The changing of the guard was taking place in the city centre. Department stores, shops and commercial organisations were closing down after another busy day. Straggling daytime shoppers lugged their bags up and down the precincts heading towards the car parks, taxi ranks, bus and rail stations. The pubs, restaurants and bars were readying themselves for the evening onslaught. Early incoming traffic included the first waves of evening drinkers, and the more sedate and sophisticated fine diners and theatregoers. It was calm and peaceful, a lull in proceedings before the city centre started banging. The time of day when the street people felt relatively safe in the Briggate doorways. There were still pickings to be made courtesy of the benevolent Leeds public. A couple of quid, a pre-packed sandwich or a meal from Maccy D's, a hot drink. The savvy street population knew that within three or four hours the ambience mightn't be as cordial. Large groups of piss-heads out for trouble had been known to turn on them, perceiving them as, 'scrounging bastards', the scourge of the city centre. They knew when best to melt into the background and when it was safe to come back out again. At this time of day though, all was good as they occupied their pitches and doorways in relative peace, quietly enjoying the fruits of the day's takings and settling down to the commencement of their weekend shenanigans.

The hyenas, headed by Foxy, were camped in their usual lair, the doorway of the vacant shop unit next to Maccy D's restaurant at the bottom end of Briggate. They'd relocate over the road to the larger doorway at HOF's in the early hours to bed down when the bustle of the street started to simmer down a little. For now, they kept themselves to themselves as did the remainder of the city's community of rough sleepers dotted out along the full length of Briggate and throughout the town centre. On the opposite side of Briggate, a further thirty yards up in another doorway slumped the lumbering hulk of Mitch. He swigged on a two-litre plastic bottle of Cider taking in the sights.

It had been almost a week since Mitch had acquainted himself with an inebriated and drugged up Yazz. She'd opened up to him a little and shared her secret of the cage, but their relationship had flourished no further than that. He hadn't uttered a word to her since. He'd hoped he might have bumped into her during his two visits back to the cage to check his baggage. Not that he trusted her. There was nothing left in the cage that was of any value. Everything he owned of any worth he'd made sure was on his person, at all times. In the week since meeting up with the pack, he'd been keeping a close eye on them, of their movements, on Foxy's treatment of Yazz. He assumed that the sly leader had specifically kept her under his strict control just to keep her away from him. As far as he could make out, she'd been either pissed or drugged up for the whole week as he'd skulked in the dark alleys and doorways awaiting the chance to catch her on her own, and sober. Thus far his efforts had proved fruitless, but he'd bide his time. He hoped if he could prise her from the clutches of the controlling Foxy then he could muscle in and maybe win her over. He had made only tenuous connections during his first week in Leeds and these were more with the sympathetic security guards and street cleaners. The only contact he'd had with any of the hyenas was when the trouble toting Pikey had pulled up on his bike, sent by Foxy on an intelligence-gathering mission. He'd left with short shrift, but that apart, he'd made little impact on the rough sleeping fraternity and he knew he'd have to integrate if his time in Leeds was to become more permanent. He saw Yazz as an integral cog in the wheel of his strategy, and as he patiently awaited his opportunity he simultaneously maintained a close eye on the animated pack of wild dogs opposite.

*

Little be known to Mitch, he too had been the subject of covert surveillance. Foxy had had his beady little eyes glued to the movements of the giant Scouser since their first encounter. He didn't trust him. Foxy didn't trust anyone. He had eyes and ears all over the city, far beyond the boundaries of Briggate. His connections kept him abreast of all the comings and goings of rough sleepers, commuting beggars, bother causers (police and street support groups) and anything else that may be happening within the city centre. Although it wasn't a direct stare, Mitch was permanently fixed in his periphery line of vision, he wouldn't be going anywhere without him knowing about it. The standoff between the two had been simmering all week and tensions were rising. The difference was that although Mitch was a six-and-a-half-foot giant and could more or less take down anyone he wanted on a one-to-one basis, he was no match for the pack of hyenas nor their extensive network of connections throughout the city centre.

Yazz slouched up next to Foxy, her head resting on his shoulder. She was already out of her skull having been drinking since early morning and topped up with crack cocaine courtesy of her beloved partner.

'He's still there,' said Woodlouse to Foxy quietly.

'I know, I've got me eye on 'im don't worry about that. Dunno if 'e's trying to put the frighteners on us or what, but we'll see.'

He whipped out another can of cider, ripped off the ring-pull and carried on supping. Woodlouse was already working through a crate of lager. Scotch John, older than the rest of the pack, was slumped up against the glass frontage with his feet laid out directly onto the street. He slurred and smacked his lips as he guzzled away at a bottle of wine,

'Whazze? The f'cker!' he said.

'What yer on about Scotty ya daft cunt?' piped up Woodlouse, 'just be quiet and finish yer drink.'

'Eee ah fuckin' will anorl ya bashdards,' he replied, casting a blurry-eyed sideways glance.

'He's fuckin' gone,' grinned Pikey who as usual was perched on his bike ready for a whirl should anything kick-off. Pikey didn't drink that much but he got his highs from crystal meth which kept him animated and energised for most of the day. The quiet and reticent Jester didn't do much. He wasn't into drugs and couldn't handle drink. He'd found himself ostracised from mainstream society and fallen in with Foxy and the hyenas. They'd become his family on the street and looked after him. He was only small and not yet twenty years of age. He wasn't a talker and just hung out with the group for protection, doing a bit of running for Foxy to earn his keep within the pack.

'Well, tonight's the night for you Jester, ya little bastard,' proclaimed Foxy.

'What?'

'What d'ya think lads. Is he up for it or what?'

'Up for what?' asked Woodlouse.

'What?' repeated Jester.

'The old lass,' said Foxy quietly. Pikey and Wood-louse raised their eyebrows and grinned.

'Go on, you can do it ya little twat!' cried Pikey, as he sped away with a grin as wide as the inner ring road, circling around and back again. 'Whoop whoop!' he screamed.

'Come on old lad. You can do it. You've watched us do it enough times 'an't ya. Come on, show a pair and go do 'er.' demanded Foxy. 'You've gotta start somewhere.' Jester had little resistance and took a deep breath to calm his nerves.

'Okay,' he said, his voice wavering, 'I'll do it. But what if she wakes up?'

'Well, just act daft, ask 'er if she's alright or sum-mat. Use yer loaf,' replied Woodlice tapping his head, 'it's all part o' yer apprenticeship.'

Foxy laughed. 'You up for it then young un?'

'Yeah, okay, I'm in,' he replied after a short pause.

'Good lad, now remember, just keep calm, keep your wits about yer and wait 'til 'coast is clear. Got it?'

'Got it.'

*

Pikey's animated hollering had alerted Mitch to the com-motion opposite. He hadn't grasped every word they'd spoken but he'd heard enough to work out that something was afoot and it involved 'the old lass'. The only old lass that he could think of was the one that Yazz had referred to as Betty. The one with the shock of white hair, the one Yazz had said went nowhere else except the bottom end of Briggate. He'd felt sorry for her after that first encounter and he'd been keeping tabs on her during the last few days. He'd even tried to engage with her in his desperate and futile attempts at trying to build up a network of contacts. He needn't have bothered as she'd totally blanked him. Yazz had been correct though, as far as he could make out the strange old woman never ventured far away from the bottom end of Briggate and was always either stationed in one of the shop doorways or heaped on a bench with her bags. As Mitch looked up and down the street, he could see that, even at this early hour, she'd bedded down in a mobile phone store doorway, now closed for the day, on the opposite side of the street, just further up from the M&S store and about fifty or sixty yards up from where the hyenas were camped out. She appeared out cold as there was no movement and was already covered in a blanket. He watched as the annoying Pikey had stormed up the street on his bike and then whirled around. As he did so he'd pointed a mimicking finger over at Mitch before returning to the pack. Mitch murmured, 'Prick!' as he sped past on his bike. He would love the opportunity to smack the little bastard in the chops, he thought, but for now, he kept his own counsel and maintained his policy of observation only.

*

Jester sat just outside the doorway with his legs crossed and his back up against the glass frontage. He watched the comings and goings. No security guards, no street support officers or other fucking do-gooders doing their rounds. Certainly no coppers. Once he was sure the street was free of all bother causers, and not before, then he could make his move. After a couple more minutes, he turned towards Foxy.

'Just hang on a minute,' said the pack leader holding his hand up. He nodded to Pikey. 'Just one more,' he said, 'and for fuck's sake no fucking screaming. D'y'ear?'

'On it boss,' said Pikey quietly before setting off and pedalling his bike, slower than usual and up the side of Briggate. He coasted past the doorway where the old woman lay, out cold. After a quick turning circle, he turned back and stopped in front of her. She lay wasted, incapable and vulnerable. The scouting dog hovered over her, his narrow eyes scanning every square inch of the nest which was full of junk and debris. Once the surveillance was complete he whirled away in typical style. He couldn't resist screeching like an agitated Great Black-Backed Gull on Bridlington Quayside as he flew down Briggate to re-join the rest of the pack.

'She's good,' he said quietly as he skidded to a stop in front of the lair.

'What bit o' 'no fucking screaming' do you not understand yer fuckin' prick?' said Foxy firing a stern glare at his insubordinate pack brother, 'for fuck's sake!' Pikey ignored him.

'An' both bags are opened. Good to go.'

The eyes of Foxy and Jester met as Foxy gave a hint of a nod.

'Go on lad, do the business,' said Woodlouse with a smirk on his face.

'Go on Jester lad, do it for England,' declared Pikey loudly.

'Fuck ye inglish bashdads,' countered Scotch John.

'Shut the fuck up Scotty, ya silly old cunt,' demanded Foxy as he once again glared at Pikey, 'And will you be quiet ya prick, give the lad a fuckin' chance!'

Pikey got the message as he backed off and watched as a nervous Jester took in a large breath of air before easing himself up and onto his feet. With his head lowered he then slowly made his way up Briggate towards the mobile phone shop doorway. From across the road, Mitch looked on.

As he approached the woman Jester slowed down and looked around. There were still people milling about but no one that would have any interest in his extra-curricular activities. Once he was sure the coast was clear he calmly entered the doorway and sat down beside her. Here, he sat still for two or three minutes, arms and legs crossed, keeping an eye on his hostess lest she wake up and rumble him. After a while, he slowly and methodically began scouring through the woman's belongings which were strewn around the doorway. The nest contained everything the woman owned, the total sum of her worldly possessions and which were lugged around wherever she went, 24 hours a day. They were unguarded now though, as she lay unconscious and incognizant to the rummaging little thief sitting right beside her.

It didn't take him long to find what it was he was looking for. A full bottle of scotch whisky in one of the bags and, as he calmly rifled through the remainder of her stuff, he found another half-bottle, already part-consumed but which was still three-quarters full. It was partially underneath the body of the woman and so he gently eased it away from her whilst all the time watching for any signs of movement or any indication of her stirring from her brain-pickled coma. He calmly stood both bottles up and remained seated next to the woman. Nothing untoward in that for any passer-by looking on. The enterprising little bastard wasn't done yet though. He looked around and began further rummaging. He saw it. It was wedged under her arm but on the other side as to where he was sat. He remained seated and calm for a few seconds before getting up to his feet. Again he looked around and over his shoulder before moving to the other side of the woman. He bent down on one knee and feigned to straighten up the blanket that loosely covered her. He then reached over and gently pulled the cream-coloured plastic purse that was almost stuck under her elbow. He eased it out bit by bit but the woman roused. She didn't open her eyes but she shifted her position and emitted a guttural grunt. Jester stopped dead in his tracks and remained silent, his heart thumping. Only when he was 100 per cent satisfied that she'd fallen back into her senseless state did he continue his objective to openly steal her purse. Once he'd eased it into the open he checked over his shoulder. All was good. He placed the purse into the pocket of his hoodie and calmly and quietly lifted both bottles of scotch taking care not to clink them together. He then set off with his booty, back to the lair where the pack of hyenas eagerly awaited his return.

Mitch could hardly believe what he'd just seen. He came from a shitty background himself where it had been dog eat dog, survival and all that. But to see a group systematically plan and execute such a despicable act towards a vulnerable and defenceless fellow rough sleeper was beyond even his comprehension. He sat there and simmered. *What a fucking shit-hole this place is.*

As Jester returned with the whisky he was high-fived by all the gang except Scotch John and Yazz who were both still incapable.

'Nice one Jester lad, 'ere lets 'ave a sup,' said Wood-louse, grabbing the half bottle from him. The full bottle was passed over to Foxy.

'That's mah boy,' smiled Foxy, 'proud o' you lad.' Jester beamed with delight, but he wasn't finished yet.

'And as a Brucie bonus,' he said as he pulled out the purse from his pocket.

'Wow! Ya little bastard,' said Foxy, his eyes bulging with delight. 'Ere, gizzit 'ere,' he demanded and grabbed the purse from the little thief.

'Top lad Jester, ya little fucker ya nowt else. You can come again lad.' He yanked the purse open and inspected the contents before pulling out three crisp twenty pounds notes. 'Result!' he said unable to disguise his absolute delight and beaming from ear to ear. 'Ere y'are, you can 'ave 'change for being a good lad,' he said throwing the purse back at Jester who was equally chuffed to bits at the way he'd impressed himself onto the pack leader. He set about retrieving three pound coins and a handful of coppers in change from the purse. Once he'd removed the coins there was nothing of any value left, the purse was empty.

'Right, you know where to take that don't ya?' said Foxy. Jester nodded and embarked upon the task of getting rid of the evidence. 'The drinks are on me tonight lads,' grinned Foxy as he stuffed the sixty quid inside his trouser pocket. The fact of the matter was that the drinks weren't on him. The drinks were on the vulnerable old woman, the one that as a group they'd just callously robbed of every penny she had. And of her medicine, the only medication she understood, and which her exhausted and depleted system required, just to get her through the night. From across the wide boulevard, Mitch looked on. He was disgusted.

Jester calmly walked onto Boar Lane and round the back of Maccy D's where a small passageway lead to the rear of the three-hundred-year-old Holy Trinity Church. In a dark corner was a drain. He silently slipped the purse through the foul-smelling grill. The evidence had been disposed of, whilst back on Briggate the pack devoured the whisky with Scotch John aggressively making sure he got his fair share. Even Yazz got in on the act as she eventually came round and joined in the merrymaking. It was a happy pack.

*

It was bound to happen. Mitch had been waiting for it but had been unsure as to what form it would take. It kicked off just after half-past nine as dusk tumbled upon the ancient thoroughfare of Briggate. He'd been at the wine and cider himself since early afternoon and had spoken to not a soul since he'd paid the young lass in Tesco's for the day's hoard of booze. He'd just about nodded off as he jerked up his head to the sound of high-pitched screaming. At first, it sounded like a little kid crying. And then it turned into a wail. It was 'Betty' from across the road. He quickly worked out that she'd woken up and discovered the heist - no money and no booze. She now slouched on the stainless steel bench, head in hands and bayed like an injured wild beast. Her desperate and failed attempts at recovering her medicine had resulted in the remainder of her possessions being scattered around the doorway and onto the street. Groups of well-meaning revellers approached and attempted to calm her, but despite their best efforts she was inconsolable, her bewailing incoherent and nonsensical.

Patrol cops descended upon the scene and tried to

make sense of the situation but were unable to fathom out the prevailing problem, whilst the pack further down Briggate, cackled and revelled in the commotion. They knew fair well that they were in the clear. They knew that the woman didn't have the mental capacity, nor inclination to talk to the authorities, they knew that she wouldn't point a finger down their way. They knew this for certain, as it was a raid they'd carried out regularly. Tonight, due to the ingenuity of their newest recruit, they'd procured the added bonus of taking her cash as well as her sustenance. They weren't concerned for the physical or mental welfare of the silly old bag woman. They were pleased with their foolproof methodology. It was a cinch. It was easy. It always was.

The wailing continued with neither the police officers nor the street support teams able to settle her nor evaluate what the problem was. It hurt Mitch to watch the pandemonium after what he'd witnessed earlier, but of course, he couldn't intervene. As much as he hated the pack he could never turn grass. He eyed the group as they stood outside their doorway watching the commotion, drinking from and passing around the whisky they'd embezzled from her, satisfied smirks emblazoned across their smutty, dirty little faces. He watched as Pikey took off and parked up within ten yards of the brouhaha, gleaning intelligence for HQ and revelling in his own self-styled importance.

The authorities decided to remove 'Betty' from the arena, her constant howling was causing too much of a rumpus. An ambulance arrived at the scene and Mitch looked on as the team of medics backed up by police officers struggled to manipulate her onboard, with whatever luggage they could retrieve. It was a painful watch for

Mitch. He didn't know it but the street teams were accustomed to this behaviour with 'The bag lady'. It wasn't
unusual for them to have to deal with her in this way.
They'd whizz her round to Leeds General Infirmary for a
check-up and then drop her off at St George's Crypt for the
night where she could sober up and get a bite to eat. She'd
be back on the street after breakfast and would return to
her patch on the bottom end of Briggate as if nothing had
ever happened. They were used to this, she was harmless
enough, non-aggressive and just about sane enough not
to be sectioned once she was sober. This was her life, her
choice and she harmed no one. But as far as Mitch was
concerned, after witnessing the proceedings of earlier on,
it had been the pack of hyenas that had unseated the
peace and passivity of the poor old woman. The chief pro-
tagonist was Foxy and it was he who was responsible. As
the ambulance headed towards the bottom end of Briggate with 'Betty' and her bags in tow he'd decided he'd had
enough. He was pissed up and now couldn't give a fuck. It
was time he had a little chat with Foxy, the leader of the
pack.

*

The ambulance drove out of Briggate and turned left onto
Duncan Street. The automated stainless steel bollards
rose smoothly back into position and a sense of calm once
again descended onto the bottom end of Briggate. Not
for long though. By now it was around ten o'clock and
the crowds of drinkers were just beginning to swell. It
would be no good causing a scene with groups of unruly
drinkers roaming about. It was now or never for Mitch.
Although shit-faced, he was still aware at the back of his
mind that he shouldn't be going anywhere near the group
opposite. But he felt compelled to do so. Fuck 'em, he

thought, *fuckin' pricks*. He'd taken just about as much shit-housery from these feral shit-bags as he was prepared to take. He finished the dregs of cider and crushed the can in one hand before throwing it to the ground. He then stumbled up to his feet, brushed himself down and looked over towards the hyenas. He'd only taken one step when Foxy's radar observations picked up on his intentions.

'Ey up,' he said. 'He's 'ere, the fucker's coming, brace yersens.'

The rest of the pack looked up to see the lumbering Giant slowly amble towards them. Jester melted into the shadows of the doorway as far as was possible. Woodlouse held his ground, he wouldn't be sacrificing his street credentials for anyone, not for now anyway. Pikey reacted as if he'd been plugged into the national grid. Super animated, he zoomed away on his bike and whooped it for all he was worth. Although conscious, Yazz was still too far gone to appreciate the situation or even what had occurred earlier on. She was still high and was giving not one fuck to anything nor anyone. Scotch John continued to glug and sway, oblivious. But Foxy was far from oblivious. As he sat in the dark shadows of the doorway, with Yazz leant up against him, he was as conscious and alert as his highly charged senses would allow. His sunken, pinprick eyes scanned the giant as he slowly approached. He could see the glint in Mitch's eyes that told him that whatever his intentions, he wasn't crossing the road to borrow a cup of sugar.

Mitch reached the pack and stood a couple of yards in front of the doorway, eyeballing Foxy. Just as he stopped, Pikey returned from his circuit and pulled up right next to him. Too close for comfort as far as Mitch was concerned as he immediately handed him off almost shoving him off the bike.

'Fuck off, dick 'ead,' demanded Mitch.

'You fuck off,' replied Pikey, 'ya big twat, I'll fuckin' nut ya.'

'Any time pal,' returned Mitch as he turned to face him square on.

Pikey ducked down and dragged the bike and himself out of reach. Only then did he answer back. 'Fucking wanker,' he fired but Mitch wasn't interested in Pikey who he could have easily knocked senseless with one backhander. He looked back towards Foxy, totally ignoring Woodlouse, the only pack member who he thought might be able to handle himself.

'You.'

After a short silence, Foxy replied. 'Me? What about me?'

'I wanna word wi' you.' Another silence. Foxy's little clockwork mind ticked away. Chess, a game of chess. Each move and answer to be measured, designed to keep the pressure upon his opponent. Let him make the first move, let's see his hand, see what he's capable of, how far he's prepared to go. Avoid being put on the back foot at all costs, keep calm and keep in control.

'Oh Aye...well...what's this word you want wi' me then pal?'

'Well, why don't you stand up an' face me? Like a man, an' I'll tell ya.' Another standoff ensued. The pack looked at Foxy. How would their leader respond to that ultimatum? They knew Foxy wasn't a street-fighter but they also knew there was no one better on the street at turning around a situation when the chips were down. Right at this moment, Mitch had the slight upper edge. They watched on as Foxy slowly got to his knees and began to straighten up.

'Gaa'n smash 'im, f'kin bell end,' slurred Scotch John who was still swiggin' and swaying the bottle, but had no notion as to the circumstances behind the current stand-off. 'Geeim one f'me the fucker,' he garbled whilst swinging a half-hearted fist about six inches in the air.

'Shurrup John, ya pissed up get. Ya don't even know what they're on about like,' laughed Yazz who thought it was all a big joke.

Foxy now stood up straight and he took two paces towards Mitch. The two were now standing face to face. Woodlouse stood up and moved next to Foxy. Now there were two of them facing up the Giant hulk. Pikey wanted a piece of the action but having just been manhandled he didn't want to risk further disgrace by moving any closer. He improvised and rang his bike bell twice, just to let them know he was there. He received a fierce glare from Woodlouse. With the force of the pack behind him, it was Foxy who had now gained the upper hand.

Mitch leant over and lowered his head down to Foxy until their noses almost touched. 'I don't fuckin' like you Arkid. I saw what you did to the old lass. Out of order pal. Out of order. I don't fuckin' like you.'

Foxy saw the cracks immediately. His policy of keeping the pressure up and passing the baton straight back to his adversary was beginning to pay off. If the only thing he could come up with was the fact that he didn't like him then it was plain sailing from here on in.

'And why don't you like me then pal?' came his next measured response. This caught Mitch a little off guard. His response was hurried.

'Cos, you're a twat, that's why...a slimy little twat.'

This brought a crooked smile to Foxy's thin mouth.

'D'y'ear that lads. He thinks I'm a twat.' Both Pikey and Woodlouse smiled. 'Fancy that. A twat on the streets eh? How bad is that, eh?'

'Smash the f'ker,' said Scotch John with his head lolling all over the place. 'Giy the cant one f'me... '

The participants of the faceoff ignored him. 'Why don't you all just chill out,' said Yazz, 'lets all just 'ave a nice little drink together.'

'Shut it bitchlet,' fired in Foxy as he looked over his shoulder. Yazz raised her eyebrows and rolled her eyes as she took in another glug of 'Betty's whisky.

'An I don't like 'ow you treat 'er neither,' said Mitch nodding towards Yazz behind him.

'So what,' replied Foxy, now clearly in his thinking, in the ascendency. 'What the fuck 'as it got to do wi' you?'

Again Mitch was caught short for words and when they did arrive they lacked impact. He was slowly losing ground.

'I'm just tellin' yer. I don't like you and...you'd better just watch it...just watch it Arkid...that's all I'm sayin'.'

Foxy immediately took the initiative. He leaned even closer to Mitch, his eyes narrowed.

'And I'm telling you, pal...don't drop in 'ere from nowhere, land on our patch and start laying the fuckin' law down. We don't like it. So keep your big fuckin' bent nose out of our affairs and fuck off. And now...I'm telling *you*...you watch that big sweaty back o' yours and watch it carefully...so get the fuck outta my face and fuck off...now there's a good lad.'

With that checkmate parting shot Foxy stood away and sat back down in the shop doorway with Woodlouse following suit. There was no more eye contact and no more posturing. The bubble had burst and the confrontation was over. Foxy had won hands down. Mitch didn't have the wit nor intellect to take on Foxy in the verbal stakes. Sure, he had the muscle but he'd been put in his place by the street wizardry of the pack leader. He stood there in front of the whole group for a while until he began to look and feel a fool. He turned to walk away with Woodlouse shaking his wrist at him giving the wanker hand gesture. Pikey wheeled away and once out of range shouted over his shoulder, 'Fuckin' big cunt!' Mitch turned and gave him a stare but the showdown was over. He'd said his piece, made himself look a twat in the proceedings and lost hands down, but at least he'd made a stand against them. He walked away, down past Maccy D's and turned right onto Boar Lane.

'You can come out now Jester, you soft little bastard, 'e's gone,' laughed Woodlouse, 'Fuckin' prick 'e is.'

'Gaan, smash the f'ker te bits,' slurred Scotch John,' A'll 'ave the cant meself.'

'He's gone ya daft old twat John,' giggled Yazz.

'Eee, wha th' fck.'

*

If the confrontation with Mitch had taught Foxy one thing, it was that Mitch wasn't a threat. He was a bit dim, he thought, about as sharp as a piss-stained sleeping bag, easy meat, easy to manipulate. And if he was easy to manipulate then that gave him control, gave him the upper hand. His devious little mind didn't stop ticking over. It never did.

For Mitch, once he'd sobered up he realised his mistake in approaching Foxy and the pack. He couldn't afford to be getting emotionally involved in street business, it was counterproductive. He needed to be making connections, not enemies. He decided to ditch his aspirations of hooking up with Yazz, that wasn't going to happen any time soon. His best bet, he decided, was to stay away from Briggate for the time being, give it a wide berth, keep out of the spotlight. He needed time to re-evaluate his strategy.

*

Had Mitch not taken the decision to lie low for a while after his confrontation with the hyenas, he would perhaps have witnessed a couple of extra-large geezers dressed in black who'd been sloping around Briggate and the surrounding precincts. Starting at the top they'd wandered down, casually chatting to the rough sleepers and street workers. After being pointed in his direction they eventually reached Foxy in his lair and realised straight away they'd got what they were looking for. They needed the eyes and ears on the street, the local intelligence. They were looking for a large Scouser who they'd heard might have landed on the streets of Leeds. They were big guys, huge, athletic, black-skinned and certainly not street folk. Dressed in black, smart casual sportswear they looked the part, with designer shades and stylish baseball caps. They meant business. They held strong Birmingham accents. The slightly taller and wider one stood silently and confidently with his arms in front of him as the smaller one calmly grilled Foxy. The rest of the hyenas kept quiet. They always left the talking to Foxy, apart from Scotch John who, in his usual half-cut self, had already told the pair of them to fuck off. They'd ignored him and listened to Foxy as he claimed no knowledge of such a character landing on his patch, but agreed, that if their descriptions were accurate he wouldn't be too hard to pick out. There'd be a financial reward should he be able to help them in their search and five hundred quid on the street was not to be sniffed at. They exchanged mobile numbers and parted on amicable terms. The two strangers knew for certain that Foxy knew of the Scouse giant they were seeking, but they decided to play things cool. They weren't in a rush and there was a lot more at stake in it for them than the five hundred they'd tempted Foxy with. Foxy was also aware that they knew that he knew about Mitch, but he too was playing his cards close to his chest. The pack leader was as shrewd as they came on the street. His much-prized moniker had been well earned.

CHAPTER 9

It was over a week since Phil's mauling at the hands of the Scissor Sisters and his subsequent eviction from the house at Kentmere Avenue. Zoe had shed a deluge of tears since the early hours of Saturday morning. Her emotions had been ripped open and laid bare, she'd felt violated and vulnerable. This wasn't her core disposition, nor was it a predominant family trait. Exposing this soft underbelly was alien to her, it didn't feel right. She'd spent the whole day of Sunday at her brother's house where his down the earth manner and quirky sense of humour, along with the company of his family, had taken the edge off the situation. It was when she was back at her mother's and found herself alone that it all came flooding back, hitting her hard and low. The humiliation, the sense of betrayal. But now, a week later, she'd decided she needed time away from the house, to take stock - alone.

Having left Sophia in the capable hands of her mother she'd taken the short bus journey up to Temple Newsam. The Estate was a local authority 1500-acre parkland site that combined stunning Capability Brown landscaped gardens and lakes with the addition of the jewel in the crown, the historical 500-year-old country mansion. This magnificent house was termed by some, in the relevant academic quarters, as the Hampton Court of the North and the Park was just what Zoe needed. Here she could wander around the exquisite gardens and open landscape in perfect solitude enabling her to reflect and contemplate on the recent traumatising events. It gave her the opportunity to think calmly and rationally about her future, her next move.

It was a beautiful tranquil morning. A small cluster of rogue clouds gently aired their way across the blue skyscape as a pair of majestic Red Kites soared high above the estate, searching for breakfast. Vibrant Song Thrushes competed with the gusty Blackbirds in nature's version of the X-Factor as the electric blue flash of the resident Kingfisher darted in and out of the still, calm waters of the ornamental lake. As the temperatures gently rose, Zoe wandered the length and breadth of the park. She ventured up into the wooded glades, as far as the footpaths and natural track ways allowed. She ambled around the 300-year-old walled rose gardens which included an eighty-metre long south-facing greenhouse. It was bursting with colourful and exotic blooms and shrubs, buzzed by an army of industrious bees and gently docked upon by hundreds of delicately silent but strikingly beautiful butterflies. The sweet profusion of aromas tenderly washed her soul, stimulating her senses and reducing her jangled thought-waves into a gentle whirlpool of peace and tranquillity. She made her way up to the imposing Tudor-Jacobean mansion, encircling the full circumference twice before deciding to pay the entrance fee and take a look inside.

The Estate of Temple Newsam is named after the Knights Templar who owned a preceptory on the grounds some 900 or so years ago. The house endured a turbulent early history but is perhaps most famous as the birthplace of Lord Darnley who would become the second husband of Mary Queen of Scots before succumbing to an untimely and mysterious death in 1567. Zoe had visited the mansion many times as a small girl with the family, but this was the first time she'd ever been in the house alone. The place was virtually empty of visitors but stewarded by several wardens peppered around standing guard over priceless objets d'art, furniture and other artefacts. The building was a museum but set out as a historical country house in various stages of its history. There had always been stories about the mansion and its resident spirits, from the Blue Lady to the Ghost of Phoebe Gray. The stories of these hauntings and phantoms had been etched into Leeds' culture over the years: whether or not there was any truth to them they'd be forever embedded in local folklore and passed on through the generations.

As she walked serenely around the ground floor she was taken by the total silence save for the sound of her own footsteps which echoed off the ancient polished-oak floorboards. There was an odour that oozed a sense of great age, and an atmosphere of depth and richness found only in ancient buildings and places of worship. Although the setting gave an ambience of peace and tranquillity, there was also a definite edge. Not quite sinister, but just a suggestion of a presence from an alternative dimension, perhaps another realm. She sensed there were many pairs of ethereal eyes observing her every move, wherever she ventured. She picked up on this psychic voyeurism all over the place, but it didn't trouble her. She had entered their place of existence, she was on their patch and so she adopted an attitude of respect. There was no attempt to tune in to anything, her mission for today was to clear her headspace of all the shit she'd been through and get her head sorted for the future. But she did wonder if her father was there watching over her. Her dad had always loved coming to Temple Newsam with the family, he'd loved taking them around the house and educating them in his own way. He'd loved reciting the tales of the old estate and the ghosts that were purported to stalk the corridors and wander around the deserted floors and rooms at night. Perhaps he was now there with them, on their level, fraternising with them. She decided in her mind that he would be with her in some shape or form, which gave her an inner glow of confidence as she continued her tour.

She lazily scaled the old Oak Staircase to the first floor and began to pick up subtle impressions from the very fabric of the building. The oak panelling, the wall tapestries, the paintings, the furniture, all emitting a faint, subtle vibration, an energy. Zoe didn't try to evaluate it or work it out. She just enjoyed it. She felt privileged as if the house was accepting of her, on a one to one basis, a mutual respect.

She entered the Long Gallery, named due to its length at over a hundred feet and began slowly walking right down the centre. The ancient floorboards creaked and groaned and echoed with each tentative step. The huge space spanned the whole width of the North wing on the first floor. Magnificent paintings and priceless furniture adorned both sides of the huge gallery leaving the centre of the vast room free and unencumbered. She began to envisage the hall as it might have been during the late 1700's, with the upper classes drinking, dancing and merrymaking. The sentiment of long-dead masters and occupants focussing their attentions on her made Zoe shudder. Zoe, the little local woman, nothing more than a peasant from their era, but a special peasant, one with powers that could link their parallel existences. She tuned in to the delicate tunes of harpsichords and violins and flutes as they harmonised into the popular dance melodies of the day. She was aware of chatter and laughter, the hum of a room full and bristling with activity. Domestic servants, impeccably dressed, attending to the needs of the master and his guests, scuttling around fetching and carrying whilst keeping a professional low profile. As she continued her slow walk she sensed the flamboyant costumes of the pretentious guests, wig-adorned chivalrous male suitors and delicate ladies with beauty spots and white powdered faces. Dutiful footmen held out trays of wine and sherry, bowing and nodding to VIP guests, maintaining a stiff upper lip and a serious manner at all times. And all of this just three miles from Seacroft. She felt a pressure in her head. The noise increased, the music, the chatter, the laughter, the clinking of glasses, the swishing of costumes, the dancing footsteps, the eyes, those piercing eyes lasering into her vulnerable soul, all merged into one huge frenzy, a cyclonic whirlwind of senseless psychic junk. It became unbearable. She stopped dead and shuddered letting out a small cry and lifting her hand to her forehead. Deathly silence once again. She looked up and turned her head. All alone. The watchful eyes from the numerous portraits fixated on her, awaiting her next move. The oak floorboards behind her creaked. She turned around. Nothing. A soft waft of scent. She stood still, taking in the fragments of information her senses were conveying. The room was empty. And then she smiled, and relaxed. She noticed the huge ceramic vases throughout the gallery, filled to bursting with fresh flower arrangements. They were beautiful bouquets of powder blue freesias and brilliant yellow lilies cut from the estate's own nursery. The colours were vibrant, the fragrance delicious. She realised that the floorboards were probably 300-years-old and that it would be almost unthinkable that they didn't creak of their own accord now and then. She shook her head and carried on towards the top end of the Gallery which lead into the old Library. She was happy. She was at one with herself, something that Ruth had mentioned during their first meeting. Perhaps the events of the last few days had been meant to be.

A barefoot blond-haired little girl dressed in a white nightdress silently followed Zoe at a distance, as she had done throughout her time in the huge, historic mansion.

*

Zoe spent a good hour in the house. It had had a calming and soothing effect on her. Apart from the brief moment in the Long Gallery, the whole experience had been a positive one. Alone and free to wander around it felt as though she'd brushed souls with the wise and long since departed owners and residents of the beautiful stately home just a stone's throw from the Seacroft council estate where she lived. Her muddled mindset had been cleansed, she realised that she had never really loved Phil and the only person she cared for now, apart from her mother and brother, was her daughter Sophia. She wandered down the slight incline past the open amphitheatre and into the stabled courtyard which had been converted into a shop and cafeteria and where she ordered coffee. She sat outside and she watched, she observed, she envisaged. The cobbled courtyard transported her back 300 years with the rustic handmade bricks under a Yorkshire stone slate roof and Georgian styled, white painted windows. Handcrafted planters, window boxes and hanging baskets spilling with locally grown colourful annuals gave the little setting a calm, relaxed atmosphere. She spent the next hour sitting in the courtyard, enjoying the historic ambience - contemplating. The weather was calm and warm. She decided to ditch the bus ride back home and walk instead. It would only take her an hour at a steady pace down Selby Road. It would give her more time to think and to come to terms with her situation. The day of solitude at Temple Newsam Park and Mansion had done her the power of good. She was ready to rumble.

*

'Right Mam, I'm off to town to see Ruth,' said Zoe with sharp, succinct assertion. There was no wavering in her tone, no half telling, half asking. She was going to town to see Ruth and that was that. Despite the overcast and dull weather, she was chipper, confident and stoic. Linda had picked up on the more positive disposition and was glad that her only daughter was getting back to her confident old self. Although there was just a hint of rebellion in her tone she was happy to let it slide over her head if it meant that Zoe was getting back on her feet. She could always reel her in a bit if she started getting too cocky.

'Okay love, don't worry about Sophia if you're not back in time for school I'll sort her. I told you din't I, we'll stick together and get through this, we'll manage,' she said half smiling. They'd stick together up to a point that was, but that didn't stretch to her clearing up the dog shit in the back garden. That was a job that she'd leave for Zoe, but not wanting to burst her bubble she let it lie, just for now.

'Thanks, Mama,' replied Zoe. 'And, by the way, I've decided to ditch the therapy. I was coming out of those sessions feeling more depressed than I did before I went in.'

'You sure about that? It took a load of effort to get you them in the first place. What about the medication?'

'I'm positive. I know what I'm doing. Me 'ead's as clear as it's been for years so don't worry. I'll still be seeing 'doctor so she can sort 'tablets out. I've made an appointment with her for a week o' Tuesday.'

Linda wasn't exactly worried but she remained cautious. She was happy that Zoe seemed to be getting over the Phil thing but hoped it wasn't a false alarm. She'd hate to think her daughter would suffer a relapse. God knows where they'd go if that happened.

*

Zoe had called into Kirkgate Market for a wander. The market hadn't changed much over the years, apart from the huge open-spaced eating plaza created by the council. An abundance of food stalls served delicious dishes from all over the world with tantalising aromas arousing the nostrils into a frenzy. There was authentic cuisine from South Africa, South America, North America, every European country you could think of plus Indian, Chinese and Cantonese. British Fish and chips, Italian pizza, Spanish tapas, Mexican fajita. It was all there. The food court illustrated the true cosmopolitan society of the city, rich in diversity and integration, and was located in the 'new' section of the market. A large part of the original had been devastated by fire in the mid 1970's, but Zoe's favourite area was the section that had escaped the ravages of the blaze, the original 'old' market. It was here, amongst the scores of little shops and stores and snickets and odd little booths that held some of her fondest childhood memories. The huge uneven and worn York stone flags, laid well over a century ago, mazed around the stalls in a haphazard and shambolic order, overlooked by dusty balconies of painted cast-iron fretwork. She remembered, as a tot, her visits to the market with her dad. He'd buy her junky, brightly coloured toys from the cheap hardware store that would last less than a day before being jettisoned to the dustbin. The little pie and peas stall was still there where they'd always stop for lunch on a Saturday afternoon, where Dad would perch her on the high stools so she could watch the passing throng of activity. The menu was the same as she remembered. There was no place like Leeds' Kirkgate Market to invigorate the senses if one was feeling a little under the weather. The sights and sounds, the smells, the patrons, the tramps and oddballs, the vibrant atmosphere battered one's soul into the present, real-life world. There was no pretence here, no room for self-pity or doubt or hesitancy. She left the market energised and rejuvenated with her senses bristling. She cut along Duncan Street and turned right onto the bottom of Briggate.

Her meeting with Ruth was at the usual coffee shop on Albion Place and she found herself walking up Briggate towards the planned rendezvous. As she walked past Marks & Spencer's she came across the old woman with the shock of white hair, the same one she'd seen on the Saturday night when volunteering. She was slumped over on the bench and the sight of the pitiful woman brought the whole episode with Phil and Katie rumbling back. She felt hurt. She stopped and looked down whilst those around her carried on with their daily assignments. The woman was asleep, or at least she appeared to be. Her face was pale and she listed over slightly, half laying on the large laundry bags bursting with worthless belongings. Zoe stooped forwards just to make sure that the woman was alive. A slight movement of her chest and a random twitch of her hand eased her mind, but what a way to live she thought. The buzzing started. Like a fine electric current running through her head to start with. Then the pressure built up, the buzzing became more aggressive to the point that it started to hurt. She stood back. Her heart beat faster, her breathing became laboured. She took a further backwards step, away from the woman, bundling into an unapologetic shopper. She began to perspire and then shuddered as the sense of someone standing directly behind swathed her mindset. She turned. There was no one. She became spooked and walked away at speed. The vibrations eased up the further she moved away but her heart continued to race and her hot forehead made her feel lightheaded. She made her way up to the coffee shop, a little shaken, but certainly no less resolute. She composed herself and prepared for her meeting with Ruth, more determined than ever to crack this psychic, mediumship thing. It wouldn't beat her.

*

Zoe was already sat in her favourite corner as a flustered Ruth entered the shop. She wore half-mast bright green baggy trousers and a knee-length pink and cream checked coat. Her usual back-to-front flat cap completed the somewhat unconventional style of outfit. But that was Ruth. She approached Zoe in panic mode.

'Oh, Zoe love, can you help me out? How are you love? I'm sorry. I've only gone and lost me blooming purse with me bus pass and me bank card in love. I had it on me when I got off the bus, but I must've dropped it somewhere. I can't find it anywhere, I've been back and looked. Can you lend us summat to get us both a coffee love? I'll give you it back...I'm sorry—'

'Bloody hell Ruth! stop apologising. Here,' she said handing over her debit card, 'just go get the coffees in. Your purse'll turn up somewhere, stop flapping woman, what yer like?' But Ruth was flapping. She dropped her shopping bag onto the table, thanked Zoe and apologised profusely before bundling her way over to the counter, almost joining the queue at the wrong end once again.

It took Zoe ten seconds to find the purse, tucked into an inside pocket of the bag. *She wants a swift slap around her lug-'oles that one...knock some bleedin' sense into her, the gormless cow.*

'It's 'ere you dotty old bugger,' said Zoe, shaking her head and waving the purse in the air as Ruth returned with the drinks. 'What yer like?'

'Where? What?'

'In yer bag, in the pocket on the inside, yer daft bleeder. Listen, just sit down and chill out will ya. You're supposed to be mentoring me not the other way around.' Ruth heaved a sigh of relief and did as she was told. The first five minutes were spent composing and calming down the excitable Ruth, amid a multitude of apologies. Once Zoe had settled her she then got down to business. She explained the episode with Phil and Katie and why she'd left in a hurry the other night. She described how it had felt like being hit square in the face with a brick. How she'd come to terms with the situation and that she'd kicked both Phil and therapy into touch. She then detailed how much she was now determined to throw all her energies into the pursuit of mediumship, it was all she had left, her last throw of the dice. Ruth sat quietly and listened, it was all a little dramatic for her. Last roll of the dice and all that, but Zoe was coming across as very ardent over the matter and she didn't want to deflate her. She was genuinely upset at the way she'd been treated by Phil and Katie. Up to now, Zoe had presented herself as troubled and vulnerable, but today she seemed much more assertive, not quite aggressive but perhaps a little more abrasive than she was used to. A different person. But Ruth erred on the side of caution.

'I'm so sorry for what happened Zoe. I can't imagine what you went through love and I'm glad that you seem to have come through it all the stronger. But still, in this field, it can be dangerous to try and run before you can walk. You definitely have the gift, there's no doubt about that, Paula wouldn't be sanctioning me to work with you if you didn't. But you can't just go running in there and start contacting the other side without proper training. Believe me, love, it can get dangerous.'

Zoe listened, but she was headstrong. She agreed with Ruth to a certain extent but buoyed by the recent vision of the woman in the yellow dress plus the encounters with the Briggate lady and her experience in Temple Newsam mansion, she was ready to go.

'You haven't even joined the circle yet, and yes I know, before you start, you won't be singing and stuff but I'm talking about the closed circle, with Paula and her select group. This is where we connect to each other's energies and tap into each other psychically, we protect each other and go about the business safely. You've only just starting to practice meditation and it's good that you're feeling more confident but —'

'Bleedin' hell Ruth, you're beginning to sound like me mother. Just chill out a bit, will you? All I'm saying is that I'm ready to push on a bit harder, I'm fully on board, it's what I want to do.'

Ruth looked at her with a hint of suspicion. 'Okay love, well I'm here for you, you know that, so just let's tread with caution. If you get things wrong it can really play with your mind you know. And if that happens then I'm not doing my job right.'

'I know, I know, but listen, there's this old tramp wom...homeless person, on a bench down 'bottom end of Briggate. I've seen her a few times now, she's usually slumped, pissed up just outside Marks & Spencer's, in fact, she dun't look well at all and looks as though she's just about to tail it... '

Ruth shook her head and tutted at Zoe's turn of phrase. 'Yes love, what about her?'

'Well, on two occasions now when I've approached her I've got a buzzing in me head. You lot might call it vibrations, but this morning on my way up 'ere to meet you I went right up to 'er and the buzzin' got worse and started paining me. I panicked a bit and came away but I were sweating and me heart were going ten to 'dozen. What do ya think?'

'Well, this is what I'm talking about love. Now you've started meditating your mind's going to be opening up to this sort of thing and you're gonna have to know how to deal with it.'

'Well what should I do then? Just ignore it?'

'Well no, we don't have to ignore it love, but we've just got to go through the proper channels. If spirit has got a message for this poor woman and they're trying to use you as a medium to channel that message then you need to be fully equipped to convey that message—'

'So? Should I be doing summat about it or just let it go?'

'Well,' replied Ruth, getting a little flustered at the

pace Zoe was pushing the matter, 'what I'd advise you to do...is...this. Tonight, when you're practising your meditation. When your mind is still, open up the airwaves... don't forget the little prayer—'

'What little prayer?'

'The one that I told you about, the one you need to recite when you start meditation and one of thanks when you've finished. They're in the information pack I purposely made up for you!'

'Oh, yeah, the prayer, yep, got it.'

'Well...when you've settled down and your headspace is empty and quiet, just take the image of the lady and bring it forward into your mindset. Just concentrate on the image of her and see what comes to the fore. It's important that you instil compassion and love in your emotions when you're using this technique. It'll help keep you safe and promote positivity. If not, negative energies can invade and take over. And don't forget the little prayer to thank spirit for looking over you afterwards. You might not think so but just using that little tried and tested routine can make all the difference. Do that and just see where it takes you, see what comes up. No expectations, just go with the flow. Nice and positive, compassion, love and prayers. Ok, lady?'

It was a lot for Zoe to take in but she'd got the gist of the message. It wasn't as exciting or dynamic as she'd hoped it might have been, but she reluctantly agreed that it was perhaps best that she didn't jump straight in. She had faith in Ruth.

'There's just one other thing,' she added. 'I don't know how to explain it...I—.'

'Take your time love, what's up? What's bothering you?' replied Ruth in a soothing reassuring tone.

'Well, I feel that there's summat holding me back. Summat negative, inside me. I've had this feeling since all that shit at East Moor Park...and I've just kind of tried to ignore it.'

'Well it's in your head love, it's not anything residing inside your body so let's put that one to bed for a start off. Listen, you've been through a lot of late so there's bound to be negative stuff flying around inside your head. Maybe the fact that Phil wasn't exactly supportive of you might have something to do with it, but he's gone now, you're past that and you say you're getting on better with your mum. Maybe the feelings will just slowly dissipate now that you've got your mojo back.'

'Hmm, maybe. But I can't help thinking that this...thing...whatever it is, is evil, and it gets stuck in my throat like a lump of coal. Whatever Phil was I don't think he was evil. Ok, he couldn't keep 'is slippery little dick in 'is knickers, nor his mucky little mitts out of 'ers, but that makes him a twat, not evil. This is something different as if it's a part of me and it's eating me away, like a sort of cancer...but...not of the physical me...but of the psychological me. Does that make sense?'

'Of course, it does love. But let's just take stock. I don't think it's anything to worry about, we can take steps to banish any suppressed negative emotions if we need to in due course. But this is the new you so perhaps these feelings will diminish as we go forward. In the meantime, I'll speak to Paula and see if it's worthwhile getting you involved in the higher circle. There's no singing, just prayers and it's all positive, so don't worry, we're making good progress, trust me.'

'Okay, Ruth. I'll put me trust in you but don't you let me down. Don't know if I could handle another betrayal.'

Ruth looked her in the eye and slid her hand over the table and onto Zoe's, just as Katie had done all those weeks before. 'There's no chance of that love,' she replied, 'we're in this together. And don't forget Simon.'

'Simon? Tidgey Squidgey Simon? Bloody 'ell, 'e dun't say much does 'e? You don't know 'e's there 'alf o' 'time, 'e's harmless enough but 'e is a bit geeky you must admit Ruth.'

'No love, he's a lovely lad is Simon, and I've told you before, I think he likes you, he's very intelligent.'

'Can't be that brainy if 'e likes me now can 'e? Listen, after that two-faced bastard I've had it wi' men for now, an' anyway, I generally like me men with a bit of beef on 'em, don't you Ruth? Y'know what I mean love? I've seen fatter legs on spiders than old Squidgey, 'e needs to get down and dirty at the nearest Gym does the lad.'

'Ooo you are rotten Zoe, he's lovely and sometimes opposites attract love. I don't know, what are we gonna do with you?' Both smiled and continued their light-hearted natter over the pros and cons of poor Simon whose ears, no doubt, were sizzling in the heat.

CHAPTER 10

It was a drizzly start to the day as Mitch mooched around the tight aisles of the Tesco Express store at the top end of Briggate. He was cold and damp and needed a modicum of respite against the rain, just to warm up a little. This and to replenish his supply of alcohol. The security guards wouldn't allow just any old street person into the store at this time, half-six in the morning. Known trouble causers were often turned away, but Mitch was good. During his time in Leeds he'd caused them no trouble and, to their knowledge, had paid for all his stuff in cash. He was in no rush and so was taking his time to browse around. It was a week since his latest confrontation with the hyenas and he'd avoided their end of Briggate, using the Tesco store at the top end only when he needed to. He'd found two or three safe little hubs away from the centre and had made a couple of tenuous connections with other rough sleepers. But on the whole, he was finding it tough. His face didn't seem to fit around these parts. Or maybe it was just that he wasn't trying hard enough. His daily consumption of cider and wine helped ease the pain and it was this he had in mind as he pondered over the selection of cheap booze.

He yanked a 2litre bottle of cider from the shelf. He knew it was only medium strength at five per cent, but checked anyway. At two nicker a bottle you couldn't go wrong, just right to get the day started. He turned towards the checkout and bumped into a slight figure peering up and over his shoulder. It was Yazz.

'Sorry Arlass,' said Mitch before realising who it was. 'Oh it's you...er...what are you doing 'ere?'

'Just on me way over to 'cage an' I saw you sneak in 'ere. Had enough o' that little bastard. I'm done with him. What you up to?' Mitch held up the bottle and raised an eyebrow. 'Fancy coming down to the cage for a bit?' she continued.

He hesitated. He'd grown to trust no one on the streets of Leeds and that included Yazz. Though she seemed relatively sober this morning he knew that wouldn't last. On the other hand, he hadn't spoken to a soul for the last couple of days and it was beginning to grate on him. He looked her in the eye and sighed, deciding that he'd nothing to lose. 'Aye, go on then, why not? Just let me pay for this.' Yazz didn't move, she looked at the bottle and then at Mitch. He got the message and shook his head as he grabbed another from the shelf. She followed him to the checkout and stood behind him as he reached the counter and then watched as the cashier grabbed and bar-coded the bottles. The scene that Yazz witnessed next caused a shiver to run down the entire length of her backbone. Mitch reached into the inside pocket of his combat jacket and pulled out a rolled-up wad of twenty-pound notes as fat as a baby's leg and bound by thick elastic banding. Her knees almost buckled as her eyes widened, she'd never seen so much cash in one place. She quickly composed herself and looked away just as Mitch realised he may have let his guard down. He peeled off a note before hastily ramming the wad back into his pocket and out of sight. The cider was paid for and Mitch moved on with Yazz right behind him. The cashier glared at her.

'I'm with 'im,' she fired to the young girl on the desk. They walked out of the store but Yazz was again given close attention by the security guard who looked at her quizzically, unable to work out how she'd slid past his attentions in gaining admittance into the store.

'What? I'm with 'im, and we've paid for us stuff,' ask that silly cow behind the counter,' she said confronting the guard head-on before moving away and firing him another hostile sideways stare. The guard remained unmoved and nodded his head in the direction of Briggate, 'Go on, piss off,' he said quietly.

'Fuckin' wankers,' said Yazz as they stretched away from the store, but still unable to resist scowling back at the guard over her shoulder. "Ere, do you want one?' she said to Mitch as she eventually turned round to face the way they were walking. She handed him a chocolate bar.

"Ave you just nicked that you thieving little cow?' he replied.

'Only fair, you got the booze in...d'ya wannit or not?' she repeated. Mitch looked down at her and then grabbed the bar. He shook his head.

'You've got some fuckin' front you 'ave,' he muttered. Yazz ignored him and lead the way down Briggate towards the cage.

They entered Harrison's Yard, passed The Old George pub and checked the coast was clear before ducking into the dingy little ginnel and gently closing the door behind them. They headed down towards the narrow passage. Only after they'd wrapped the chain back around the iron gate and made their way into the dark square did they feel any sense of sanctuary. They quietly made their way up the stairs to the landing gantry. As he reached the top Mitch heaved off his backpack and shoved it up against the old wooden door to use as a backrest. He lowered his giant frame onto the deck and spread his legs out in front of him. Yazz pulled out a battered camping chair and checked it for bugs before standing it up next to Mitch and collapsing on it. She held her hand out. Mitch looked at her and handed one of the bottles over.

'You don't fuck about do ya?'

'No,' she replied, twisting off the top and guzzling for all she was worth. Her first 'fix' of the day. '...I don't!'

Mitch opened his bottle and slowly gulped his first swig of the day but taking a much more measured approach in doing so. He was trying to weigh Yazz up. She'd put her trust in him, she'd shared the location of her secret little seat of sanctuary, but then sided with the hyenas when push had come to shove. Now they were drinking side by side in the cage once again. He couldn't work her out. He decided to do a little probing.

'How is it with the hyenas and yer little Foxy mate?' he asked.

She looked at him and sighed, interference with the consumption of her liquid breakfast didn't sit easily with her.

'He's a cunt!' she replied after a brief hesitation.

The sharp abruptness of her answer made Mitch smile. 'Tell me summat I don't know. Would you like to expand on that a bit? You got any of your money back?'

'Huh, no chance o' that. I've told 'im I'm not going with any more of his slimy clients. I don't get owt for it, you'd think at least 'e'd go fifty-fifty wi' me wun't yer like. But no, well 'e can go bollocks cos I ain't doing it anymore. Unless you wanna quick un? Just a tenner to you,' she added looking up at him.

Again Mitch looked on in disbelief before emitting a little chucklet from the back of his throat. He didn't know if she was being serious or not. It was only an hour ago that he'd woken up miserable, contemplating his future, thinking about moving on. His time in Leeds hadn't been good, he'd failed to hook up with anyone of any substance and had spent the last couple of weeks more or less on his own trying to find his feet. And now here he was, with the lass that he'd given up on, propositioning him for sex, albeit at the cost of a tenner. He wasn't interested in getting his end away, his foremost efforts were channelled towards forging some kind of connections on the street and if not in Leeds then somewhere else. But perhaps he wasn't finished in West Yorkshire just yet.

'A tenner for me? How much for anyone else?' he replied.

'Fiver,' she replied with just the faintest trace of a smile on her pale features.

'I'm good thanks. And anyway I got you some cider so what do I get for that?'

'Fuck all mate, for two quid you'll get a kick in the knackers, minus the chocolate that I got you, so that's down to a quid and that's a double kick in the knackers.'

'Right...we'll call it quits then,' said Mitch, sensing the tone of the conversation was beginning to nosedive. He proceeded to shift track and try to catch Yazz on the back foot. It wasn't easy though, as soon as he got anywhere near her she'd become defensive and abusive. But he wouldn't be giving up that easy. He let her guzzle away in peace for a while and then had another stab.

'So where do ya see yerself in say, five years then?' he asked.

'What do ya mean?'

'Well, you don't plan on spending the rest of your life on the street do ya? Ending up like that woman, what you call 'er? Betty, the one you all robbed blind the other week.'

'No, I don't, this is only temporary, just until I get on me feet that's all. And I wouldn't worry about Betty. She's no idea what the fuck's going on. She's back on 'street in no time...'an't got a clue.'

'It wan't nice what you did though was it? And taking her money wa' a right shitty thing to do, wannit?'

'I din't do owt mate.'

'No, but you watched, and supped her stuff and that din't ya?'

'Well I'm not gonna stop 'em like am I? An' that's your problem mate, judging everyone. Who the fuck are ya? Just let 'em get on wi' things, there's nowt gunna change around 'ere just cos you've arrived is there? Just shut the fuck up and maybe you might be teken in rather than being on your own all the time. I've seen ya, always on your todd, probably going round laying the gospel down to everyone. It dun't work like that round 'ere bonny lad.'

Mitch remained quiet. He could half see where she was coming from even though he didn't agree with it. He tried to steer the conversation back on course.

'So how you gonna get out of this hellhole then, how you gonna escape from Foxy? He has you round his little finger.'

'Does he fuck! No one tells me what to do, I could walk away today if I wanted.'

'Well, why don't you then?'

'Cos I don't fuckin' want to that's why...just yet anyway...I'll get mesen sorted one o' these days...don't you worry about that...I'll get a job, get me own place, in me own time. Then I'll get our Lilly down and away from them bastards up there.'

A silence ensued. Mitch had managed to tear just a tiny hole in the fabric of the tough abrasive exterior of Yazz. He looked her in the eye and she turned away. He knew he'd hit a soft spot and played it cool, not wanting to barge in too quick.

'So what is it between now and when you move on then? Just mooching around on the street, selling yerself for Foxy, enjoying a nice little drink, shooting up?' He nodded. 'Nice.'

Yazz stared at him. 'Fuck you!' she sneered. 'Anyway, Mr Big, what's your fuckin' story then? What's your plan? Why 'ave you ended up on 'street if you're so fuckin' full o' yersen?' She looked at him. 'Well? ...I'm waiting.'

'You wouldn't wanna know,' replied Mitch. 'You don't need to know...it's a long story. Me mam an' dad split up when I were a lad and I got mixed up wi—'

'You're right, I don't wanna know, I'm bored already, 'eard it all before mate. Just sup yer drink and shut the fuck up.'

Mitch looked at her. He smiled and shook his head, he just couldn't weigh her up. There was definitely a malfunction somewhere along the line, as if a section of DNA was missing or damaged. He couldn't work her out, nor could he work out why he felt a need to fraternise with her. There was an attraction but he didn't know what it was. As far as he could make out it wasn't a sexual one, perhaps the decency in him felt a need to protect her vulnerability, from the sly devices of Foxy, he wasn't sure. And he wasn't sure he could trust her. In any case, he did as he was instructed and carried on drinking. He held the bottle up to her. 'Cheers,' he said. She held up hers to him but remained silent as she stared up to the grey Leeds skies.

They spent the following half an hour in silence, quietly drinking, thinking, plotting and planning, though neither knew even what the next twenty-four hours would hold. The damp, grey clouds gradually lifted to reveal blue skies. The silence was suddenly broken. With no warning, Yazz turned to Mitch.

'Anyway, he wants to see ya.'

'Eh? Who does?' he replied, 'What yer on about?'

'Foxy.'

'What the fuck does that little bastard wanna see me for? I'll ring his fuckin' neck if I get chance.'

'I dunno. You can ask him.'

'I'm not going anywhere near the little twat. You should stay away an' all, he's nowt but trouble.'

'Well, 'e told me to tell you if I saw you so I'm telling yer. They were on about giving you a second chance seeing as you 'an't caused 'em any more trouble since 'other week. It's up to you, stay on your own if you want, it's your choice. I'm just passing 'message on.'

Mitch could hardly believe it. He couldn't think of a more deceitful, manipulative cretin than Foxy who, no doubt, was scheming or hatching some plot or other. On the other hand, maybe it was time to ease up a little. If you can't beat 'em, join 'em, as the old saying goes, he thought. He let the matter lie.

'What yer doing today? he asked.

'Probably go down to Briggate an' hook up with those skanky bastards,' she replied, 'what else is there to do?'

'I thought you'd said you were done with him.

What you going back for?' Yazz didn't answer. 'Why don't you hang out with me for 'day? Worse things 'ave 'appened at sea.' She continued to ignore him and guzzle away at the cider, but at least she hadn't curtly dismissed it out of hand.

The sun began to peep over the rooftops and as it did so it neutralised the early morning chill which had hung around the dank little square. Before long the elevated gantry was bathed in sunshine as the temperature slowly nudged upwards. Yazz had been right, it was a great little sun trap up there and as the air temperature increased it took the edge off her demeanour as she allowed herself a rare moment of wistful peace and solitude. It was times like this in the cage that just for a short while she could sit back and reflect. Perhaps life on the street wasn't so bad. Here, she was dry, warm, secluded and safe. Just for a brief period, she let go of her negative thoughts, allowing them to drift away on the warm breeze. Being hunched up in doorways pissing wet through, freezing cold in sub-zero temperatures, rummaging through bins for food and provisions. Barbaric practices such as defecating behind waste bins and wiping her backside on anything she could lay her hands on and doing the deed with Foxy's grubby little clients. Just for a minute, these thoughts were jettisoned from her headspace allowing an incoming flow of happy and positive thoughts. She dreamt of Lilly and the little flat that she'd get for them to share. She'd cook food for her and buy her nice clothes and they'd call in at Maccy D's for a proper sit-down meal. She'd tuck her into bed and leave the bedside lamp on for her. She'd stroke her hair and kiss her forehead. She'd make sure she was warm and cosy and safe, away from the drunken molestations of their lousy father. Granddad could come down to see them when he got out of the nick. Granddad was a good man.

The warm sun also radiated through to Mitch's inner self. He took a deep breath and closed his eyes in a sea of contentment. He thought about the sun and how beautiful it was. Not just about the heat and light from the burning gases millions of miles away. But the positive effect it had on his mindset and how it seemed to energise every living cell in his body, uplifting his mood beyond all the shite of everyday life on the street. A recalibration of the soul is how he thought of it. Priceless. Within a couple of minutes, he dozed off, warm, satisfied and as contented as one could be as a rough sleeper on the streets of Leeds.

*

Mitch woke up abruptly. He saw a hazy blue sky with a fuzzy ball of golden fire in the top corner. His face was red and sweaty as he squinted and looked around him. He was still in the cage, but he was now alone. As his brain booted up he realised it was the clanking of the chains on the iron gates that had stirred him. Yazz had sloped off. He searched around for his cider but both plastic bottles lay empty and discarded on the metal decking. He tried to work out whether he'd finished his or if Yazz had polished it off on his behalf. It was gone in any case, but Mitch always carried emergency provisions and grabbed his backpack for a top-up of cheap white wine. It was then his heart sank. He'd let his guard down in the Tesco store when he'd pulled out his roll of 20's. In a moment of panic, he slammed his hand into his inside pocket but the burst of anxiety was short-lived as he grabbed hold of not one, not two but three thick rolls of notes. He heaved a sigh of relief. *Maybe she didn't see...Just my bad mindedness.* He yanked out the wine and spent the rest of the morning in the cage in the warm sunshine. He was alone, as he had been since he'd moved over to Leeds. Perhaps it was time to move on. He was getting nowhere with Yazz, she'd obviously found the attraction of Foxy and the pack of hyenas more alluring than the prospect of spending a few hours with him. His mind ran amok, he didn't really know how honest Foxy's intentions were in wanting to see him nor how much he could trust Yazz. His intuition told him to trust no one, but his inclination had always been to give people the benefit of the doubt. This conflict between intuition and inclination had caused him real problems in the past.

*

Yazz made her way down to the bottom end of Briggate. She approached 'Betty' who had claimed the whole bench just further up from Marks & Spencer's, baggage included. She sat at one end with her head lolling to one side and grasped a paper cup of coffee, provided for her by the kindly shopfloor manager of the store. 'Y'all right pet,' said Yazz as she jaunted past her. She received a nod of sorts in return and nothing else. She could see Foxy and the pack already slouched in and around the vacant shop doorway next to Maccy D's. She was the bearer of news. News for Foxy anyway and good news at that. She loved it when she pleased him, it gave her a thrill, it made her feel special, he made her feel special when he was happy with her. When she did right, and he appreciated her, there was no better feeling. She was spilling over with eagerness as she approached the doorway and surprised to see Scotch John in non-paralytic mode, though still far from sober.

'Aye wee lassie,' he croaked as she joined the group. It was the most coherent she'd ever heard him and it made her smile.

'Howay John,' she replied. A glint of emerald green light flashed from the narrow slits of his eyes. Under normal circumstances, his peepers were dulled, greyish-hazel and focussed into another dimension. Today they were razor-sharp and flashed in the sunlight like two rare green diamonds set deep into his rutted complexion as he scanned the length and breadth of Briggate. Somewhere buried deep beneath that dishevelled, whiskered and re-cidivous object was a person, a human being. A person born into a loving family and who, during those first few days and weeks of his life, was cherished, coveted, loved and adored. He was rocked and fed and sheltered and kissed, a tiny but precious addition to the growing assem-blage of God's creatures on earth. It didn't last long. Poor John was born into a dysfunctional family unit and into a broader society that cared not for its poorest citizens and sat by whilst those who fell through the cracks were left to rot and fester. There was no safety net. John was one such character, who now spent his life hundreds of miles away from the land of his birth slowly eking his life out and heading towards a premature demise. There were souls that stalked the earth who still loved John dearly but they may as well have resided on the other side of Mars for all the good they served him.

Not so Foxy. One could be forgiven for thinking that Foxy hadn't been born at all. He'd been knocked up and created in a deep, dark cavern by non-other than Be-elzebub, the prince of devils himself. No one loved Foxy apart from himself, but there were plenty on the street who served him, who went out of their way to please him, to court his favour. Yazz was one of them.

Jester laid in the back of the doorway, he looked

scared, not because of any impending tribulation but because that was his countenance by default. Pikey's bike lay discarded and prostrate outside the doorway, with the public having to work their way around it while Pikey lauded himself with his usual over the top exuberance to a group of fellow desperados outside the Greggs store opposite the lair. His manic, screeching impression of the Great Black-backed Gull was improving with practice, though not necessarily to general endorsement. Woodlouse was absent, having been locked up overnight for causing a fracas during the early hours. That wasn't unusual for Woodlouse, he was the only member of the pack who was always up for a scrap. His disposition, if provoked, was to smack the antagonist in the face and ask questions later. No doubt he'd be joining up with the rest of the pack in due course subject to the usual bail conditions or court orders.

Foxy looked up at Yazz. 'Where've you been ya little cow?' he asked. He was surprised to detect a slight smirk on her face. Normally if she'd done one after a fall out her return would be fuelled by rebellious insubordination, smattered in a spray of obscenities. Today was different. She couldn't hold back a small smile as she pointed to Foxy and then flicked her index finger towards herself, an indication for him to follow her.

'What?' he replied. She walked away towards the Briggate Minerva sculpture, known also as the 'Draped Woman', but termed the 'Rusty Bitch' by the street people. This metallic plinthed work of art, commissioned to a brethren of Scotch John's, Glaswegian artist Andy Scott, stood five metres high and about thirty yards away from Maccy D's, outside the entrance to the Trinity Centre. It was used by the street people as a quiet place, away from the doorways, to talk business. She turned around and again beckoned him to follow her. He reluctantly agreed and heaved his lazy carcass from his resting place and followed her, albeit with his usual cynical scepticism. On reaching the Rusty Bitch he folded his arms and listened to the message Yazz had for him. Through lowered tones, raised eyebrows and a host of hand gestures she proceeded to explain the news she was so eager to share. Her eyes widened as she attempted to describe the sheer size of the roll of cash she'd seen in the possession of Mitch, the Manchester Scouser. Foxy was not one for showing his emotions but Yazz could see by the colour in his cheeks that he was pleased with her, she'd done good and she'd done the right thing in sharing the intelligence with him. She beamed with pride as he promised her she'd be well rewarded for her loyalty and integrity. But she hadn't finished there. Anticipating that Foxy may want her to set up a meeting of sorts she explained that she'd already set the wheels in motion. She could tell by Foxy's face that he approved. His devious nature, at last, brushing off on his gullible street partner.

The situation was getting complicated. The two Brummie heavies, nick-named 'Big Fucker' and 'Massive Fucker' by Foxy, behind their backs, of course, were still dropping in for the occasional chat. And now this. Foxy had some thinking to do. He lead Yazz back to the lair. 'Come on bitchlet, let's 'ave a drink and a smoke, I've got some good stuff for ya. You deserve it.'

*

It was later on that same evening that Mitch lumbered down Briggate, the first time since the altercation he'd been down this end of the precinct. He saw the hyenas flaking around the lair but was a little reticent to go over and start fraternising straight away. He slumped into the shop doorway next to House of Fraser and whipped out a tinny. He was unsure if he'd done the right thing in coming back onto Briggate in the first place, never mind the wisdom in approaching the pack. They'd made him look and feel a bit of a twat on both previous occasions he'd met them on their patch. As it happened he needn't have worried.

He'd only been in the doorway for five minutes. He looked up to see Foxy, not an errand lad, not Pikey or Jester, but the lead hyena himself, making his way over towards him. With a slouching gait, Foxy kept his hooded head bowed and his hands in his trouser pockets. He reached the doorway and looked down at Mitch before dropping down beside him and slouching up against the glass-fronted shop door.

'Ey up pal,' he said, avoiding eye contact and looking straight into the middle of the street. "Ow's it going?'

Mitch hesitated as he eyed up his adversary. 'Not bad,' he replied.

'Fancy joining us for a few tonight? Bitch says you're alright, you're sound.'

'Dunno,' replied Mitch.

Foxy clasped his hands together and dropped his bony chin onto his knuckles. He sat there for a second, looking like a dishevelled Plato deliberating between a Big Mac and a Big Tasty.

'Listen,' he said, 'Forget all that crap the other day. You've gotta be careful when you get newbies springing up from nowhere. Yer never know what they're up to, or why they've suddenly appeared. It's a fuckin' warzone out 'ere pal, yer don't know what's coming at ya next. Some o' these bastards out 'ere on the street are pure evil, fuckin' mercenaries. You've gotta be careful. You know where I'm coming from?'

Mitch wanted to smash his skull in for the way he'd referred to Yazz as 'Bitch', but he played it cool. There was nothing to gain by resisting Foxy, nor his pack of hyenas, or their ways, and he had nothing to lose by going along with them, just for a while. Just to see how things worked out.

'I suppose so,' replied Mitch

'Truce then?' said Foxy as he turned and faced Mitch square on. He held his hand out. It was the first time Mitch had been able to look Foxy in the eyes at close quarters whilst relatively sober. They were deep, dark and unnerving. He took the scrawny, bony-fingered hand into his ham fist and gave it a good solid squeeze. They shook hands, the spell was broken. The two entered into an uneasy conversation, strained at times but a communication nevertheless. Mitch watched Foxy's every move and every mannerism. Foxy watched the street, never taking his eyes away as they flicked left and right, scanning the whole panorama of Briggate. After a while, once both were good, they eased themselves up and lumbered over to join the rest of the pack in the lair.

*

'Now then you scruffy bastards, this is Mitchell from Manchester. Be nice to 'im,' pronounced Foxy as they reached the doorway.

'F'ck eem, th'big kent,' slurred Scotch John, back to his usual inebriated state.

'Scotty, shut the fuck up,' said Foxy, 'Just fuckin' ignore 'silly old piss 'ead.'

'Y'are ken feck y'sen anorl,' he snarled back. The remainder of the pack had been well briefed. They ignored

Scotch John and shuffled around to make space for the large bulk of their newest recruit. Before long they were drinking, snorting, smoking and getting high together. Just a normal evening down the bottom end of Briggate.

CHAPTER 11

The light in the room slowly dims as a soothing velvet-blackness descends onto the tiny sitting room. The sound of the TV, the tick-tick-ticking clock and the tempest of the outward prevailing storm dissipate, leaving the atmosphere shrouded in an ice-cold silence. A chink of light emerges in the dark far corner of the ceiling and slowly draws to the fore, gradually increasing in size as it reaches the centre of the room. A spotlight from above now focuses a harsh light onto a figure in the pitch-blackness, a life-sized figure. The figure of a haggard old woman. The figure is centre-stage and sits upon a revolving barstool. The stiff-backed figure is slumped to one side, emaciated limbs hang loose and its unkempt grey hair is scraped back into a bun. The figure sits stock still on the slowly revolving barstool. The head hangs loose, with eyes closed. The grey face is wrinkled, embellished with ugly scarlet-red lipstick and heavy black eyeliner. The figure is clothed in a grey tutu and bodice with loose-fitting tights and scuffed ballet slippers. The listing, stiff-backed figure is dead. It sits on the revolving barstool. Zoe witnesses, she scrutinises, she observes. She sees. Slowly revolving, dead, spotlight, soothing blackness, front, side, back, side, round and round, over and over, silence, revolving, slow. The dead figure raises its head. It opens its liquid-black eyes and stares at Zoe. Limp-limbed and stiff-backed. Dead.

A sharp scream pierced the stillness of the night as Zoe sat bolt-up, wide-eyed. Panic-stricken, she searched the room for a correlation between her earthly surroundings and the macabre images still swirling around her muddled headspace. The digital bedside clock told her it was three twenty-two in the morning. The bedroom door opened and Linda cocked her head around the corner.

'You okay love? What's up?'

'Jesus!...It's you,' she sighed. 'I'm alright Mam...just a nightmare that's all, sorry, go back to bed.'

'You sure? You were screaming. You want a cup of tea or a glass o' milk or owt?'

'No thanks, I'm alright. Sorry for waking you up- ...go on, go back to bed...Night.'

'Alright love...night night.' Linda turned away and gently closed the door behind her.

Zoe clicked on the bedside lamp. A dark and multi-dimensional image of a dead woman on a revolving barstool saturated her thoughts. Although her breathing remained free and unimpaired she had the sensation of constriction in her throat. She'd previously described it to Ruth as being like a lump of coal lodged in her windpipe, jagged edges digging into her gullet. The dead woman on the barstool was a recurring nightmare she'd first experienced during her time at Reginald Street in East Moor Park. Not only was she experiencing the dream more frequently, but it was now appended by these physical manifestations, which was far more worrying, especially as the intensity was gradually increasing. She recognised the aura of the setting, it was the tiny living room at Reginald Street. The dead woman was anybody's guess, but she surmised that she must be connected to the house in some way or other. Then there was the ballerina factor.

During the few months that she'd lived in the house, she'd often been woken, in the early hours, to haunting but beautiful orchestral music. They'd found an old portable record player in a corner with a few dusty singles from the 50s and 60s in the case. *Lonely Ballerina* by a bloke called Mantovani had been one of the records, but even though the record player and discs had been cast to the bin-yard, the music from this particular record continued to play out of thin air - at any time of day or night - and only ever for the attention of Zoe. It felt as though the music had been part of the fabric of the tiny house and was somehow reaching out to her, for whatever reason. Of course, Phil had never bought into it, he insisted it was all nonsense and that she should be seeking further medical evaluation rather than fretting over 'incarnate' renditions of Mantovani and his orchestra's *Lonely Ballerina*. But now Phil was gone, he'd done one. Unfortunately for Zoe, however, the recurring nightmare had not.

Each episode left her with an overwhelming sense that the pathway to her future was being blocked by obstacles which she somehow had to overcome. She had a gut feeling that she'd left something behind at Reginald Street, part of her soul perhaps, or maybe she'd brought something from Reginald Street with her to Seacroft. She was unsure, but adamant there was unfinished business at the house. Somewhere within these nightmares was a memorandum, a directive, a message, the significance of which was lost on her. The truth of the matter was that she was out of her depth. On one hand, she had such a powerful internal hankering to return to the house to bury these feelings, and on the other, the message from Ruth, her trusted mentor, was to take things steady, to go easy. The conflict was causing intense anxiety, her head hurt and she felt like crying. She was supposed to have 'the gift', to be 'special', but she had no one to turn to on this one. No spirit guide, no father helping her from the other side. Just the house from East Moor Park beckoning her from one end and Ruth from the spirit circle holding her back on the other. It was a tug of war and something had to give. As the swelling sensation in her throat began to ease she continued to ruminate over her predicament. By the time she eventually dozed off the first rays of sunshine had already squinted over the Seacroft horizon.

*

The few hours of sleep that Zoe managed since the nightmare had left her feeling refreshed. Her senses were sharp, her thought process crystal clear and positive. She felt physically energised and mentally rejuvenated, rebuking herself for wasting so much mental energy worrying and ruminating during those early hours. She couldn't wait to get going. She showered and dressed and with Linda taking care of Sophia's school run she had the house to herself. Coffee and toast and then into the sitting room to make the call.

'Hi Ruth, it's me.'

'Hello love, everything okay? You alright?'

'I'm fine,' replied Zoe, 'are you okay to talk for a bit?'

'Yeah, course I am love, what is it?'

Zoe spent the next twenty minutes explaining her predicament. The recurring dream, the house at Reginald Street, the cellar, the oversized leather armchair, the haunting music and the sense of unfinished business. She told of the choking sensation and the headaches. The overwhelming sense that there were issues to be addressed and hurdles to clear, before she felt she could continue with her development as a psychic, and her life in general. It wasn't something that she could hang up on, leave to fester. Ruth listened patiently. She knew that Zoe could be impetuous at times. She remained calm.

'Okay then love, I agree. It sounds as though perhaps there is something that's holding you back and if you feel that strongly about it I can talk to Paula—'

'No!' replied Zoe, 'You don't understand Ruth. I need to go down there myself, in person, back to the house. I can't think of a more horrible, negative space on the face of the earth than that shitty little bastard cellar. What I went through down there will be with me for the rest of me life. I need to go back. There's summat down there, summat's telling me I'm not finished with the place yet.'

'Well you can't just go around banishing demons or confronting evil spirits love, it's not what we do. You've been watching too many films, Zoe, believe me. We're a million miles away from that kind of thing love. Even an experienced psychic or medium wouldn't do that sort of thing without proper planning and forethought and through the proper channels. We're just trying to develop your gift love and we've only just started. You're not even up to speed with the meditation yet. We're not Ghostbusters Zoe, we can't just go around messing with spirit and other negatives, it's dangerous.'

'Oh Ruth, get off your bleedin' high 'orse will ya? It's summat I just need to do. We'll need Squidge's help as well.'

'Listen, Zoe, I don't think this is a good idea love, I'll have to put it to Paula

'Don't do that Ruth. You know she won't sanction it. It needs to be just us, me, you and Squidge—'

'But I could lose my job, Zoe. It's this kind of thing

that amateurs get involved with. Paula's highly respected in her field. It could do her a lot of harm if this goes wrong,' replied Ruth, her voice beginning to waver a little.

'Listen Ruth. The other day you asked me to put my trust in you didn't you? Well now, I'm asking you to put your trust in me. I need your help love, as a friend...but if I don't get it I'll still 'ave to go down there...even if it's on me own...I need to banish this once and for all. I'm asking you to help me on this one. You're all I've got left.'

Zoe had put Ruth in an almost impossible position and after much cajoling, some of it outrageous emotional blackmail, Ruth eventually succumbed, though she regretted it as soon as she'd put the phone down. Zoe had played on her easy-going nature, she'd worn her down, eroded into her sense of empathy and taken it hostage. From her perspective, she needed this to happen and she didn't mind dragging Ruth and Squidge down to East Moor Park with her. She was on a roll, she was taking no more shit, no more tears. She was taking control of her own destiny, with the extorted assistance from her two psychic circle buddies.

*

It was about five o'clock in the afternoon, or tea-time as they like to say in the North. There was a knock on the front door and a rattled Shelley bundled her way in.

'Linda! Where are ya?' she cried as she clicked the door closed behind her. 'Look, I've got summat to show ya.'

'I'm in 'ere slack 'ole, where else would I be?' shouted Linda from the kitchen as an excitable Shelley burst in. 'What's up? Calm down ya silly bugger, what is it?'

'Look!' she said, thrusting a piece of card right in

front of Linda's face. 'Look! What do you think?' Linda pulled her head away.

'Hang on a minute, just calm down, what is it?' She grabbed her glasses from the table and snatched what looked like an old dog eared photograph. Shelley, still slightly flustered, sat down at the table as Linda checked it out. It was an old, coloured photograph of a pretty young lady. The figure wore a full length 50's swing dress, canary yellow in colour.

'Hmm, lovely, but what are you getting excited about? An old photo of a lass in a yeller frock. Go on.'

'Well just look at the back,' replied Shelley. Linda flicked the card over and read a message written in pencil.

'September 5th 1956. And some message from someone called Beryl to an Ada and Bill saying she's gonna visit in a few days. So, what yer getting all het up for yer daft get?'

'Look closer,' said Shelley, 'look at the little printed line, not the handwriting, the bit about the photographer.' Linda re-scrutinised the back of the card. Down one side in fine but easily identifiable print were the words: *Thos Alice. Photographic studio. Briggate LEEDS.* Linda appeared stunned as she read out the text. She stared at the postcard and then handed it back to Shelley.

'Well?'

'Well what?' replied Linda.

'Well...the other night with your Zoe. That's what she said din't she. A woman wi' a yella dress and the name...bleedin' Alice! ...din't she? ...and she said summat about Briggate...din't she?'

'Don't tell me you believe in all that bollocks Shelley, it's ridiculous, it's just a coincidence ya silly bugger. Where'd ya get it?'

'We were just going through some old stuff from Dennis's family box. It's put the shits up me I can tell ya. It's uncanny. Apparently, this Bill were some relative of 'is granddad but it's the Alice bit and 'yellow dress, an' then when I saw 'Briggate bit I came over all funny and came straight round here. Dennis says I'm overreacting but it's bloody spooked me I'm tellin' ya.'

'Ere, let's have another look,' said Linda snatching it back. Again she scrutinised the photo and pored over the back before looking at the image on the front. 'Listen, Shell, I don't know if it means owt or if it's just coincidence but don't mention it to Zoe. She's got some bloody important meeting or summat going on tonight and she's been getting stressed out over it. She's been doing that meditation stuff and getting bleedin' grouchy all day so just put it in your pocket will yer love? I don't want 'er to see it, it might send 'er 'aywire. I don't know if this thing she's getting into is right for 'er, Im a bit worried to be honest. Anyway, let me put 'kettle on, I'm just doing Sophia an' 'er mate some tea, they're having a picnic out in 'back garden.'

'Ok love, but I'm still baffled by it all, I've got to say.' replied Shelley sliding the photograph back into her cardigan pocket. 'Who's the little mate anyway, anyone I know?'

'You might know 'er mother, it's little Bethany, Bethany Gobshell, they live at 'top o' North Parkway.'

'Bethany what?'

'Gobshell, do you know 'em?'

'Gobshite?'

'No, it's Gobshell ya slack get and be quiet will ya, she'll hear ya, 'door's open.' Shelley couldn't help but start sniggering.

'Gobshite? I've never heard o' that one afore in all me life,' she chuckled, 'you takin' 'piss or what?'

'It's bleedin' Gobshell, an' be quiet ya silly cow, she'll hear ya.' But Shelley was off, she slapped her hand over her mouth in a futile attempt to stifle her chuckling, which soon morphed into uncontrollable laughter. Her large frame convulsed and her eyes welled up. It was too much for Linda who shook her head in dismay but couldn't help being drawn into Shelley's infectious cachinnation. She succumbed and was soon reduced to tears herself as she held onto the kitchen sink to steady herself.

'You're a silly bleeder you are,' spurted Linda in between her cackling and uncontrollable belly laughs.

'Bethany bleedin' Gobshite! I've never heard o'... ' was all Shelley could manage before she collapsed once again and slapped the tabletop with her hand. This fuelled Linda's laughter even further as she lunged for the door to close it before the two little girls outside got wind of the facetious shenanigans. The two women spent the next few minutes coming to terms with the odd surname of Sophia's little schoolmate. Their merriment was abruptly interrupted by Zoe who walked into the kitchen unannounced.

'What's up wi' you two?' she enquired dourly as she wearily trudged over to the back door. Her serious demeanour immediately expunged the exultant gaiety out of the moment.

'Nowt love, just having a laugh, like we do, y'know,' replied Linda. 'You okay?'

'Yeah, I'm off now. I'm going for a walk and then meeting Ruth and Squidge at MacDonald's at Killingbeck. They'll be dropping me off later.'

'You sure you don't wanna tell me owt about it?'

'No, it's best not, I'll be okay don't worry. It's just summat I've got to do that's all. I'll just go and say tara to Sophia.' She opened the door and went out to see her daughter. Linda and Shelley looked at each other with raised eyebrows. The arrival of Zoe had at least sobered up their fit of hilarity. They descended into serious mode once again.

Having given Sophia a cuddle and a kiss Zoe she re-entered the kitchen. 'Right, I'm off. Wish me luck and don't forget Bethany's mam's picking her up at about seven.'

'Alright love, and good luck wi' whatever it is yer doing. Keep safe. I'll be waiting up for ya.'

'Thanks, Mam, see you then, see you later Shelley,' she said as she brushed past the pair of them looking pensive and nervy.

'See ya love. You look after yersen,' replied Shelley. They listened for the front door being closed behind her before they spoke again.

'I'm worried about that one Shell. She's a stubborn little bleeder though, there's not a lot I can do. At least it's not drugs and she doesn't really drink owt much now, but...it's just one thing after another. That bastard Phil's got a lot to answer for—

'Don't worry love. She'll be alright.'

'Hmm, I hope you're right,' said Linda as she picked up two plates of food for the girls. There were sandwiches and an assortment of cakes and biscuits plus a large glass of fruit juice each. Linda carried the food out on a large tray and lowered it onto the blanket where both girls laid out on their fronts playing on 3DS game consoles. Princess laid aside with his tongue hanging out.

'Thank you, Nana,' said Sophia.

'Thank you,' replied Bethany.

'Just let me know if you need owt else girls and don't forget, no going out o' 'garden, okay?'

'Okay Nana,' replied Sophia once again. Linda looked up at the skies. It had been a lovely day and the sun was still shining hot through the blue skies, but on the distant horizon, black, ominous clouds were beginning to gather. Could be a storm in the pipeline she thought as she made her way back into the house.

A couple of minutes later the kitchen door was pushed open and Bethany quietly walked in holding her plate of sandwiches at arm's length. Her eyes met with Shelley's.

'Oh hello luvvie, are you Bethany?'

'Yes. Is Sophia's Grandma here?' replied the little girl.

'She's just in the other room love, why what's up?'

'Would she mind cutting away the crusts from my sandwiches? I don't eat crusts. Mummy always cuts the crusts off for me.'

'Bring 'em 'ere love, o' course we can cut the crusts off for you, that's no problem at all.' She passed the plate over to Shelley just as Linda re-entered the kitchen.

'Oh, 'ello love what's up?'

'It's alright. She just wants the crusts cutting off 'er sandwiches, don't ya love? Her mummy always cuts them off for her,' replied Shelley on behalf of the little girl. Linda turned away and rolled her eyes.

Shelley grabbed a knife and started to trim the sandwiches. 'Now then love, it's Bethany in't it, and what's your second name luvvie?'

'It's Bethany Gobshell,' she replied.

'Ooo, Gobshell, that's a lovely name, I think I might

know your mam... ' Linda looked over the little girl and shot Shelley an icy stare. She knew what her game was. She silently mouthed a string of obscenities. *Don't you fuckin' dare. I'll fuckin kill you.* Shelley continued unabated. 'You live at 'top of North Parkway don't you love?'

'Yes, that's right,' beamed the little girl. 'It's the last house at the top of the hill. We've got a Jaguar.'

'Have you luvvie? Ooo that's nice, we've got a Tomcat called Geoff.' Bethany looked bemused as Linda continued her silent charade behind the little girl's back. She lifted her fist and shook it at Shelley.

'Well there you are look, all the crust cut off love, is that alright for you?'

'Yes, thank you very much,' she replied.

'You're very welcome me little love, any time,' smiled Shelley at the little girl.

'Oh yes, there is just one other thing, Princess has poohed on the blanket. Could someone please come out to move it as it's very unhygienic to be eating food next to it?'

Shelley just about managed to stifle her laugh. Linda looked down quizzically and silently mimed the words, *What the fuck!*.

'Of course love, you can't be having your tea next to that, can you? You're right about the hygiene luvvie, you can't be too careful where that's concerned can you?'

'No, you can't. That's what Mummy says.'

'Well, your mummy's spot on my little love, but because this isn't my house I'm not allowed to touch Princess's pooh, so Sophia's grandmamma will have come out and move it for you, won't you Linda?' she said looking up at her. Bethany also turned to face her now red-faced and bewildered hostess. She'd been cornered.

'Er...yeah, I'll sort it out Bethany, just you go out love, I'll be out in a minute,' replied Linda, stony-faced.

'Thank you,' replied the little girl.

'Okay Bethany love? Is there anything else we can get for you?' asked Shelley, revelling in the muted exasperation of her dearest friend.

'No thank you,' replied Bethany, 'that will be all for now.' She took her plate of crustless sandwiches and went to re-join her friend in the garden. Linda clicked the door closed behind her.

'You fuckin' bitch! I'll fuckin' kill you...I don't fuckin' believe you,' cried Linda. Shelley was in hysterics and banged the table. Linda stood and watched, dumbfounded. 'And grandmamma, I'll fuckin' grandmamma you ya silly old bitch!'

'Stop your bleedin' chelping and go an clear up the friggin' dog shite will ya? Do as you're told. It's very unhygienic you know!' Linda stood with her arms folded and stared down at her mate, before reluctantly retrieving the poop scoop and a plastic 'doggy' bag from under the sink. The sight of this caused Shelley to crease up even more.

'It'll do you 'world o' good lass...it'll build character, and while you're at it take her a little bell out so she can give it a shake if she needs owt else.' Shelley doubled over in hysterics. 'Gobshite by name... '

It was too much for Linda to bear. Her poker-faced countenance morphed into one of mirth, she couldn't hold back a little smile no matter how hard she tried.

'There's only one Gobshite round 'ere lady, and that's you, ya silly old twat,' she said. 'Wait 'till I get back, I'll show you 'ow to build character!' She opened the door, wiped the smile off her face and attended to the needs of her granddaughter's posh little guest.

*

It was D-day for Zoe. She'd steamrollered Ruth, and to an extent Simon, into doing something they weren't entirely happy with, but there was no way she could back out now. It was more Ruth under duress than Simon, he was happy to go along with anything for Zoe, but Ruth was nervous, she was definitely the god-fearing type when it came to rule-breaking and dishonesty. Although she hadn't spoken any direct untruths to Paula Jackson she hadn't exactly been honest and upfront with her either and she'd wished she'd never agreed to this whole 'mad charade' as she described it, but Zoe's steely determination had forced the issue.

The arrangement was to meet at MacDonald's restaurant on the Killingbeck retail park, just on the outskirts of Seacroft. It was on the A64 York Road into town so it was easy for everyone to get there. The long walk had given Zoe more time to think and prepare. She'd had a rough time in the house at Reginald Street. On 'that night', she'd been found in the cellar, curled up on a battered armchair, semi-conscious and rambling. They'd never quite worked out how she'd pulled a huge fridge freezer over the doorway from the inside of the cellar head, but there'd been nothing untoward she'd been told, nothing improper had occurred and everything could be accounted for. It had all been in her head, they'd said. Apart from the issue of the fridge-freezer. It was all psychological they'd explained. But Zoe didn't agree. It had been real to her but she'd no answer to the riddle of the fridge-freezer either. She had no recollection of how she came to be in the cellar in the first place never mind shifting the fridge to get in and then blocking the doorway up with it from the inside. There was no way she could have moved it alone, she reasoned. There was something in that house, something in that cellar that had latched onto her, something not of this world. Tonight, she was going to confront it, one way or another.

The blue skies had been outmuscled and overpowered, eventually capitulating to heavy dark clouds. The first drops of rain were now spitting onto Zoe's pale and worried features as she sat outside MacDonald's waiting for her corrupted cohorts. She was nervous. The prospect of revisiting the little house and reliving the horrible experiences there made her feel sick. She scratched her head and gently bit her finger-ends as self-doubt began to infiltrate her psyche. The pressure was slowly building up in her headspace. A slight tension in her throat. Her breathing distinct, more pronounced.

An equally apprehensive Ruth appeared with Simon from the direction of the car park. She looked as if she was about to burst into tears, especially on seeing the anxiety on Zoe's face. Simon remained surprisingly calm. He greeted Zoe with a hug (he would thought Zoe) and then ushered everyone inside to escape the rain which was getting heavier by the minute. They found a nice secluded corner before Simon peeled off to buy coffee.

Ruth looked at Zoe. 'It's not too late to call it off love,' she said. 'You know I'm still unsure about this don't you?'

'No, it's got to be done, Ruth. There's no turning back. I'll admit to being a bit nervous meself, but I'll get through it. I'm more concerned about you, to be honest. You don't look well at all.'

The sight of her friend, so fragile and jittery, reinforced Zoe's resilience as if she had to be strong for her mentor rather than the other way around. This added apprehension only served to crank up the uncertainty of the whole affair. Simon returned with the drinks and sat down next to Ruth.

'Right, what's the plan then,' he said.

'You've got the keys?' replied Zoe staring him in the eye.

'Yeah, I got them. So officially I'm house hunting, and I can only do evenings because of work commitments, which is technically true.' Simon smiled as Ruth closed her eyes. It wasn't a little white lie to her, it was deceit, and she didn't like it.

'The agent said the owners were gonna let it out but had changed their minds and that they were open to offers before it goes back to auction,' continued Simon. 'Might have a look around myself whilst we're there, you never know, I might even put a cheeky bid in for it.'

'I wouldn't let you buy it Squidge,' butted in Zoe, 'It's a fuckin' 'orrible place, the street, the 'ouse, the cellar. It wants pulling down, the whole place does.'

'Anyway,' interjected Ruth, 'what are we doing Zoe? I'll be glad when it's over and done with, I can tell you now.'

'Right, well we can all go into the 'ouse but I insist that I go down into the cellar meself, alone. There's things down there, nasty evil things as far as I'm concerned, things that are connected to me, and me only. I've got to go down there and face 'em, get them or it or whatever it is out o' me system.' Ruth held her head down and started shaking it. She wasn't convinced that they were going about this in the right way.

Zoe picked up on it. 'And it's alright you shaking your bleedin' 'ead Ruth, but at the end of the day, I'm gonna need your support. If you can't give me 100 per cent then ya might as well not bother because all this negativity from you is doing me bleedin' 'ead in. They had to carry me out last time and there's no way that's 'appening again, but if you don't wanna see it through just say now, the pair of ya, 'cos it's 'ard enough facing up to these twatting inner demons as it is!'

'I'm in,' spurted Simon straight away. Both he and Zoe then looked at Ruth. There was an impasse.

Ruth looked up at Zoe and sighed. 'Alright love. You're right, I said I'd help you and I will. I won't dwell on it but it's the first and last time I'll get involved in anything that I'm not happy with. But count me in. No negatives, you get my full support.'

*

It was raining heavily as they drove down York Road and turned left at the Irish Centre onto Temple View Road. They were now officially within the confines of the area known as East Moor Park and Zoe could already sense the foreboding. The rain and the dark clouds gave the area a sullen ambience. There were no trees, no lawns, no privet hedges. Just little blocks of cells, red-bricked with black roofs, separated only by dark grey tarmac roads. Traffic calming dictated their speed was kept to a minimum as they tentatively crawled down the road like a funeral hearse on the way to a graveyard burial. Ruth felt the tension, her insides churned like a half-macca in a cement mixer as the burden of guilt chewed away at her insides.

They turned right and drove down Ascot Terrace and then left onto East Moor Drive. The sight of the road in front of her gave Zoe the creeps. She'd become quite familiar with the long, straight incline of the Drive during her time in the area and the journey down towards

Reginald Street embodied a sense of dread. She hated the place. Row after row of dreary, depressing back-to-back houses. Gothic, angular, jagging gables hung over the road on either side, as far down as the eye could see. Black and grey, dismal. She looked towards the bottom, where the Drive dissected Reginald Street. Down towards the bottom, down towards the street, the off-licence, the park, the railway wall. Always downwards. Edging downward, falling, plunging. Down the old stone steps to the dark cellar beneath. Sinking into the black depths, down into the acidic womb of irredeemable existence. She shuddered.

They slowly weaved in and out of the traffic calming system. On reaching the bottom they briefly pulled up outside Sally's off licence. The place looked empty. They then turned right into the little cul-de-sac of Reginald Street. They were here. She was back. The place was just as it had been when Zoe had first set eyes on it a year ago. Dark, wet and devoid of life. There were no cars in the street, no dogs, no children - no signs of life. Peggy Bowden, the weird, little bulbous-eyed old lady who'd lived opposite at number eleven had passed to the other side. That property was up for sale along with a number of others in the street. Zoe looked down towards the end of the road where 'Racy' Tracy and the bottom street kids had lived, but there was no sign of life there either. Just the low, black stone wall, beyond which stood the patchwork of allotments and the steep embankment which plunged down towards the black railway lines.

They pulled up outside number ten. The light was fading as Ruth looked at the facade of the dreary little house. She immediately picked up on the sense of dread that Zoe must have suffered living in a place like this, she felt for her. She scanned the street up and down. There were no illuminated front rooms and the only street light was from the Drive which gave the place a murky, dark atmosphere. Boarded-up properties and for sale signs were dotted about the place with open bin yards spilling rubbish and filth out onto the pavements. It dawned on her that she was the senior and most experienced of the group, and taking into account Zoe's rather brusque attack on her earlier she decided to assert herself as best she could.

'Right, we're here guys,' she blurted out. 'I'm not being negative Zoe, but if at any time you want to bail out, do so. Only carry on with this if you're comfortable with it. No pressure.'

'Well, wouldn't say I was comfortable...but I'm not bailing.'

'Right then,' continued Ruth, 'Simon, get out and open the doors and then we'll jump out and get straight inside so we're not getting wet...come on, let's go.'

Simon did as he was told without hesitation. He got out of the car and stepped into the gloomy street as the rain continued to sling it down. The windows of the house were boarded out in plywood and the front door was protected by a wrought iron security grill. He leant forward and hastily unlocked both door and grill before leaping inside to avoid the deluge.

The door opened directly into a tiny sitting room and other than a a slightly damp odour the place was empty, dark and ominous. He searched for a light switch. He found one in the entrance just by the door and reached over, flicking it on with his middle finger. He then realised there was no central bulb, but he'd come prepared. He pulled out a torch and flashed it in all directions to get a feel for the place. He sniffed the dank air. He listened. Just the constant rain battering against the plywood. He scooped up a pile of letters and placed it in an alcove aside the chimney breast with other accumulated post and junk mail.

With the door now opened and the shining beam of the torchlight, it signalled for the girls to follow. They extricated themselves from the car and ducked to avoid the rain. The rotten timber gutter from two doors up sent a cascade of rainwater leaching onto the old stone footpath below, like a filthy urban waterfall, just as it had done during Zoe's time in the street.

Once inside the door was slammed closed and they shook off the rainwater as best they could. All three stood in the centre of the room and took stock. Zoe quickly engaged the torch facility on her phone. She'd never seen the room like this. The first time she'd set foot in the place it had been dilapidated. When she'd been carried out it had been renovated, decorated and furnished. But there was no furniture now, just dusty laminate flooring and modern decorations. She looked down at the space under the front window. She'd spent many hours staring at this spot, contemplating the history and rationale behind the giant battered armchair that had stood silent in the cellar directly below. She wondered whether it was still there and shuddered at the thought. She took a step towards the tiny kitchen and peered into the darkness. She flicked on the light switch and this time the room was illuminated, only dimly but just enough for them to see in the sitting room without the use of the torches. The new kitchen units they'd had installed were still there, minus the huge American style fridge-freezer, the one she'd always dreamed of. Having discovered the original cellar head doorway bricked up, Phil had knocked it through and the sheet of plywood he'd used to block up the resultant hole in the wall remained, albeit lying loose and propped up against the bare opening. No wonder the property hadn't sold, she thought. She turned back to face Ruth and Simon. The time was here. The pressure in her head was escalating as the intangible grip on her throat tightened.

*

Ruth, concerned that the whole affair was in danger of becoming a farce and devoid of any professional integrity, once again took charge and pulled them together. She yanked Zoe back from the kitchen entrance.

'Right give me your hands and link up.' Zoe and Simon both took deep breaths as they turned to face each other in the middle of the darkened room. They formed a small circle and held hands. Each closed their eyes and settled their minds as the storm continued its spiteful assault on the little house. Ruth recited a small prayer, addressing spirit and requesting protection from negative entities, and she prayed for God to overlook Zoe. Just as she finished a flash of light lit up the little room followed by an almighty crash of thunder. Zoe flinched as she silently mouthed the word, Jesus. The storm took her back to the fateful night when the power cut had struck the house and the whole street. She'd been left in the pitch darkness then and the sudden spike of lightning transported her back to that pivotal moment in her life. Her face was ashen, her heart sank and her energy and courage seemed to evaporate.

'You okay love?' asked Ruth. 'We can walk out now, just say.'

Zoe took time to compose herself and took a deep

breath. 'No...I'm fine.' She turned and walked towards the open kitchen. 'You two are staying up here aren't ya? You won't be leaving me will ya?'

'We're going nowhere,' said Simon.

'Just you say and we'll be down there in a flash,' added Ruth. 'We're here for you love...and Zoe?' Zoe turned her head to face Ruth. ' ...don't forget...what we do is about love and compassion. Don't try to fight the forces of evil with negativity, you won't win. Love and compassion will see you through anything if you channel them correctly.' Zoe nodded slowly. She turned into the kitchen and out of view leaving Simon, and a very nervous Ruth standing helpless in the living room.

She pushed the plywood just enough to one side so she could squeeze through and stood on the square stone step inside the cellar head. She flicked on the original Bakelite switch and looked down. Though the light was dim, from what she could see from the top of the stairs, the cellar looked just how she remembered it. Dark, malodorous and daunting. She attempted to steel herself. *Come on you silly bitch. You can do it. Fuck the cellar, fuck Phil and fuck 'em all. This is for you and Sophia.* She took a large intake of breath and began her slow descent down the worn stone stairs.

Up top, in the living room, a worried Ruth looked at Simon. 'I don't like it,' she said quietly, shaking her head. 'I'm already getting bad vibes. I should have told Paula about all this. Are you picking anything up?'

'Just negative vibrations. I'm not getting anything positive that's for sure,' he replied.

'Well, if anything happens, and I mean anything, we're straight down there, I don't care what Zoe says do ya hear me? It's only gonna end up one way is this, I can feel it, it's not good...I should never have agreed—'

'Just calm down Ruth, I can see why she felt a need to come down here and get this off her back, whatever it is, so just let's see what happens...and of course we'll be down there in a flash if we have to, that's why we're here. Just you relax a little bit, your anxiety sometimes rubs off on people without you knowing it.' He smiled at Ruth and his calming tones had the desired effect.

'Okay,' she replied. 'You're right. Just let's see what happens. I don't like this weather though, it couldn't be any worse—'

'Ruth! There you go again, you don't even realise it.'

'Oh, you're right Simon, I'm sorry love, I'm a nervous wreck. Just give me the car keys, I've left me phone in there, I might need it.' Simon shook his head and threw her the keys.

'Don't forget to lock it, I've heard it's a bit dodgy around here,' he smiled, raising his eyebrows. Simon was the only calm and reassured person in the building, fully worth his salt on tonight's performance, thought Ruth. She disappeared into the street and fumbled with the remote for the central locking button. After the third attempt, the lock released. She opened the door and had to stretch over to reach her phone which lay on the back seat. Having grabbed it she then ducked back out of the car and pressed the remote to lock up again but as she did so a massive crash echoed around the tiny rain-soaked street. She flinched, assuming it was overhead thunder, but as she turned around to re-enter the house she realised it was the front door that had been slammed closed. She immediately started banging it.

'Simon! Simon! Open the door! Simon!' But Simon didn't open the door and she began to panic. She ragged the handle up and down and slammed her tiny fists onto the door and screamed for the love of God. 'Please! Simon, open the door' The door remained locked shut. There were no signs of any activity from within the house, no light, and the only sound was of the rain pouring down, battering the plywood and which easily drowned out her wailing and screeching. There was nobody in the street to help, no assistance, no backup. She was on her own in the storm, in a derelict little cul-de-sac of depressing Edwardian back-to-backs in the desolate East Moor Park area of Leeds.

*

Zoe slowly descended the stone cellar steps, tentative and cautious. The smell was awful and made worse by the stagnant groundwater that had begun to rise through the earthen flooring. There was a fault in the far corner of the cellar where the ground had collapsed below the old foundations and it was from this point that an inky black liquid slowly filtered through into the cellar. She continued to descend the stairs, slowly and methodically. The first thing that she caught sight of halfway down was the old stone worktop standing in the middle of the little cellar. Formed from a piece of stone at least four inches thick it was supported at both ends by roughly coursed brickwork. Exactly as she'd remembered. As she continued downwards, it occurred to her that each step seemed to take her deeper into the cellar, deeper than she remembered. There seemed to be more of them, each step larger in depth, taking her deeper and deeper into the cellar. She carried on. Her head was becoming heavier, the sensation in her throat tighter. The stone steps took her deep into the cellar, much deeper than she remembered, but she bravely persevered and eventually reached the bottom. It was there. Just as it had been. She'd only ever consciously taken the journey down into the cellar once before, and other than the staircase being seemingly longer and deeper, everything on first sight was as it had registered in her memory. The oversized battered armchair sat directly under the bricked-up window which at one time would have looked out and upwards onto the street above. She'd erred on the side of caution and conditioned herself to expect it, but now, standing right there in front of her: the old, musty leather armchair. It still sent a shiver down the length of her spine. She looked around the place. The light was weak and dim. The tiny disused coal bunker to her left, the stone table in the middle and the chair under the window. And that was it. In the shadows of the far corner was the collapsed floor through which the dirty rainwater continued to bleed into the cellar. She stood and looked, she surveyed and she contemplated. But she knew what the next move had to be. The chair. To her, the single most abhorred item on the face of the planet, the one that symbolised the full horror of this repulsive little house.

The patchwork of animal hide, the hardened splints of leather, jagged and ripped. Brass studs and horsehair spilling out onto the wet earthen floor. Rusted springs poking out into the dank air. Just as she remembered. She walked slowly towards it. There was a little black and white photograph that lay on the stone table. She and Phil had discovered it the first time they'd ventured the depths of the cellar. It lay exactly where they'd left it. It was of an older lady and a sad-looking little girl. A black and white passport-sized photograph. It meant nothing to her then and even less so now as she paused to take a cursory look before flicking at it with her hand. She reached the chair, which dwarfed her tiny frame in comparison, and lowered herself into its heinous bosom of abhorrence. She shuddered as she spread her hands and arms out onto the chair's huge battered arms. Her head was throbbing as she slowly leant back. She gave herself. She prostituted her body to the chair, sacrificing her flesh and bones to the room, to the house. But not her mind, they weren't having that. She opened herself up mentally, luring, enticing whatever it was that lurked deep in that horrible little room to show itself, to tease it out into the open. She was here for a confrontation. She'd take whatever was coming her way. She was as ready as she ever would be as she closed her eyes and opened her airwaves. Her heart thumped like never before.

*

The door was locked solid as Ruth continued to batter it from the outside screaming for Simon to open it. The rain lashed down laying siege on the little street of back-to-backs. She was getting nowhere and a further onslaught of crashing thunder and fork lightning overhead spooked her as she dived back into the car to escape the rampant storm. Once inside she calmed down a little. She had a flash of inspiration and grabbed her mobile. First Simon. No answer. Then Zoe. Nothing. *So much for that brainwave. Ring the police. And tell them what? That the door's stuck? Oh God, I knew we shouldn't have come. Ruth! Why, why did you agree to this? Oh, God.* Her eyes misted up and tears began to roll down her cheeks. *The shop at the end of the street. Maybe I can get help there, but they're not gonna want to come out in this weather just to help get the door open.* She was now in full panic mode. Her only option was to call Paula but that would have repercussions. Her loyalties were divided but she couldn't work out what to do for the best. She threw the car door open and attacked the front door of the house again, and this time with even more gusto.

*

The buzzing sensation began. At first, light vibrations, just as Zoe had got her breathing rhythm going, and then a full-on constant buzz. Not only was it audible to her, but such was the physical impact, she struggled to keep her head still. Her breathing became laboured as she struggled to control it. The constriction in her throat gave her a claustrophobic choking sensation. The temperature began to drop and she watched as her exhaled breath dissipated into the cold air like white billowing smoke. She felt a numbness in her feet which slowly moved up to her ankles, then her legs and slowly encompassed her upper torso before finally rendering her totally paralysed. Although she'd been through all this before, she was petrified. Her heart thumped and her breathing became increasingly erratic. With the use only of her darting eyes and her sentient mind, she hung in there. Her senses heightened, her pupils dilated, and she waited.

As she remained anchored to the hideous armchair unable to move even an inch, she heard a soft bubbling sound. It emanated from the sunken corner where the black rainwater continued to ooze into the cellar from beneath. Her eyes flicked to her left to see the liquid now frothing up and giving off a stealthy, wispy vapour. She got a sense that things were about to kick off. She was right.

She found herself shackled to the chair by heavy rusted chains around her waist. Her arms and legs were stretched outwards, splayed open and attached to rope which pulled them tight, the ends of which disappeared into the fabric of the cellar. Flashes of memory speared into her headspace. A sense that she'd been in this exact predicament before, that she had to ride it out, that she was safe.

She was now as physically vulnerable as could be, but she'd already handed over her body, they could do whatever they wanted with that. They weren't getting inside her head though. She was scared shitless, but she held strong. *Is that it? Is that all you've got? Come on, let's see what you're fuckin' made of.*

The pain in her head was almost unbearable, The choking sensation intensified, not only the constriction of her breathing but also the sharp shards that felt like swallowing broken glass. Her heart raced, but the ice-cold cellar rendered her paralysed body freezing and lifeless. But she remained resolute and mentally strong. Though she'd been unsure as to what form it would take or down which dark corridors she'd be dragged down she'd spent the last few days steeling herself for this. Last time she was weak in the head. Not so now, this was the new Zoe. *Fuck em!*

The wispy vapour from the sunken corner, a luminous mustard yellow-green concoction, began to slowly condense into an indistinct form. Zoe watched through the narrow slits of her eyes and sensed a consciousness in the dark, a negative conscience. As the form grew in density a gut-wrenching stench pervaded the tiny little cellar. The light dimmed as the electrical energy was sucked in and consumed by the entity, fuelling the manifestation as it grew stronger, increasing in tangible malevolent intent.

She remained bound to the chair and physically incapacitated as the misty form moved closer and closer. The faceless materialisation enveloped her face and body, so close, so intimately close, but she wouldn't be bowed. She was now in unchartered territory and terrified but she kept her mind strong, for now. Whatever it was, it was knocking on the door. She wasn't ready for what came next.

*

Ruth desperately beat on the front door in the pouring rain. She was getting nowhere. She felt helpless. She looked around but there was no one to be seen anywhere. In panic, she rushed around to the shop at the end of the street but its doors were locked, its lights out. She looked up the long incline of East Moor Drive but there was no one. No evidence of any life anywhere. She was desperate. She'd have to ring the police, she'd no option. She walked back to number 10 and looked at the house. Not a sound, just a little dark house in a dead street with the door slammed closed and locked tight. The whole street, the whole place was devoid of life, of activity, no lights, no nothing. She may as well have been stuck in the middle of the Yorkshire Dales. She rang 999 but nobody answered. She rang Paula Jackson but no answer. *What the hell is going on?* Physically shattered and mentally drained she was drenched from head to toe. She got back into the car and cried.

*

Zoe felt like crying, but she wouldn't give in as the ghostly formation explored her whole body, searching the very core of her intimacy. The foul-smelling, heinous mist curled around her neck and face before reaching for and infiltrating her open mouth. As the vapour slipped in it funnelled around her dry cavity and wrapped around her tongue. She felt the sensation of the mist sliding down her throat, the feeling of violation, the contamination of her intimacy, she was being raped by an evil spirit. She felt gut wrenchingly sick inside and for the first time, it occurred to her that she might not make it, that she'd bitten off more than she could handle. She felt so tired, exhausted. Her mental resilience began to waver. She felt the first pangs of surrendering her mind to whatever it was that now violated both her soul and body.

She watched in horror as the tail-end of the vapour disappeared fully inside her. She could feel the entity pushing and probing around her innards, and with it the stench emanating from her mouth became unbearable.

She began to feel dizzy, as if she was about to pass out and then she began to slip away. She slumped downwards, a falling sensation. And then it was as if the whole ground beneath her disappeared as she began to plummet, downwards through the earthen cellar floor and down towards the deep echelons of the earth. Deeper and deeper through the crust of the earth, through solid rock. Far, far away from the place where she'd been born, where she lived, far from the land she called home, from the ones she loved. Deeper she plummeted, downwards towards the hot cored centre of the earth, she hung on for dear life before crashing to an abrupt halt. The armchair and chains had vanished.

She found herself backed into the corner of a small, dark claustrophobic pit, chiselled out of rock, deep beneath the surface of the earth. On a niche carved out of the rock face, a burning, glowing red cross dripped with blood. Zoe was no stranger to this place, she'd been here before, she knew that much, but until now it had been eradicated from her memory. Directly in front of her was a crude stone altar over which materialised the luminescent and levitating figure of a small girl. The girl was covered from her neck down in a white sheet and her head slowly turned towards Zoe. Again, she'd witnessed this setting in the past but the memory had lurked deep within her subconscious and only now chose to surface. The eyes of the girl were liquid gloss-black, as they had been before. They stared hard at Zoe. She hung on. She knew she was been tested to the very limit. And whatever 'they' were, they were now on the brink of defiling her soul. The entity continued to circle her innards, seeping around every organ, infiltrating every cavity and every millilitre of her bodily fluids.

Though every cell of her physical body had been corrupted Zoe just about retained, by the thinnest of threads, her mind. She'd been reduced to the very basic essence of humanity, but her mind, her sanity, hadn't yet been breached. She retained her consciousness, her memories, her mind, her thoughts. It was all she had left, but it was becoming more and more difficult for her to retain focus. The physical pain was unbearable as she felt the entity knocking, probing, attempting to get in, to gain access to her mind. As she looked at the figure of the little girl, it morphed, before her eyes, into an image of Sophia, her innocent little daughter, her eyes turning blood-red. *It's not Sophia. They're testing you. Keep strong, ignore the bastards!* But she couldn't, it was too much. *Fucking leave her alone you filthy bastards!* Each time she mouthed obscenities in her head she received a fork of pain in her heart as if the very life was being squeezed out of it. *Filthy piece of shit...leave her!* The grip tightened, expunged more life, more energy. Her heart felt as though it was almost bursting open. She was losing consciousness but she continued to hang on by a thread as the far-away cries of her daughter pleading for mercy rang around her head,

crying begging for mummy and daddy, screaming piti-
fully. *Bastards! Fucking leave her!* More pain. Zoe's pitiful
remonstrations were becoming weaker.

She was now teetering on the edge, her life slowly
petering out, she was losing the battle. They'd taken her
body and were on the verge of taking her mind. The altar
and the levitating girl dissipated to nothing as a lump
of flesh and matted hair slowly emerged from the dark
corner of the pit. This was no materialising vapour. This
was solid, the solid head of a creature, which grew and
grew until it took up the whole space of the claustrophobic tiny cavern. The huge horned head was scarlet-red
with matted strands of black hair, a grotesquely missha-
pen hooked nose and luminous bright-red, pin-pricked
eyes. The leathered skin was wrinkled, warty and rough,
its lips cracked and bloated. The temperature had now
turned upside down, the space was hot, red hot with the
crackling sounds of fire and the clanking of heavy chains
echoing around the tiny chamber.

As the snout pressed against the nose of a terrified
Zoe the entity opened its mouth to a rush of rancid breath
and a mouthful of jagged animalistic teeth. Her face was
licked with a wet, dripping slab of stinking tongue, as
its deep-inset eyes bored into her soul. She was on the
brink as the debauched demon pushed its engorged nose
up against her, salaciously rubbing it into her face as it
pinned her up against the rock face amid a wanton guttural moan of pleasure. She felt the immense power of the
entity as her wretched struggle for life ebbed away. She
resorted to the only thing she could, blasphemy. *Cunt!*
The demon pressed her further and harder against the
rock face with the excruciating pain increasing by the
second. *Bastard!* Again, the force was cranked up and with

it, the level of pain heightened.

She felt her bodily fluids draining and the last vestiges of her sanity slowly being transmuted over to the negative, evil aura of the demon as it slowly consumed her. One last desperate surge of electrical activity fired through the neurons of her brain. The last thought, perhaps, she would ever create as a human. But the impression which fired up in her head activated another, and then another, and then she was on a roll. Sophia. Her daughter Sophia, her face, her image, her voice, the day she was born, her first cry, her first smile, her first birthday. Her fucking daughter. This intense love she held for her daughter stabilised her mind. It gave her time, only a second, but time to think. *Fight like fuck! Never am I going to let this bastard creature take me away from my daughter!* The last words that Ruth had spoken to her rang through her head.

"Don't forget...what we do is about love and compassion. Don't try to fight the forces of evil, you won't win. Love and compassion will see you through anything if you channel them correctly." She let the words sink in as she clung to life. No more profanity. She composed herself.

And then the battle began. She slowly brought the image of her beautiful glowing daughter to the fore of her consciousness and allowed the powerful love that existed between them to flow. There was an immediate alleviation of the force being thrust upon her giving Zoe just enough wiggle room to mount her challenge. From the brink of oblivion, she now had a chance, and she went for it. In her headspace, she envisaged harnessing the power of the whole universe, and she converted that power into love for her daughter. And as her energies re-booted up so the strength and powers of the demon diminished. She visualised millions of billions of streams of millions of billions of particles, every single one bristling with life, love and positive vibrations. The imagery conjured up a shaft of brilliant white light being channelled into her soul empowering and re-energising her conviction to overcome and conquer.

The physical power of the huge satanic beast was immeasurable, but its psychic capacity was even more formidable. It sensed the desperation of Zoe and the strategy she now employed. Amidst the continuing sounds of a crackling, raging fire and the ominous clanking of heavy chains and bullwhips the demon stepped up the onslaught, it wasn't giving up his prey this easy.

Zoe's positive energies of pure white light initially took effect but her tiny comparable frame could only harness so much power as her whole body shook and vibrated with the immense strain being placed upon it. The Demon sensed this frailty and again upped the ante. Its colossal strength and power slowly forced his adversary backwards, back towards the damp rock face of the cavern. She fought with all her might, her fighting spirit from the estate in full swing but it was still no match for the powerful demon. Once again, she felt that the battle was slipping away as the beast slowly impressed its vastly superior forces upon her. She continued channelling the power of love but was slowly becoming weaker and weaker, teetering over the edge of a deep black abyss. Total darkness. A distant low hum. Nothingness. And then, just a spark, a seed of thought, a distant memory firing up from the deepest recesses of her convoluted mind. She'd done it before. She could do it again. She had experience. Somehow, from somewhere, she found the mental fortitude and strength to delve deeper than she ever could have imagined.

She visualised Jesus Christ on the crucifix, high up on the top of a hill, silhouetted against the blazing sun. He looked down at her from afar before drawing closer as his vision became surrounded by light, white light, brilliant white light, which grew in intensity. Zoe and the vision of Christ connected. The energies that were now being channelled through Zoe were 100% utterly pure, white and unblemished and they met those powerful energies of the demon. Good against bad. Jesus Christ against the demon of the deep. Almost unconscious, the pitiful listless body of Zoe was the conduit for the battleground bringing the supreme powers of good and evil together. It was a mismatch.

An explosion of pure, brilliant white light shook the whole cavern. The intensity of the light was unworldly as the psychic blast hit the demon like a stun gun sending it reeling to the far side of the pit, its powers immediately zapped, its size diminished. Zoe slumped to the ground. The negative mist that had been probing Zoe's innards flew out of her mouth and dissipated into thin air. The Demon, defiant to the end, roared an almighty guttural outcry before receding into the fabric of the deep cavern and out of sight. Pitch blackness. Silence.

*

The front door released and opened just a few inches of its own accord. Ruth, who had been lamenting over how wretched her life had turned out, jumped out and ran into the house as soon as she realised. She discovered Simon curled up on the floor in the centre of the room.

'Simon! Simon are you okay love?' she cried, with tears in her eyes. She rushed to his aid. Simon stirred as if he'd just woken up from a deep sleep.

'What? What's happened?' he said, 'yeah, I'm alright, where's Zoe? What happened?' Ruth helped him up.

'Come on,' she said, 'we need to—.' As they turned around to face the kitchen, Zoe was stood in the doorway. A physical and mental wreck, her face was white, her eyes red-rimmed and her hair bedraggled. She was in a shocking state and fell into the hands of Simon as he rushed to assist her. The ordeal was over. They thanked God, carried Zoe into the car and eventually got her back to Seacroft. It took three days of complete rest and recuperation before she was able to contemplate getting back to normality.

CHAPTER 12

Zoe, along with Ruth, had been summoned to meet the big cheese, Paula Jackson, at the Kirkstall and Meanwood Spiritualist Church. It was just a week since the harrowing return to East Moor Park and having initially taken to her bed for a couple of days her physical energies were just about restored. She'd decided not to dwell on the mental images which were now branded into her headspace. What was done was done, however, the overall experience had lifted that niggling encumbrance that had been psyching her out for months. She couldn't forget the experience, she never would, the memory of the ordeal would stick with her for life, but the heavy weight of anxiety that she'd harboured for almost a year had been offloaded. She'd emerged a stronger woman both mentally and physically, and proved her mettle in standing up to the horrors of the cellar. Whether they'd been mental demons or actual physical manifestations, she didn't know or understand, but she'd faced them head-on, she'd confronted her fears. When it mattered, when she was backed up against the wall this spiky little Seacroft lassie was as tough as tungsten carbide, just like her mother. The house and the area no longer symbolised fear and horror, nor did it send a current of revulsion scudding down her back at the very mention or thought of the place. Her head was clearer, she was much more positive and confident. She was now ready to take the next step in her development not only as a potential medium but onto the next phase in her life. Life after Phil.

But before that, she had to face the music with Paula Jackson. The prospect of the meeting had left her a little apprehensive. She'd only met Paula the once back at the open circle and though she'd seemed a down-to-earth type, the fact that she'd requested an audience so soon after the event at East Moor Park had left Zoe feeling that she might be in for a bit of a roasting. The two bus rides from Seacroft to Kirkstall had given her time to mull the whole episode over and she now just wanted to get the meeting over and done with before she could set about mapping out her future.

*

'Come in Zoe love, it's nice to see you again,' said Paula Jackson as she looked up and offered a comforting smile. She stood up. 'Journey over ok?' she continued as she reached over to shake Zoe's hand. She then rounded her and closed the door before gesturing her nervous visitor to take a seat. The little room was modern, bright and airy. The decor was calming and the simple furnishings comprised of comfortable tub-style armchairs, a small, polished-oak coffee table and matching shelving units. A crystal vase bursting with fresh flowers stood on the windowsill. It was the room where Paula conducted her one-to-one private sittings. Zoe had been directed down the corridor to the little side-room by Ruth who would be joining them shortly after preparing drinks in a side kitchenette.

'Er, yes thanks it was good,' replied Zoe cautiously, as she analysed the manner of the woman who, up until now, she'd regarded as some far-reaching figure of authority. Paula was well manicured with short, dark hair.

With just a hint of cosmetics, she was dressed casually in stylish brushed jeans, a white loose-fitting blouse and flat white sandals. Zoe estimated her age to be late thirties or early forties.

'You know what the buses are like,' continued Zoe in such an awkward tone that Paula felt obliged to nod and smile just to make her feel at ease. Both sat down in the armchairs and faced each other with Paula crossing her legs and clasping her hands in front of her.

'Now Zoe love, don't look so worried. I think you might know why I've asked you to come along for a bit of a chat.'

'Yeah, I think so,' she replied, 'but please Paula, I don't want Ruth to get into any trouble. It was my idea and I forced her and Squidge...er...Simon into coming with me...it was all my fault.'

'Okay love, don't worry. No one's in trouble. You did what you thought you had to do under the circumstances, and I know you leant on Ruth to help. And she helped because she's a good person, maybe too good for her own good sometimes. You'd have still gone down there alone if Ruth hadn't gone along with your little plan wouldn't you?'

'Yeah, I think I would.'

'So it was right that she was there for you in the end, you'd have been in a right pickle if she hadn't have been, and don't forget Simon. I've had a word with him also. But what's happened has happened, so we need to look to the future. I know you're a strong-willed woman, I know that because I've been told. I've also been told that, potentially, you've got a great gift, a special gift, and it's that I don't want to see go to waste and so it's important to me that if you're serious about this, and according to what Ruth says I think you are, then from here on in we have to go about things through the proper channels...haven't we love,' continued Paula staring Zoe in the eye.

'Yeah, I know...it was just that...I just had this bad experience down there and I just... '

'I know love. I know. Well, let's start as we mean to go on shall we—' At that moment Ruth burst in through the door with three hot drinks on a tray.

'Sorry about that ladies,' she said as she attempted to apportion the drinks. 'Oh, wait a minute, you said you wanted tea didn't you Paula?'

'No love, it's okay, it's fine.'

'No, well look if I give you my tea, and then I'll have this coffee, will that work? You wanted coffee didn't you Zoe...er...did you want sugar though?' She scratched her head whilst the other two looked on in muted amusement.

'I'm fine with whatever Ruth,' said Zoe a little relieved that the confusing drink scenario had shaved off the edge from the gravity of her conversation with Paula.

'Right, you take that Paula and I'll go change this and I'll bring some sugar for you, Zoe. Sorry about this, I won't be a minute,' she said as she scooted out of the room through the door, and disappeared back down the corridor.

Paula allowed herself a surreptitious eye roll and a sideways smile.

'Wouldn't have her any other way,' she whispered, as she slid a little wink towards Zoe.

*

They were soon rejoined by the scatterbrained Ruth and over the next twenty minutes, they listened intently as

Paula outlined the dangers of meddling in matters they were unqualified to deal with. Both Ruth and Zoe kept quiet as it was rammed home, in a nice way, that they'd had a close call.

'Right then,' said Paula, 'that's my didactic rant over, now we've got some unfinished business to attend to haven't we? And we need to bring this whole episode to a swift conclusion so that we can all get on with our lives.'

'What unfinished business?' asked Zoe.

'Well, my guide is telling me that there are still some issues that need resolving here, with you and the house and other things.' Zoe and Ruth exchanged a glance. 'Don't worry, you won't be needing to go back down there, and you've got me on board now so don't be fretting. Right, give me your hands.'

The two of them quickly complied as they took hold of each other's hands and formed a small circle. Paula recited a little prayer. It wasn't a scenario that Zoe had been expecting and her heart began to flutter, but she went along with the instructions, not daring to contemplate anything to the contrary. She took a deep breath.

'Now, close your eyes and empty your minds of all your day-to-day thoughts...let the soft breeze enter and gently blow them away and out of your headspace...nice and softly...think of nothing, emptiness...allow your breathing to be deep and resourceful...out with the negatives and in with the positives...harness each other's love and positive energy...keep the breathing going, nice and easy.' There wasn't a sound to be heard from within the little room as Paula tuned into her psychic airwaves and attempted to connect with her spirit guide. After a minute or two of total silence, she began to speak.

'Right, yes I understand Sean thank you. So there's

a link between Zoe and the house at East Moor Park. She landed there by chance...and then...an opportunity arose for spirit, for a reason, a purpose...hijacked by elementals and demons through a portal...but...they no longer have a hold on her...yes, we've discussed that Sean, she knows...but the purpose remains...a girl...what's her name, Sean? Do you have a name? No name? A girl with no name? Okay, that's a bit odd...and what? No name and no voice? Yes, I can pass that on... '

Paula continued her exchange with the invisible spirit guide for quite a while, some of it pertaining to Zoe and the events at Reginald Street and some on other matters, most of it incomprehensible nonsense as far as Zoe was concerned. Paula eventually drew back and conveyed her thanks to Sean. Another silence ensued as the spiritualist medium re-tuned her mental airwaves to the present environment and again recited a little prayer of thanks. She then broke the link and heaved a sigh of relief, feeling more than a little weary as she addressed the two women opposite. Zoe looked on spellbound.

'You can relax now ladies. Did you get the gist of that Zoe?

'I think so. Who's Sean? Is he your guide or summat?'

'Yes, love. Sean's my spirit guide. He was a Hindu Rishi in a previous life. His name's Shaunaka but I call him Sean for short. He's very wise and calming but he also has a lovely sense of humour.'

'And what did he mean, 'the purpose remains'? and who's this girl he's on about?'

'I think he means that you still have a job to do for someone in spirit, the reason that spirit cottoned onto you in the first place, at the house, before all the nasty stuff started. That's the problem with these things, they can get complicated and it's like trying to untangle a spider's web. The portal to the dark side, the elemental shape shifters and the stuff you encountered down there just complicated the whole thing, but now that's out of the way, we can concentrate on what we do best. And that's getting the message from spirit to their loved ones over here. That's what the task is Zoe, that's what we have to work out, that's what we do. No more Bonnie and Clyde stuff from you two.'

Again Zoe and Ruth's eyes met and neither one could repress just a tiny smile etching over their otherwise serious countenance.

'What he did say is that you need to contemplate the whole situation, look at the bigger picture. If you practice your meditation and open your mind the answers will come. The answer to the problem will be in your head, stored in your memory somewhere or it will come via spirit. Go over the stuff you might have thought or dreamt about. Some of it might be relevant and things may start to fall into place.'

'And the girl? He said about a girl with no name and no voice. What's that all about?'

'Your guess is as good as mine on that one love,' replied Paula.

'Is she deaf and dumb or summat?'

'I don't know love. Guides don't always have all the answers, but if anything does pop up then Sean will get the information to me one way or another.'

'There was a photograph of a little lass in the cellar, with an older woman. It was still there from when we had the house. And in that underground cave thing, there was a young girl floating above the stone table thing, but she changed into Sophia...so does that mean she's involved in all this?'

'Don't even think about anything that happened down there love. These negative entities have ways of making you see stuff, of getting into your mind and making you feel bad. Sophia has nothing to do with any of this, she's safe love. So please don't worry about that.'

Zoe resigned herself into the capable hands of Paula. She liked Paula and she trusted her. Along with Ruth, and even Squidge, she was building up a small group around her she could trust and who she felt at ease with. They weren't her usual type. They didn't drink or do drugs or even swear. They didn't curse or bicker or employ a cutting sense of coarse humour like the Scissor Sisters, but she enjoyed being around them. They gave her the security which perhaps since her father had passed away she'd been denied.

'And just one more thing before you go,' said Paula as Zoe and Ruth stood up to leave. 'Sean says they're trying like hell to get you lined up with a suitable guide.'

'What?' replied Zoe, 'What do ya mean?'

'Nothing to worry about love. Some of these potential guides from the other side, well, let's say some of them are snowflakes, they get a little bit upset at bad language and stuff like that,' Paula laughed. 'There'll be someone perfect for you out there, don't you worry, but maybe just think a little more positive. Learn to love not to hate, it's harder than you think, but don't for one second think about changing who you are love. They're working on it and your dad's on the case, don't think he isn't, in fact, he's telling me he's looking forward to getting his feet up for a rest when he's fixed you up.' She laughed again. 'Now you two get yourselves off because I need a rest myself, I'll do some more work with Sean on this and if anything crops up I'll call you, and in the meantime, you take on board the stuff we've discussed here and we'll have another chat in a couple of weeks.'

'Thanks, Paula,' said Zoe as she reached over and hugged her. Ruth followed suit with a hug first for Zoe and then for Paula.

'What?' said Paula, 'I'll be seeing you in half an hour, Ruth, what are you like lady?' She smiled and embraced her PA in any case, they were very fond of each other.

'Oh yeah, sorry.' Ruth couldn't help but smile at the situation. Both girls left the room and closed the door behind them leaving Paula to rest her head in her hands. She was exhausted and needed to recharge her batteries before her afternoon engagements. The door burst open and Ruth rushed in.

'Sorry Paula,' she said as she retrieved her cell phone from the coffee table before shooting back out of the door. 'Bye.'

'Bye Ruth, see you soon love.'

CHAPTER 13

Yazz sat slumped and wasted in the shop doorway. It was late morning. Scotch John was in an even worse state than her and young Jester sat quietly in the shadows of the furthest corner. It was a miserable day. Even though smack bang in the middle of summer, 15th July to be exact, this Friday morning was chilly, overcast and dour. Not the kind of day that would instil a sense of optimism or provoke expectations of a positive nature. The type of morning when one resigns oneself to writing the day off. Perhaps tomorrow will be better.

For Yazz and the pack, the routine was just the same. Of a morning they'd sniff it up, piss it up and shoot it up until one or two in the afternoon before sleeping it off and starting over again in the early evening. And then heads down for a few winks in the early hours.

Today, Yazz's world was hazy, indistinct and uncomplicated. The doorway was quiet. Woodlouse and Pikey were nowhere to be seen and to anyone who didn't know Jester, they could be forgiven for thinking of him as a dumb mute, such was his contribution to any sporadic line of conversation. However, on this morning, debate on any subject was thin on the ground with the only exchanges, verbal or otherwise, being incomprehensible grunts as and when the eyes of Yazz met those of Scotch John. A lulled atmosphere of apathy hung thickly over the bottom end of Briggate.

Thirty metres from the lair, leaning on the marbled plinth of the Rusty Bitch was Foxy, speaking in earnest to Big Fucker and Massive Fucker. They were deep in conversation, or at least Big and Foxy were. Massive took a back seat and was more a lookout than a negotiator. His huge and intimidating frame ensured that any potential eavesdroppers kept their distance, should anyone harbour thoughts of sidling up and attempting to pry on the furtive deliberations.

As Yazz gaped over through dulled eyes she could just about see Foxy and Big gesticulating, looking up and down the precinct. It wasn't confrontational, that would have been a mistake on Foxy's part, but it looked like a constructive discussion. Not that Yazz took any of it in. She sat in the doorway with a crooked smile on her face, her head bobbing about like the proverbial nodding dog.

The low, morose tones of Foxy could be heard concluding business as he referred to the Fuckers as '*lads*' and further added that he'd '*see them later,*' before offering his hand. Big and Massive took it reluctantly as if slightly embarrassed at being forced to do business with such a coarse and nondescript street urchin. But business was business, they nodded and turned away, slowly walking up Briggate before turning left into Commercial Street and out of sight.

*

It was later on that evening with the whole pack in attendance as a weary Mitch trudged his way down Briggate towards them. He was already half-cut and since his recent pact with Foxy, he'd spent almost every evening drinking with the group. Never during the daytime, he liked his own company and preferred to move around under the radar, including lone trips to the cage, than be stuck in one place all day with this crew. He tended to join up with them in the evenings and hang out until the early hours, and then when the hyenas were sky-high, he'd slope off alone to get his head down somewhere a little more discrete.

At last, he felt that he was making inroads with the regular streeties. He now regarded the pack as his mates, not close mates, but matey enough that he could talk to them on a one-to-one basis. He'd never become one of the pack, he was far too aloof for that, but he could live with them, side by side. He didn't have to condone their shady practices to be able to chill out or fraternise with them. He'd learned that much from Yazz, and overall he was in a much better place than he had been. He felt part of the crowd and his affiliation with Foxy had opened new opportunities to make even more connections in other areas of the city centre.

'Ey up, it's bleedin' Mitchell from twatting Manchester,' chirped up Foxy, 'come on ya big fucker, get yersen sat down 'ere...Jester get out o' 'way ya little shit.' Jester shuffled up to make room for Mitch who lowered his giant bulk into the doorway, wedging himself between the young lad and Yazz. The usual pleasantries were made with the usual unpleasant language but Mitch had learned to take the piss and to have the piss taken. There was no other way on the street.

Amongst a profusion of 'twats' and 'cunts' and 'fucks' and 'bastards' the banter rolled along with only Jester reluctant to contribute to the lively small-talk. The input from Scotch John was reduced to his usual slurring references to various members of the pack being of large proportions in which the word 'big' was sandwiched between the f, the c and the b words. But at least he made the effort. Pikey was at his most excitable, his shrill and screeching tones echoing around the far corners of Briggate. Woodlouse was Woodlouse, morose and sullen, the Clint Eastwood of Briggate. Yazz was a little quieter than usual although the exuberance with which she necked the booze remained unaffected. Foxy had handed over an almost full bottle of 'voddy' to Mitch who in return had distributed his offering of ciders and wine to the group. Very convivial. It was a happy little setting as the group tucked into their evening sustenance. The conversation was crude, the laughter at times raucous, but the tone was positive and harmless. Mitch had finally made the transition from outsider to trusted and accepted streetie.

*

The group were still at it by nine o'clock. Pikey had disappeared for an hour on his trusty little bike but had since rejoined the group. Mitch had offered the vodka around but had no takers, the others preferring his cider and wine and so he'd more or less the full bottle to himself. On making an enquiry to Scotch John as to whether or not he'd like a swig of the voddy, John had thanked him but said he preferred his scotch whisky, or as it came out: 'Fick ya big c'nt, no suppin tha shite, ahm f'kin whisky man me, yeee f'kn prick!'

It had put a smile on Mitch's face as he continued to work through the vodka, seemingly all to himself. Yazz remained a little reticent but there was still lively banter between Foxy, Woodlouse and Pikey with Mitch chipping in and giving as good as he got.

Foxy's phone buzzed. He grabbed it from the inside of his jacket, looked at the screen and then looked around at the group. He got to his feet and ambled up towards the Rusty Bitch deep in conversation with the caller. The group took little notice and carried on drinking with Mitch necking the last few dregs of vodka from the bottle. He then grabbed a tin of lager from the stash stacked in the middle of the doorway. He'd been steadily drinking for most of the day and now, topped off with an almost full bottle of vodka, he was as well slaughtered as he had been since his arrival in Leeds. But he felt easy with the group and easy with getting lashed on the street with them. He'd tried engaging Yazz in conversation but got nowhere, suspecting that she was only being quiet in his company in front of Foxy. But he was cool with that also, he was in a good place due in part, no doubt, to the fact that his head was as pickled as a froglet in a vat of vinegar.

After five minutes Foxy returned looking quite serious. His head was bowed as he stared directly at the ground, his hands stuffed tight in his pockets,.

'What's up wi' you ya silly cunt?' asked Woodlouse, 'Who were on 'phone?'

'Hmm. We've got a problem lads an' lasses,' he replied as he eased his thin, wizened frame back into the doorway and slouched down next to Yazz.

'Why what's up?' she said.

'It's 'im,' he said nodding towards Mitch.

'Me? Why what 'ave I done?'

'Well...nowt. Y'an't done owt, but I've gotta square up wi' ya, ya big fucker.'

'Square up wi' *me*? What for? Go on then,' slurred Mitch, 'What?'

'Well, there's bin some geezers going about asking about ya?'

'What geezers?'

'Calm down,' said Foxy holding his palms downward towards Mitch. 'There's two big fuckers from Birmingham been looking all over 'place for ya.' Mitch's eyes narrowed, his cheeks flushed up.

'How do you know it's me they're looking for?'

'Well, how many six an' 'alf footers from Liverpool have just dropped on us doorstep ya big daft twat? I know ya say you're from Manchester but ya can't hide your scoucey accent can you? We're not all thick fuckers over 'ere ya know.'

The revelation sobered Mitch. There was genuine fear in his eyes as he looked at Foxy and then scanned the whole street. He started breathing through his nose, his nostrils widened and his brow creased up.

'Well, where are they?' he asked,' 'ave you told 'em owt?' He made to get up but Foxy grabbed his arm.

'Just chill out will ya?'

'Where the fuck are they?' protested Mitch, 'did you tell 'em I were 'ere or what?'

'Well, that's the problem we've got Mitchell. Just sit down a minute and shut the fuck up will ya? Just 'ear me out.' Mitch settled back down and hard stared Foxy with doubt and suspicion. 'When you first got 'ere you were acting like a bell-end, some kind o' fuckin' self-centred street defender, and I'll be 'onest wi' yer, when they first came askin' I told 'em I'd seen ya on 'streets.'

'Fuck me, ya little bastard! I've gotta go—'

'Just hang on a minute. As I wa' about to say...since you've come into our little family, you've proved yersen to be a decent bloke, so that's us problem. They think you're on 'streets 'ere and we've gotta convince 'em that you've packed up and fucked off. I've just 'ad a call from Yardie Geoff up at Little Queen Street saying that they've rang 'im and they're on their way to Leeds again, looking for ya. They're about 'alf an hour away and they're gonna meet up wi' 'im and then come over 'ere. I've told 'im to stall 'em as long as 'e can to give us time. So you, ya big gormless get, 'ad better get going afore they get 'ere. Fuck knows what you've been up to or why they're chasin' yer down, ya, you can fill us in wi' 'details later, but they're big fuckers, I can tell ya that. Proper big fuckers, so you just get the fuck out of 'ere an' we'll cover for ya. Understand?' Mitch was frozen. He couldn't think.

'I ... I'll go straight to 'station and fuck off,' he said.

'Don't be a twat, that'll be 'first place they land, and don't forget they've got eyes all over 'centre, so whatever ya do, do it undercover.'

Mitch looked at Yazz. 'Well where the fuck? ...I don't fuckin know... '

Then Foxy turned to Yazz. 'Listen bitchlet, you know these streets and alleys better than anyone. Fuck off with 'im and squirrel the big cunt away somewhere, and don't come back 'ere till I give the all-clear. Come on, the pair o' ya, fuck off...now!'

A worried Yazz stood up and shook her head. 'Come on, let's go,' she said as she and Pikey helped the stunned and lumbering Giant to his feet. Propped up by the slight figure of a worried Yazz, he then staggered up Briggate as fast as he could. Just when he needed a clear head, they'd tracked him down, right at the point when he'd been at his most vulnerable. At least he'd got Foxy and the pack on board. Again, Yazz had been right for him to bury the hatchet. In the meantime, even though his thoughts were hazy and his lumbering gait haphazard, both he and Yazz knew exactly where they were heading.

*

It was only by the time they'd reached the little dark square with the chain secured around the metal gate be-

hind them that they both relaxed just a little. The journey up had been traumatic, especially for Mitch who had
regarded everyone they passed as a possible assassin. He
was unable to speak such was the panic that had taken
possession over his whole body and which was clearly
etched over his tormented features. Yazz, under orders
from Foxy, was almost as bad. However, once they had
reached the high landing area they allowed themselves to
exchange a few low whispers. The moonlight offered only
partial illumination as the intermittent clouds drifted
across the dark Leeds sky.

'Get yer 'ead down and get some kip,' whispered
Yazz. 'By 'morning they'll 'ave fucked off and we can sort
summat out.' Mitch looked at her and nodded. He was
breathing heavily and sweating profusely. His head was
fuzzy, his thought processes slow and cumbersome. He
knew he was pissed and he just needed time for the
effects to wear off and then he could plan. But one thing
he knew for certain, this would be his last night in Leeds.
Fuck Foxy, he thought, I'm off. First thing, first light.
He lay down and rested his head on his backpack. Yazz
bedded down next to him. His head was spinning and
eventually, the effects of a full day's drinking finally took
effect. He was mentally shattered and after some stubborn resistance he finally drifted off into a deep troubled
sleep.

*

It was sometime later that Mitch stirred to the clanking
sound of the chain. The moon cast a bright surreal light
onto the gantry as he opened his eyes and saw the jum-
bled silhouette of the Leeds skyscape in front of him. He
knew as soon as he sat up that it was Yazz who had left
the scene, he needn't go looking for her. In any case, he

thought, best she was out of the way so he could make a good clean getaway in the morning, with no questions asked. The drifting cloud once again obscured the moonlight as the gantry plunged back into blackness. He closed his eyes once more and waited for daybreak.

*

Yazz crouched in the dark on the other side of the iron gate in the fetid little ginnel. She'd been there for almost an hour and even though she was scared shitless and wanted out, she knew she couldn't renege on the arrangement. The prospect of incurring the combined wrath of Foxy plus the two big fuckers from Birmingham was too much for her to contemplate. The chain hung loosely from the top of the open gate.

She heard a shuffling sound and then muffled whispers coming from further up the ginnel. Nearer and nearer. They were here. The pair of Birmingham brutes had arrived, as planned, and she heard one of them curse as he cracked his head on the low brick arch. *Serves 'im right, the big thick bastard!* Although he'd been warned of the low arch it was Big Fucker who transmitted a cacophony of profanities under his breath as he crouched further down to avoid any other obstructions. And just a moment later, perhaps an indication of an even lower intellect, Massive Fucker followed him up and cracked his skull on the same arch.

Big reached Yazz first and nodded to her whilst still rubbing his head. Massive soon caught him up. It was pitch black as the two looming figures dwarfed the slight configuration of Yazz. The three of them crouched motionless. Three sets of white eyes flitted around the dark stinking ginnel. Two pairs determined, cold and sober. The other, uneasy and fearful. Yazz stood up as Big leant over to whisper something to her. She didn't hear the exact words but she got the message clearly and concisely. Something to the tune of that if she was setting them up she'd get her fucking throat slit. Asked if she understood she nodded, wide-eyed and compliant. She pointed down the narrow passageway through the gate. Big went first, crabbing down the narrow alley sideways attempting to minimise the scraping sound of his jacket against the ancient brick walls. Massive came next, he didn't say a word to Yazz, but he didn't need to, his glare was enough to convey the same message as his associate. As soon as he entered the passageway and started huffing and puffing his way sideways she took off, her job was done. She moved as fast and silently as she could, ducking under the bricked archway and feeling her way up the dark ginnel. By the time she reached the entrance into Harrison's Yard, she was in tears as she flew out into the arms of Foxy.

'Whoa, what's up?' he said, 'Calm down.'

'Just get me away from 'ere, I wanna go,' cried Yazz who was gripped with fear and shaking like the hind legs of a shitting dog. Foxy forcibly restrained her. He was having none of it.

'Just fucking calm down will ya. We've started this ya silly bitch so we've gotta finish it, we're seein' it through so stop the fuckin' blubbing.'

*

Mitch woke up to the sound of shuffling and whispering. But by then it was too late. The full weight of Massive bore down on him as he started to struggle, throwing his arms and legs in the air. Even though his huge bulk was of immense proportions he was no match for the muscular frame of Massive who held down his arms and knelt on his chest. Big crouched down in between them and slammed his left hand over Mitch's mouth and brought his face close to his. There were no words spoken. Just a brief moment of respect. Then down to business. Within a second he'd produced a short sharp blade with which he slit Mitch's throat with clinical precision. In full control, he then waited a second before cranking his victim's head further backwards by pushing up on his stubbly chin, which opened the fresh wound gaping wide. He then repeated the firm, sweeping motion to cut deeper and wider. The throat was now wide open and began to leach blood copiously. The efficiency in which the despicable act was carried out, in pitch blackness, was a testament to the professionalism of the assassins. No doubt the act of such heinous intent had been executed many times enabling them to fine-tune their clinical methodology. Mitch didn't move. The only sound, a sickening gurgling coming from his throat as the blood leached out and dripped through the meshed gantry onto the squalid ground beneath. The hitmen remained still and silent for a full minute. As Massive eventually removed his bulk from the listless body, Big moved in and again crouched over Mitch. He was still conscious but didn't move or attempt any form of communication, just a stare, fully aware of exactly what was going on but unable to do anything about it. He felt the cold, flat blade of an eight-inch knife punctuate his skin and slide deep into his stomach, right up to the hilt. And then out again. Once, twice and the third time each inflicting excruciating pain as his perpetrator cruelly twisted the blade. He lay there and took it without a murmur. His victim now well and truly nullified, Big removed the blade from his steaming hot, sliced open guts and wiped it clean on the victim's combat jacket. The assassins work was done and they retreated from the crime scene as stealthily as they'd entered it.

*

Big and Massive emerged from the dingy little ginnel into Harrison's Yard, brushing themselves down. The area offered little illumination, just a few dim wall lights over the full length of the yard made it only slightly less dark than the ginnel from which they'd just emerged. The place was deserted save for the scruffy little couple who stood waiting. Yazz wouldn't look them in the eye and stared down at the ground, but Foxy faced the pair of them and nodded. From their perspective, they could have easily have walked away from him or even smacked the smug little bastard down. But the price on Mitch's head was far too great to risk any kind of comeback. Big reluctantly pulled an envelope out containing five hundred pounds in cash and shoved it into the chest of Foxy, ensuring a little push as he did so. Foxy grabbed the package and briskly shoved it straight into his inside pocket. Big stared him out for a second and then turned and walked away. Massive followed him, delivering an equally ominous stare as he did so. The pair were never seen on the streets of Leeds again.

*

'Can we just go now?' whimpered Yazz as the Brummie hitmen disappeared into the distance. She snivelled and wiped her runny nose, a by-product of her constant blubbing.

'No, can we fuck just go!' replied Foxy looking down at her. He grabbed hold of her by the shoulders and stared deep into her eyes. 'Listen, you're into this as much as anyone, don't forget that. Now, we've got a job to do and we're gonna see it through to the end. D'ya fuckin' 'ear me?' he said shaking the girl. 'Now, fuckin' get going back down there,' he said turning her around and pushing her through the open doorway and back into the dark ginnel, 'You've gotta get your stuff, and I've gotta get mine. Go on...now!'

He shoved her again and she had no choice but to go through with his demands. He was right, she'd been as complicit as anyone in the whole thing. There was no way out now. Just finish the job and have done with it.

She lead the way as Foxy followed, silent and ardent, down the dark ginnel in the dead of night. Fuck him, she thought as she approached the low brick arch and ducked under it.

'Ow! Fuckin' thing!' muttered Foxy as he smacked his head into the brickwork. 'Jesus! Where the fuck did that come from. You could 'ave told me ya little cow.'

'Sorry,' whispered Yazz in response.

The pair of them followed in the footsteps of the hitmen and shuffled their way up the narrow passage until they reached the square with the iron staircase in the corner. They didn't notice the black viscous liquid which dripped from the high gantry onto the ground beneath. Foxy indicated for Yazz to lead the way but she refused point blank and so it was he who gingerly made his way up with Yazz creeping up behind him. As they reached the top they could see a large dark bundle laying prostrate on the meshed gantry, stock-still with no signs of life. As they stood side-by-side staring down at what they assumed to be the body of Mitch the clouds parted and allowed the moonlight to light up the pitiful little scene. The light confirmed that it was Mitch, with his sliced open throat, smothered in and still seeping thick, black blood. Mitch looked up at them as his dulled but sentient eyes moved from one to the other. He was still alive. The sight caused Yazz to almost collapse as her heart dropped. Foxy took it in his stride and turned around to ram home some rationality.

'Just get yer things,' he said as he fired a determined, no-nonsense glare. She turned away and started collecting her belongings from the gantry including the family snapshots still pinned to the old timber loading doors. Whilst she was doing this Foxy lowered himself and looked Mitch in the face.

'Listen pal. I'm sorry it's ended like this,' he whispered, 'but we're gonna get you an ambulance as soon as we can. Hang in there pal.' Whilst he was uttering these narcissistic words of comfort his grubby little mitts were exploring the insides of the dying man's blood-soaked clothing. His sweaty little digits swarmed all over the stomach wounds as the blood continued to leach out, but he didn't care. He eventually struck gold as he grabbed hold of a large, wet roll of cash. He pulled it out and scrutinised the loot as brought it up to the light. The blood from the wad of cash dripped back into the open wounds of the lifeless body of Mitch, from whence it came. He then dived back in and retrieved a further two wads. He was ecstatic, his face emblazoned with a crooked grin, almost as wide as the gaping open gash to Mitch's throat. He squirreled the cash away before again dipping his head down to address Mitch at close quarters. 'Hang in there pal,' he said and delivered a sickly wink as the life of the Manchester Scouser, slowly ebbed away right there in front of him. Without any further pomp or pageantry, he shot up and made for the staircase.

'Come on, we're done,' he said to Yazz in a low tone.

'I can't find the photo of our Lilly,' she stammered.

'Fuck it, come on...now!'

She quickly stuffed all she needed into a backpack and turned to follow Foxy down the stairs. She hesitated and looked over her shoulder to see Mitch look up at her. Their eyes met, and even though she whispered to him that she was sorry and that they were going to get help there was a deep mutual understanding. With tears streaming from her eyes she turned away and followed Foxy down the stairs leaving the hulking, pitiful Mitch stranded on the gantry, stabbed three times in the guts, his throat ripped to shreds.

She almost threw up as they squeezed out of the passageway. Foxy wound the chain around the gate and secured it with a cheap padlock he'd nicked from the pound shop.

'Shut the fuck up blubbing will ya and come on. We need to get out of 'ere.' He frogmarched her to the top end of the ginnel, prodding her and poking her into moving as briskly as she possibly could. As they stumbled out into Harrison's Yard and quietly closed the heavy, steel-lined door behind them, Yazz eventually found her voice.

'Foxy,' she said in a low voice and through her tears.

'What?' he replied.

'Can we call 'im an ambulance. You told 'im we would. Can we call one? 'E's fuckin' dying for fucksake.'

Foxy turned around and glared at her. He shoved her up against the wall, wedged his left elbow into her throat and pushed his face tight up against hers. His eyes were ablaze with evil as he pushed the index finger of his right hand straight up against her lips as tears ran down her cheeks. He then removed his finger and used it to cut across his own throat whilst staring her down with those pernicious deep-set dark eyes of his. She got the message.

CHAPTER 14

It was in the early hours of Saturday, July 16, when Zoe got the call, 12.30 a.m. to be precise, just days after the showdown talks with Paula Jackson. Since that face-to-face meeting, Zoe had buckled down, taking fully on board the advice and guidance thrown her way. All kinds of threads needed mulling over as she attempted to get to the root cause and the supposed 'purpose' of all this. The girl, the recurring nightmare, the Shelley photograph with its reference to Briggate, the stuff she'd been through at East Moor Park. She hadn't been sure that any of these threads or any of the other little odd occurrences she'd experienced were connected, but she'd got her head down, done some research, made some phone calls and had conjured up some loose theories in her head. She'd done as Paula had suggested and worked on her meditation and explored ways in which she felt she could extend out to spirit. Although she felt positive about the overall situation she was still not confident enough to divulge her conjectures and theories with Paula, or even Ruth for that matter. She'd continue in the same thread, practising, fine-tuning, honing her psychic skills, sticking to the book until the next meeting, after which, perhaps, she could move on to the next level. That had been the plan. And then her mobile had rung at half twelve in the middle of the night. Events were about to gather pace.

'Zoe, is that you?'

'Er...yeah...who the 'ell is it? ...It's gone twelve.'

'Sorry to call you at this time love, it's Paula, Paula Jackson ... '

'Oh, er...Paula...er...what's up? Is there owt wrong?' replied Zoe, sleepy-eyed and still half dazed.

'There's been a development from the other side. I don't know what it is but there's a situation which could result in a passing unless we act fast—'

'A what?'

'A passing, from this side to spirit.'

'What? Someone's gonna die?'

'Believe me, Zoe, we don't normally engage with this kind of information, it's a definite no-no under normal circumstances, but the message is so strong that I've had to contact you. And please don't be alarmed, it doesn't involve anyone in your family love, it's to do with what we were discussing, you know the stuff from East Moor Park, the issue, the mission.' There was a silence before Zoe responded.

'Oh God, I don't know if I'm ready for all this Paula. Deaths and bleedin' riddles and stuff...can I just take time to think and ring you back, I've just woken up and I need to get me 'ead clear, it's all getting a bit 'eavy again.'

'I understand Zoe, by all means love have a little think about it and you have the right to totally disregard what I'm saying. You don't have to do a thing, you can roll over and go back to sleep love. But just take a minute and think about it. Does this message make any sense to you? If it does and you want to act on it then please, call me back. I don't want you messin' about on your own again so if you decide to see it through then I'll be right there by your side. Just have a think and give me a ring back. But there is an element of urgency in this Zoe, it's not every day we get stuff through like this at this time of night, it looks like on this occasion we could make a difference, I won't say between life and death, but spirit has urged me to make this call to you. And if you want to get into this field of work, well, welcome to the weird and the wonderful...just let me know love. I'm gonna hang up now and put the kettle on so I'll be up for a bit yet.'

Zoe didn't reply but turned the phone off just as Linda came barging into the bedroom. 'What the bloody 'ell's up lass, who's that at this time?'

'It's nowt Mam... ' she replied as Princess bounded into the room and jumped up onto the bed yapping and fussing.

'Oh piss off will ya?'

'Well, I'm only asking—'

'Not you, the bleedin' dog! Oh just get out the pair o' yer!' Linda shook her head and grabbed the excitable little 'Yorkie'.

'Come on lad, back to your basket. Let me know if you want owt,' said Linda as she exited the bedroom and closed the door quietly behind her, puffing her cheeks and shaking her head once she'd done so.

Zoe dropped her head into her hands. *What the fuck. I'm not cut out for this, it's just not me. Life and bastard death! Jesus Christ!* She thought how easy life had been with Phil. He'd sorted out all their problems, she'd had to do nothing. There'd been no stimulation in her life, no reason to do anything, but then again she hadn't had a life. Now she had, and she couldn't face the prospect of giving up, of not seeing the thing through. The return to Reginald Street, was that to be a futile exercise? She couldn't quit on everything now, if this was to be her life she couldn't be backing down now surely, but on the other hand...was she up to it?

Her mind ran amok, her thoughts indistinct, her nerve, her resolve tested to the limit. The right thing to do, the wrong thing to do, where the fuck was her dad when she needed him? *Where's me friggin' guide?*

She spent five minutes trying to piece everything together. And it did make sense, well, a sort of sense. She didn't want it to, she'd hoped it hadn't, but the more she pondered the matter the more pieces began to fall into place, though the last piece, the one she desperately sought, the piece that would bring everything together and give the whole thing meaning, still eluded her.

'Right, stop fucking about and grow a pair, ya twattin' lightweight,' she said aloud to herself. She threw herself out of the bed, got dressed and then grabbed her phone. She made the call. A difficult call, but one that she knew had to be made. Once finished she hung up and then rang Paula.

'Right Paula, it's me. I think might I know what this is all about but I'm not 'undred per cent sure so I hope you've got my back if this goes tits up.'

'I'll be there with you Zoe, don't worry.'

'Is Ruth coming?'

'Yes, I've already briefed her and she's getting ready, I knew you'd call me back.'

'Good, I need Ruth to be with me. So meet me on Briggate in town, say at the junction with Albion Place, near 'coffee shop me and Ruth meet at. She'll know where I mean. You know Briggate don't ya?'

'Of course I know Briggate, I was born and bred in Armley,' replied Paula in mock indignation. 'Right, I'll pick Ruth up, you sure you don't want a lift?'

'I'll get a taxi down and meet ya there. There'll be someone else joining us who I've just spoken to on 'phone but I'll fill you in when we meet. But Paula, there's just one thing.'

'What's that love?'

'I'm new to all this, so if I've got it all wrong I'm gonna look a right prat. Whatever happens, I just want ya to know that I've done everything with the best intentions, I've really tried hard on this, ya know, what ya said...about love and compassion and all that rather than being negative, I've even tried to tone down me language. I've given it me best shot.'

'I know you have love, and don't worry. I'm getting positive vibes from this end so I think we must be on the right track, but I must emphasise again Zoe that we haven't got much time so we really do need to get down there as soon as possible.'

*

The look on the faces of Paula and Ruth said it all as Zoe rushed down Briggate to meet them at the Albion Place junction. Ruth could hardly look her in the face as Paula hugged her and shook her head, conveying her sorrow and sympathy in soft warm tones. Zoe didn't need any explanation. The blue lights of the police car and ambulance flashed in unison outside the entrance to Harrison's yard, just a few yards further up Briggate from Marks and Spencer's. She hung her head and looked down at the ground. She took full responsibility. They were too late. She was too late. Her first assignment, job, case, call it what you will, and she'd blown it. She'd fucked up. They could see from where they stood that the ambulance response team had exhausted their efforts of resuscitation. The body was now covered in a white sheet, as the usual procedures and protocol, required under such unpleasant and grisly circumstances, slowly gathered pace. The police had already cordoned off an area of Briggate and were ushering piss-heads and rubberneckers away from the scene.

The three of them linked arms as they walked towards the cordon. As they approached the police tape Zoe burst into tears. Ruth and Paula did their best to comfort her but it was such a sorry spectacle, especially to Zoe who was unused to the concept of death, the sudden demise of her father being the only time she'd experienced the loss of life first hand. Zoe felt hopeless and culpable, she was broken. Her iPhone rang and she wiped the tears running down her face as she held it up. She looked around and spotted the couple walking down Briggate towards them. Ashen-faced, she looked up at Paula who nodded, indicating that she best go over and meet them.

Paula and Ruth looked on as Zoe slowly trudged up to intercept the couple, a short woman in her mid-twenties and a tall dark-haired male. They watched as Zoe attempted to spell out the situation. She embraced the female who then wiped her own tears before burying her head into the chest of her partner. He stroked her hair and gently rubbed her back. Zoe then walked them back towards Ruth and Paula where they were solemnly introduced. The sorry couple thanked the group and then left them as they walked over and grabbed the attention of the attendant police officers guarding the scene.

Debbie Richards' request to see the body of the woman whom she believed to be her mother was declined. Not that she could back up her claim with hard proof, not yet anyway. The young female officer was unable to sanction any viewing of the body but did offer the couple a place in the police vehicle where they could come to terms with the incident. They could sort out the formalities in due course. It was the last time Zoe ever set eyes on Debbie Richards, but she did receive a letter of thanks some weeks later.

The dead body of the weird homeless woman, the one with the shock of white hair, the one that was consistently robbed and ridiculed by her fellow rough sleepers, the one who had spent almost her entire adult life alone on the street, now lay cold and dead. She was covered by a white sheet on the bench just further up from Marks & Spencer's, the spot where she'd spent so many hours of her earthly life and the very spot where she'd drawn her last breath. In life, she'd boasted neither a name nor an expressive voice. She was just a label, a number. Her existence could not even hold a seat at the table of society's lowest forms, but now, in death, just for a short time, she was the centre of attention. The hard life on the street had eventually caught up with her as she lay cold and stiff on the stainless steel bench. Another pitiful victim of the shameful underbelly of a caring society. To all those gathered around the scene it struck home the dangers and the brutal fragility of life on the street, and how limited were their own efforts to help, to make a difference. A sober few stood around the police cordon sad and pitiful of the poor soul. Their pity too late, their sadness of no consequence.

The three of them looked on, not knowing what to do or what to say. Paula suddenly fixated her stare on an area just to the side of the stiffening corpse. Had Zoe's self-pity not overtaken her psychic awareness she too might have picked up the glowing spirit of a little blond-haired girl standing next to the body of the old street woman. The barefoot child wore a white nightdress and bore a smile as she looked down at the deceased woman. The spirit girl acknowledged the presence of Paula and then turned towards Zoe with a look of love and compassion, of gratitude. She then turned and walked away from the scene, up Briggate, serene, at peace, and unencumbered with the conflict and pain of physical life. And then, as if walking on air, she gradually rose higher and higher as her spirit form glowed in increased intensity. A beam of pure white light appeared which stretched up high into the dark Yorkshire skies and into which the little spirit girl entered. Paula watched as the ethereal figure slowly rose upwards into the brilliant shaft of light. She silently observed the splendorous vision of the luminous spirit of the little girl, shining and radiant, as she gently slipped into an alternative realm. In the blink of an eye, the light zapped down into the twinkle of a star, which sparkled for a second before vanishing into a dot of nothingness.

Zoe had been too upset to witness Paula's interest, her gaze lay on the covered body of the dead street woman, but Ruth had. She sensed that her mentor had endured a psychic encounter of sorts. They exchanged glances. Now wasn't the time to explain to Zoe, decided Paula. She suggested that their work was done, they could do nothing more and that it best they return home for some rest. She proposed that they meet up for coffee the following morning when they could attempt to tie up loose ends.

*

The team had agreed to meet at the Parkway Hotel on Otley Road. It was halfway between Seacroft and the ancient market town of Otley, where Paula lived. Simon had kindly offered to pick up both Ruth and Zoe and was keen to get the lowdown on the situation having missed all the action the night before. It was around eleven-thirty as the three of them walked into the large coffee lounge and through the open french windows to see Paula already seated outside on the terrace. She'd secured a nice little secluded table in the far corner where they could talk in private. It was a warm, calm morning with clear blue skies as they shuffled around the table and jostled themselves into their seats. The stunning backdrop of Golden Acre Park with its well-stocked wildfowl lake and beautiful wispy, weeping willows set the scene. The scent from potted lavenders pervaded the tranquil little terrace of pergolas, hanging baskets and planted tubs. The group settled down and once the drinks had arrived Paula took the lead.

'Well thanks for coming everyone and thanks Simon for picking the girls up. I just thought it'd be nice if we met up this morning just to go over the events of last night and to reiterate, especially to Zoe, that we don't normally get involved in any passing, as it's God's will and we have no part to play in any of that. However, this was a one-off situation with Sean getting involved and I was forced to call poor Zoe late on and she very bravely, given the circumstances, stepped up to the plate and took on board the responsibility that comes with having such a precious gift. So I think we need to start with you Zoe love, what's the story from your end? You obviously took on board what we'd discussed at our last meeting and must have done some good work for things to reach the stage they did. So...go on girl...over to you.'

The focus of the small group now fell on Zoe. Being the centre of attention didn't sit well with her, but she went along with Paula's directive.

'Well, as I said last night, I'd tried to do everything

right as you'd suggested, and for 'right reasons. You said there was a mission or a job to be done and I just felt...a sense of responsibility to see it through. I tried to think about everything and bring it all together, I was bricking it if I'm being honest. I'm still not sure about the recurring dream from the 'ouse at East Moor Park, 'one wi' 'old woman on 'barstool—'

'Well maybe I can shed some light on that one love, but go on,' interjected Paula, 'I'll come back to that.'

'Well, I started thinking about the times when I'd come across people and started to get the head buzzing, or vibrations as you lot call it. Sometimes when I go near people I just get a buzzin' in me 'ead and then it eases off when I walk away from 'em. Other times if I'm talking to someone I can start going dizzy an' stuff like that. So I'd seen this 'omeless woman in town, on Briggate, a few times and every time I went near her me 'ead started din't it. Sometimes just a fluttering and other times a full-on buzzing. I get it sometimes wi' people I don't know but it was every time with her—'

'It's probably because you haven't yet learned to open and close your psychic airwaves Zoe love. It can send you mad if they're open permanently, believe me. No wonder you've been struggling over the past couple of years.' Paula nodded for Zoe to continue.

'Well, there was another time with an estate agent that the same thing 'appened, when me and 'dick-'ead... sorry Paula...Phil, were looking for a house. I went all dizzy and felt sick and went all funny, but afterwards, I thought nowt more of it. Then I remembered her saying that she'd been an orphan or summat or she'd been fostered and remembered how sad she'd seemed about that. I remember...it was as though...I could feel her sadness. And it was just as I was thinking about the estate agent that...it was almost...like a flash in me 'ead as if the two were fused together, a connection between the old woman on Briggate and the estate agent. It freaked me out, I din't know what to do. I remember her tellin' us that it wan't her who was supposed to be meeting us but summat had cropped up and she'd had to step in at the last minute. I'm thinking, was that a coincidence or what? Then me mam told me about a photograph that Shelley, her mate, had brought up. To cut a long story short, I'd had a vision, the first that I'd actually initiated meself. I described it and asked either of them if it meant owt to 'em. Well, typically they were 'alf cut and took the piss at the time but then a few days later Shelley brings this photo up which validated what I'd said to 'em. There was a reference to Briggate in Leeds. Again I'm thinking coincidence or what?'

'All this may be coincidence Zoe, but then again spirit is always working behind the scenes love,' said Paula. Ruth and Simon remained silent as they listened in awe. Paula remained calm and receptive to everything she was hearing.

'So I couldn't get this connection out o' me 'ead,' continued Zoe. 'I caught a bus down to town and went to find the old woman, she was there, just up from M&S on her usual bench. The benches back onto each other and so I went down to sit on the one that backed on to hers. As soon as I did I started getting the buzzin' in me head and then when I thought about Debbie, that's the estate agent, I started getting these really intense emotions, it made me want to cry and after that, I knew, I just knew... don't ask me how or why but...I can't put it into words, but I knew 'undred percent that the connection was there and that the old woman were 'biological mother that Debbie, unbeknown to me at that point, had been desperately searching all her life. I had to get up and walk away and as I did I looked down and smiled at the woman with tears in my eyes. I felt a bit of a twat, crying in the middle o' Briggate to be 'onest. Anyway, she looked up at me with such sadness, but I din't get a response from her. No smile or acknowledgement, just the empty sadness in her eyes. It was as if she were just an empty shell. Her face was grey and she looked really unwell and I even told mesen that she didn't look as if she'd long left.'

Ruth could see that her friend was getting quite emotional. She put her hand on her arm. 'You okay love?'

Zoe continued. 'I got back home and I just couldn't think of owt else, it was driving me insane. I felt I had to ring this Debbie Richards up, we still had all the paraphernalia she'd left with us with her contact numbers on. The first time I rang her and told her what I was thinking she slammed the phone down on me, she thought I were a nutter. The second time she threatened me with the police, but I stuck at it, I wun't give up. The third time she broke down and admitted that she had been searching for her proper mother for years but had come up against a brick wall. After a bit o' persuasion, she agreed to meet me to go through it with her it and although she told me she didn't really believe in all this stuff she admitted that at the end of the day she'd nowt to lose. We spoke a few times on 'phone and she seemed a nice genuine lass. We were due to meet in town next week when the plan was to take her down to see the woman who I was claiming to be her mother...and then I got the call from you last night. And that's that. I cocked the whole thing up, we were too late. I sat on it for too long, I should have got back to you Paula or maybe spoke to you about it Ruth. But I din't...and poor Debbie ...well...she never got to—'

'Well, just wait a cotton-picking minute Zoe,' stepped in Paula, 'stop berating yourself, love. You didn't cock anything up at all, what are you talking about? I think you're missing the point love. Firstly the poor lady would have passed in any case, it was her time. It's not nice but it happens on the street doesn't it guys?' said Paula looking up at Ruth and Simon. They both nodded in agreement. 'We know because we've seen it, not that often, but it happens. And how do you think she'd have reacted if you'd introduced this strange woman to her as her daughter. It probably wouldn't have gone down well under the circumstances love. As it is now, subject to confirmation that they are mother and daughter, which I presume they'll confirm one way or another through DNA analysis or something, it gives her closure. She can give her mother a send-off and perhaps have a stone or a plaque to go to when she needs to. She can get on with her life now not having to carry that huge question mark on her shoulders as to who or where her real mother is. So for that my love she's got you to thank. You've given her that and so you should be proud of yourself.' Zoe didn't know what to say so she didn't say anything. Ruth smiled at her and rubbed her shoulder.

'And there is some back-story to all this,' added Paula, 'Sean and I took a vested interest in this case and spent quite a bit of time on it yesterday which resulted in the phone call to you Zoe. The old lady on the barstool who keeps visiting you in your dreams came through. She's a lady who lived in the house at East Moor Park years ago. Her name was Stella, I don't know the surname, but she died in the house with a huge sense of emotional guilt which she's been trying to put right ever since and which has prevented her from moving over to spirit. She blamed herself for the fate of her granddaughter who was subjected to abuse in the house at the hands of her grandfather, Stella's husband. She told me he wasn't her 'proper husband', they were her words, but her second husband. Unfortunately, she took matters into her own hands and committed some barbaric and dark revenge, which she regrets. In any case, the place is, or was, full of negative emotions and dark energy, which had remained in the fabric of the house all these years. It was also made worse due to the portal in the cellar, probably activated by the heinous crimes and barbaric atrocities that took place down there. And then you came along with your special gift. Stella desperately latched onto you to make the connection between her and her abused granddaughter...and...wait for it...who turned out to be the lady who sadly passed yesterday on Briggate. We'll call her Briggate lady for the sake of clarity. To further complicate things, Debbie, it seems is Briggate lady's daughter who was taken from her at birth, perhaps as she was a street person she'd no way of looking after her, I don't really know. So when you came along, it was Stella's spirit, the old lady from East Moor Park, still harbouring over the guilt she had for her granddaughter, Briggate lady, and who, through you, sought to bring Briggate lady and her daughter, Debbie, together. It's complicated but I know that Stella and granddaughter, Briggate lady, are now reunited on the other side. I saw the little spirit girl make the transition over to spirit last night whilst we were on Briggate. Her little soul was glowing and she wore a beautiful smile. She was happy and at peace. Stella can take care of her at long last. And now Debbie can get on with her life on this side. It was only by you going back down to the house and getting the negative spirits off your back that you could be free to go forward and make the connection. That's why you were having the recurring dreams, Stella was drawing you back down there. Does that all make sense to everyone?' The three of them remained quiet. It was a lot to take in but they got the gist of the matter. No doubt Sean had been very busy over the last twenty-four hours.

'The photograph,' said Zoe, 'on the stone table in the cellar. Was that the grandmother and granddaughter? Was that the little girl you mentioned? You said something about the spirit of a little girl, but the woman on Briggate must have been in her sixties.'

'Well I don't know about the photograph, perhaps it was, and Briggate lady probably looked older than she was after a lifetime on the street. But such was the horrendous abuse she suffered at the hands of her grandfather, her poor soul never developed, it never got a chance to thrive and flourish. The result was that the tortured little soul, God bless her, remained stuck as a six-year-old for the rest of Briggate Lady's life. The soul of a lost and confused little six-year-old inside the body of a grown woman. Eventually, the two, body and soul, became detached. Probably why she could never integrate with mainstream society and ended up on the street, maybe prostitution and pregnancy, who knows? But what I do know is that this sorry little soul who spent all these years in complete misery is now liberated. As I said, last night, on Briggate, I witnessed her glowing and beautiful little spirit pass over. She knew of the connection with you, Zoe. She'd been waiting for your intervention and she'd been following you around. She's in a good place now love, don't worry. So you see, you haven't failed my love. You've succeeded in helping bridge the gap between this side and spirit, for the good. That's what we do.'

'Jesus,' replied Zoe,' I don't know what to say, I'm... gobsmacked. And to think all this started with Bowler hat woman, poor Brenda, who I took the piss out of and thought she was a crank.' She bit her lip. 'I hope you can give me her address Paula, so I can call round and apologise. I know she lives somewhere on South Farm Road, but I feel so guilty now. Looking back she was such a nice lady and I disrespected her so much, I was such a friggin' arsehole towards her.' Ruth looked down at the table as Paula raised her eyebrows at Zoe's turn of phrase but then smiled as she inwardly remembered that this rugged Seacroft diamond was still a work in progress.

'Don't worry about Brenda Zoe love, she forgives you, and don't forget that she lived on the Seacroft estate since they were built after the war so she knows everything about life on Seacroft and loves the Seacroft community with all her heart. Unfortunately love you won't be able to visit her on South Farm Road, as she passed over to spirit five years ago now...but she knows you're a good person at heart and she's been watching over you. She sends you her love.'

Zoe's heart felt like it had been pummelled with a sledgehammer, her knees buckled under the table and her face turned drip-white. The emotion involved in the whole story was too much for her to take, she burst into tears and buried her head into her hands.

*

After consoling the upset Zoe the group slowly came to terms with the situation. Gradually the mood lifted and the quartet spent the next hour chatting happily, discussing more down to earth, everyday matters. Neither Zoe, Ruth nor Simon could get their heads a hundred per cent around what they'd heard but at least Paula had. And now that was all behind her Zoe could see that her path forward was along a bright wide avenue which stretched out in front of her rather than down the narrow dark ginnel that she'd been barging her way through. She'd been thrown in at the deep end and had emerged a much tougher woman. She liked her new life. She was happy even though deep down she couldn't help sensing that she'd made a mess of things, and even harboured the sensation that there was still unfinished business back on the streets of Leeds. However, if Paula Jackson said the matter had been resolved then who was she to question that? She rode the crest and for once cut herself some slack. She sat back and enjoyed the company, the easy chatter and the beautiful setting.

*

It was subsequently confirmed that Debbie Richards was indeed the biological daughter of 'Briggate Lady'. She took care of the funeral arrangements and had her ashes scattered at Lawnswood cemetery. The remembrance plaque reads:

Mum
Only briefly connected in this realm
you brought me into this world
Our hearts forever linked
Until we meet again
Your loving daughter
Debbie

*

To this day the rotting remains of the brutally murdered Mitchell from Manchester lay undiscovered and undisturbed on the secret little gantry, in the middle of Leeds, still wrapped in his ripped and shredded combat jacket. Mitch was a trusting soul, but one whose lack of judgement cost him his life. Huge in physical stature he was struck with 'little man' syndrome, misguided in his aspirations to build his own underworld narcotics empire on the back of turning over an existing and established drugs cartel. Enterprising, but his lack of wit along with his propensity to favour inclination over intuition eventually cost him. It always had done. But it would cost him no more.

Who knows how long his stiffened and skeletal corpse will remain undetected? but few have neither the nerve nor the inclination to venture down the ancient, dark, stinking alleyways, ginnels and passageways within the very heart of Leeds City Centre, invisible to the tens of thousands of people who pass within a few yards each and every day. Foxy, Yazz and the rest of the pack abandoned the lair and dissipated into the complex, blurry world of social dropouts.

*

Ruth spotted Zoe in the usual far corner of the Albion Place coffee house. She was overly excitable even for her as she squealed Zoe's name loudly over the shop causing her friend acute embarrassment as a hush descended upon the place.

'Usual love?' she shouted, apologising to the guy stood in front. Zoe responded with a thumbs up and put her head down quickly, pretending to check out her phone. Ruth was brimming with urgent news. They'd already planned to meet this morning, but according to Ruth, she'd received some news that she couldn't wait to share and by the time she'd brought over the drinks she was bursting with elation, almost spilling the coffee.

'Calm down Ruth ya silly bugger, what's up wi' ya?'

'You'll never guess what?' she splurted out as she sat down and slid a latte over to Zoe.

'What?' she replied. 'Go on, just take a deep breath and calm down. She held her hands over Ruth's fixing them down onto the table and stared her in the eye.

'Right, deep breath, and in your own time...tell me...what's up?'

'Well, I got a phone call this morning,' gushed Ruth.

'A phone call, right, yeah, go on,' replied Zoe, releasing Ruth from her grip.

'It was from Paula... '

'Paula, okay.'

'Well, do you remember when I said that Paula had a trip to Australia lined up for some TV work, I think it might have been the first time we met?'

'Yeah, I remember, well, what about it?'

'The production company have increased the number of programmes they want to shoot over there and so the trip is going to be longer than they originally planned and the result is that they've agreed to fund the costs for Paula to take an assistant with her. And guess who that is?'

A huge smile emblazoned Zoe's face. 'You, of course,' she replied.

'Yes, me! I can't believe it, Zoe, I'm going to Australia, how crazy is that?' The two embraced. Zoe was happy for her dotty little friend, she deserved it.

'Oh, that's great Ruth, what a bleedin' adventure for you. I'm really chuffed for you love, I really am.'

'And that's not all Zoe, and here's the best bit.'

'Go on then,' replied Zoe smiling, 'What?'

'According to Paula, she'd applied to the National Spiritualist Church Foundation for a student training grant to fund one of her students to travel with us... for the experience...and guess what?'

'What?' replied Zoe a little perplexed as to where this was going.

'She got the grant and guess which student she wants to take?'

'I've no idea Ruth, who? Squidge? I don't even know any of her bloody students do I?'

'It's you ya bloomin' cuckoo! She wants to take you with us to Australia...if you accept that is.' There was a stunned silence from Zoe. She hadn't even regarded herself as a student.

'She wants me to go to Australia wi' you two?'

'Yes, me, you and Paula. Ten weeks...all expenses paid trip...to bloomin Australia! Please tell me you'll accept it, love. What an experience it's gonna be.'

'Me?'

'Yes, bloomin' YOU!'

It took a while for the idea to sink in for Zoe. She filled up.

'Bleedin' 'ell Ruth, I can't take all this in. Less than a year ago I wa' wandering around East Moor Park wi' Sophia in 'dark an' 'pissin' down rain cos I was too scared to go back to that 'orrible 'ouse. At the beginning o' this year, I was still in 'ospital, drugged up and thinking about toppin' meself. Then there was the Phil and Katie thing. And now this, it's a complete turnaround. What a bleedin' mad world this is. Are you sure about this?'

'Absolutely positive! Paula wanted me to be the one to ask you, after everything you'd been through.'

'It's bleedin' mad.'

'Well, as Paula says, spirit is always working behind the scenes love. Looks like your dad's been busy.'

Zoe smiled and worked out in her head how she could approach her mother to take care of Sophia for ten weeks. She was sure she'd have no problem there, though she acknowledged there may be an issue with the expeditious defecating traits of Princess.

'Just say you're gonna accept Zoe, that's all I want to hear from you love. Just tell me.'

Zoe smiled at her. 'You bet I'm gonna accept Ruthy baby, bring it on!' The two squealed and embraced, unable to conceal their excitement and not bothering who witnessed their elation as the coffee drinkers in the adjacent booths smiled in genuine happiness for the pair of them.

'There's just one thing Ruth, one little condition.'

Ruth went quiet. 'What's that love?'

'We go out and have a drink to celebrate, now - today.'

'Zoe, you know I don't drink love it's not me—'

'I know you don't and I'm not on about us getting slaughtered or owt. Come on you dotty bugger, have a life, you're only young once! Come on, let your hair down and kick the old maid image into touch, just for a couple of hours, let's go for a couple o' cocktails. It's not every day you get told you're going to bleedin' Australia, all expenses paid, is it?

Ruth pondered for a second and then let out a huge sigh. 'You're right love. Bellocks to it! come on then, let's go out and get drunk.' Zoe burst out laughing.

'It's bollocks not bellocks ya daft cow!' She reached over to hug her new bestie.

'Right, where's me blooming cap?'
'It's on yer twattin' 'ead love.'

*

THE END

Dazzling white-chalk cliffs stick far out into a stunning expanse of turquoise ocean which gently caresses the azure-blue skies on the distant horizon. The emerald-topped cliffs stretch as far as the eye can see forming a craggy and savagely beautiful setting. The far-away roar of surf crashing onto the rocks 400-foot below hybridizes with the incessant, echoing cries of thousands of screeching seabirds as they whirr and circle the rugged, spectacular headland. The blazing sun swathes the scene in a warm positive vibrancy, its hot rays bouncing off the dancing seas creating a luminous sheet of sparkling surf, teeming with life and vitality. White birds, huge white birds, in their hundreds and thousands glide upon the thermal currents around the cliff tops with thousands more out at sea, wild, powerful and vigorous. Huge white birds with cartoon beaks and funny eyes, screeching and screaming in their hundreds and thousands, swirling above the cliff tops. Cartoon beaks and funny blue eyes. Screeching. A black mist descends blocking out the sun and the skies. The ocean turns grey, the cliffs lose their lustre, their emerald crowns fade into a mire of sludge. The seabirds dissolve, their cries quelled. The vigour of life is expunged, expelled and displaced by the quintessential essence of death.

Zoe opens her eyes and takes a deep breath. Her palate is dry, her hot head is buzzing and her throat feels like she's swallowed a thousand shards of broken glass.

Other Books by this Author:

Lonely Ballerina

Available on Amazon.co.uk

Printed in Great Britain
by Amazon